The Amaris Prophecies: The Dawning

By Zoe Nauman

The Amaris Prophecies

Published by Qavah Publishing

Library of Congress Control Number: 2026908604

Paperback ISBN: 979-8-9880357-9-4

eBook ISBN: 979-8-9958137-3-6

Typeset by BooksGoSocial

Cover design by Masa Radanic

Printed in the United States of America

This book is dedicated to my amazing friends who have stood by me and given me unwavering support on this journey to bring the world of Amaris to life. Allyson, Mallica, Caroline, Debbie, Kathleen and Jessie: You believed in my story and in me. Thank you. You're all amazing, gorgeous, fabulous people!

Contents

Chapter 1

Arielle stood before the mirror in her ornate chamber, meticulously smoothing down the fabric of her ceremonial dress. As she swirled full circle, she caught a glimpse of the intricately stitched wings on the back of her red cloak. She winced, the silver thread of the feathers, a constant, painful reminder of the real pair that used to grace her shoulders.

Pushing down the pang of regret, Arielle screwed up her nose and dug her fingernails into her palm to calm her racing thoughts.

In her mind, she ran over the speech she would be giving in a matter of hours at the Council of the Clans. Arielle was well aware that the gathering was the most important she had hosted since her descent to Amaris from the heavenly realm of Riyon.

Her chest tightened. The Divine had made it clear that assuming the role of keeping the peace on Amaris would not be easy. Already, she could visualize the condescending frowns and raised eyebrows of the Amaris clan leaders, all desperate for an excuse to snipe and snap. Sacrificing her wings and immortality would no doubt seem like nothing compared with the difficulties that lay ahead of her.

The animosity between the provinces had escalated, and Arielle knew the older clan leaders had no respect for her. They saw her appearance, which was as barely an adult, and conveniently forgot that she, as a Kaluduta in human form, had more wisdom in her little finger than all of them put together.

She patted down the escaping tendrils of her crimson hair and swished her skirts again, admiring how the constellations embroidered in silver thread caught the sunlight. At least in this finery, she could remind them of her descent from Riyon for their good. Striding over to the table, Arielle pulled out the chair with a jerk and sat down.

She irritably drummed her fingers on the table. What was the best way to handle the clan leaders? They were like a bunch of children themselves. An exasperated sigh escaped her lips; this was not the way to think. She was the peacekeeper, one of the Divine race brought to Amaris to help the clans see sense. Not for the first time, Arielle cursed the frailty of the human shape she had been forced to assume and the freedom of thought it brought to her mind.

When she had been a Kaluduta dwelling at the side of the Divine in Riyon, she'd found it easy to see the good in everything and had known she was making the right choices—the only choices.

In His infinite wisdom, the Divine desired for the clans of Amaris to possess the autonomy to make their own decisions. Yet, as far as Arielle could see, the tumultuous emotions that the beings of this world experienced were too overwhelming for them to make educated choices. She knew this to be true because Arielle was continually grappling to harness and understand the intensity of sensation and reaction in her earthbound mind and body.

Arielle was in a continuous and annoying battle to fight against any negative thoughts that might creep into her mind toward any person, circumstance, or anything. Why *had* the Divine crafted such fallible creatures?

Leaning back in the chair, she closed her eyes, took a slow breath to calm her nerves, and tried to concentrate on the fact that her role in bringing Amaris to the light was a gift, not a curse.

"Is this everything you want, Arielle?" In the stillness, a whisper so quiet it was barely perceptible.

Arielle's eyes snapped open. She turned around but saw nothing. "Is somebody there?"

The voice came again, a rasping yet enticing whisper: "I hear you, Arielle. You aren't happy."

Arielle stood up and spun in the chamber. She was resolute in her response. "By the Divine, I command you. Who are you?"

There was an icy breath, cold on her cheek, right by her. So close, brushing intimately against her ear, caressing her earlobe. Why was the voice familiar to her but made her recoil simultaneously?

"I am the one who can give you what you deserve. I am the one your Divine does not want you to know about. I possess the power you never knew you craved. Don't you remember me, Arielle?"

"I don't know what or who you are, but I order you to leave my chambers." Arielle turned this way and that, eyes wide, a knot in her stomach. *Is this fear I am experiencing?* But she still saw no presence in the chamber.

"You hear me because you're interested in my offer," the voice rasped again. "Think on that, Lioness of the Divine. I heard you roar, and I answered your call."

Arielle brought her fingers to her cheek, a glacial wetness there. Her skin crawled. But deep in her mind, a bell rang. *How does it know I'm called the Lioness of the Divine?* That was known to only a few of the Kaluduta.

Whirling again, Arielle looked around the room. Nothing. She was alone. The sense of dread and cold that had permeated the air around her just moments before had gone.

What was that? WHO was that? She tried to arrange her thoughts, scrambling through her memories of her time in Riyon, which were now, in her Amarisian form, like wisps of gossamer. That bell continued to clang in her mind—she knew the deliverer of those words, but there was a difference somehow. The tone she recognized had once been loving. Now it was cold. The familiarity there curled around her heart, but its touch burned like ice.

Surely it couldn't be, could it? Arielle's confusion was fused with dread as the name began to take shape in the dark of her lost thoughts, which struggled to formulate in her frail Amarisian form. She was almost relieved when a knock at the door snapped her out of the pain of remembering.

Before she could answer the questions in her mind or command the visitor to enter, Tauheed strode into the chamber. The leader of the Divine Interpreters carried a voluminous bundle of papers under his arm and had a pen wedged behind his ear.

Tall, lean, and with dark wavy hair, Tauheed carried himself with a knowledgeable and imposing air, which made him appear far older than his eighteen years. He was wearing the indigo color of the lead Divine Interpreter, and his robes reflected the stars and the heavens. It was a signal to the other clans of Amaris that he and others of his kind could interpret the ways of the Divine.

Arielle's heart skipped at the sight of him, and excitement bubbled up in her stomach.

Argh, there go those pesky out-of-control emotions again!

Warmth filled her. "Tauheed! How are the Lore Scriptures coming along? Surely you cannot be far off?"

Tauheed rolled his eyes, but the light danced in the green of his irises, and the corners of his mouth turned upward. "There's not much left to complete. But there is no doubt what needs to be laid down in the final pages will be dictated by the outcome of the Council of the Clans. All we can hope for is they all have the common goal of ensuring peace."

The hardest part of Arielle's goal was getting the scriptures completed. Having free will was wonderful, but it could hinder a unanimous decision.

"Any news from the Kaluduta or the Divine?" Tauheed's look was expectant.

Arielle pursed her lips. "Not yet. Have any of the arriving clan leaders been spoken to yet?"

Tauheed shook his head as Arielle began pacing in earnest. "I want this meeting to go as smoothly as possible. Surely they understand that the Lore Scriptures are designed to bring harmony and unity. I know some of the clan leaders think it's a way for the Divine—and by extension me, as His representative—to exert control. They must understand there has to be some framework and guidance for everyone to live by. Otherwise, it will just be chaos." She gave an exasperated shrug.

Tauheed rolled his eyes; a wry smile played on his lips. "The clan leaders say they want to see our world grow in strength and continue to be unified, irrespective of our race and way of living. But some of them still make decisions that hurt and harm others, rather than help and support them."

Arielle crossed her arms. "We must show them the Divine's way; they must be in unity to move forward."

Tauheed nodded in agreement. "This is exactly what we want to achieve. To make sure we, as Divine Interpreters, can translate to the clans exactly what the Divine wants. Then they can understand they are ultimately no different from one another."

"The problem is—" As Arielle parted her lips to speak, a deafening whoosh of air drowned out her words. The powerful flapping of dragon wings rattled the window frame, and the stone flags tremored slightly beneath them. Arielle's heart raced as she caught sight of Deklan, one of the legendary Caelum Bellator dragon riders, slowing his descent into the citadel on his majestic dragon, Gideon. She watched in awe as the creature slowed its wings and gracefully landed in the spacious courtyard of the palazzo.

"I will never tire of seeing that wonderful sight," Tauheed breathed. "The dragons are genuinely one of the Divine's most beautiful creations."

Arielle nodded but turned away so that he could not see her face contorted with frustration. She had expected their leader, Harda, to attend this meeting in person. He was always so hands-on. Why was Harda delegating this task? Pushing aside her annoyance, she couldn't help but be drawn to the majestic sight before her—Gideon, the fierce dragon, basked in the morning sunlight, his multicolored scales shimmering like jewels.

She suppressed her irritation and forced a smile at Tauheed. “They truly are. The Divine says dragons are the perfect mixture of power, grace, and strength. They alone can command the aspects of the ocean and sky. The wild dragons in the Northern Wilderness can stay underwater for up to an hour, and they dine on sea creatures and land animals. Only here have they become more domesticated in their food tastes by uniting with us.”

Arielle gathered her books from the table and tucked them under one arm. She motioned for Tauheed to leave first. “I’ll join you in the garden before the council meeting. I need some time to collect my thoughts.”

Tauheed turned and gently brushed his fingers against Arielle’s cheek, a tender and intimate gesture. His face flushed slightly as he realized the inappropriateness of his actions. “Forgive me, Arielle. I know I am not supposed to...”

Without hesitation, she reached for his hand and held it tightly, staring with love and longing into his eyes. “There is no need for apologies, Tauheed.” She squeezed his fingers and ran a finger along his thumb. “But we cannot act on what is in our hearts. I must be ruled by my head. My loyalty has to be to Amaris,” she said firmly, although her heart ached. “That is why I am here.”

Tauheed nodded with understanding, but she could see the pain behind his smile, the same ache that tugged at her heart.

Arielle knew at that moment they both understood the pressure of their responsibilities. There was a deep unspoken love between them, but because of her loyalty to the Divine, it could never be fully expressed. Arielle's heart was taut with a pain and longing, which was more familiar to her with each passing day.

The Divine Interpreter nodded a goodbye and left the room, closing the ornately carved door softly behind him.

Alone in her chamber, Arielle choked down guilt for the intimate moment they had just shared.

As she did so, the memory of the rasping whisper that had circled around her like a giant serpent rose once more to taunt her. The voice had come from everywhere and nowhere.

Could it really have been Lael? Arielle's head spun as she tried to make sense of everything. Lael—his name was like a harsh wake-up call in her mind. Her body trembled with a mix of fear and confusion. Arielle had been forced to relinquish her memories of Riyon when she'd sacrificed her Divinity for an earthbound form.

Lael had been her mate, her love. Their bond bound them both for eternity—until he had turned his back on the Divine and fallen into darkness. Lael, who was now known as Abaddon—his heavenly name replaced with that of a curse. He was to be known only as Abaddon, the destroyer and overseer of the abyss—the abyss he'd been thrown into after he'd turned his back on the Divine and his brothers and sisters in Riyon.

Arielle shook her head and massaged the knots building in her neck, dismissing the thought. It was impossible. Lael, or Abaddon, she mentally corrected, was gone, never to return. Banished from this world and her old one.

As Arielle looked at her reflection in the mirror, she noticed her bright gray eyes were now stormy with worry. Something had changed within her, and she couldn't shake the unease.

Rolling her shoulders, Arielle forced herself to push aside her doubt. She had a crucial meeting to attend, and she needed to focus on that for now. But as she made her way through the stone corridors to the Jivanam garden, the unpleasantness of her experience lingered on, while she struggled to fathom the meaning and source of the voice she had heard.

Strolling toward the garden, Arielle tilted her head back and gazed up at the sky, warmth kissing her skin. Her heart fluttered with relief as she realized she had a few moments to herself before the dreaded Council of the Clans. With soft footsteps, she descended the worn stone steps that led to the garden's entrance. The sun caressed her, and wispy clouds drifted across the vibrant blue sky. The sweet aroma of jasmine filled Arielle's senses, and she paused to take a deep breath. A kaleidoscope of yellow butterflies danced, their delicate wings fluttering in the gentle breeze.

The air was filled with the soft whir hummingbirds as they darted around the flowers, their colorful feathers a blur. One tiny bird flew up to Arielle's face and hovered, its wings beating so fast, they were almost invisible. "So wonderful to see you here," it chirped. "What a beautiful day!"

Arielle smiled, and her worries slowly slipped away. "Yes, it certainly is."

The hummingbird bobbed its head in excitement. "We can't wait to hear the outcome of the clan meeting."

Arielle reached out and placed her hand on the rough bark of the Jivanam tree, its strength and vitality pushing through, into her fingers. The tree was just a sapling but was already connected to the Vanavashtha through the powerful flow of Ruach. While its parent trees resided in the mystical Forest of Myrkvior, the sapling's siblings had been gifted, one to each of the clans, as a symbol of the Vanavashtha's intimate connection to the Divine.

Arielle sat and breathed in the garden's tranquility. She loved being here in her favorite place. For a moment, she closed her eyes and forgot about the immediate pressure she faced.

The calm that had been restoring her was broken as the air rippled around her, accompanied by the rustle of wings. Opening her eyes, Arielle saw Malakai, her kin Kaluduta, whose celestial form was taking shape in front of her.

The Divine Messenger bowed deeply. The Kaluduta's wings were translucent and gleamed, refracting the light. "Arielle." Malakai appeared to be present yet not; existing on two different planes simultaneously. The messenger's skin pulled every shade of the garden into its texture and appearance. "May the blessings of the Divine be upon you."

"And also upon you, Malakai." Arielle smoothed down her robes and pulled her shoulders back, feeling that familiar sense of loss that always hit her when she was with one of her winged brethren. She was keenly aware of her nakedness—the place where her own wings had once been.

Arielle experienced a small pang of jealousy as Malakai flexed and stretched his feathers. She tried to choke down the resentment and quickly dismissed it from her heart.

Malakai, one of the most senior-ranking Kaluduta, regarded Arielle, head tilted slightly to one side, eyes calculating but kind. "What are your thoughts about the gathering of the clans? Do you think you will break through their misconceptions and current beliefs? There appears to be much dissent."

"Why, yes." Arielle's eyes widened with surprise. "Why shouldn't I?"

"Our concern is that there have been stirrings within the ether—Ruach and Resha, the twin forces that run through everything in this world. The Divine cannot prevent somebody from turning to the darkness. But now it appears that a great adversary from before the Dawning has made himself known and is threatening the equilibrium of Amaris."

Arielle raised a hand to her mouth, and there was that stirring, that memory. She asked, with a neutral tone, "I thought Abaddon had been banished to the depths of Naraka?"

"Yes, the Divine cast that damned creature from the Kaluduta and our heavenly realm of Riyon when he defied Him. Abaddon is now trying to take hold of Amaris through nefarious means."

This must have been the voice I heard. By the Divine, my suspicions are true! But I don't know for sure. Not yet.

Arielle raised her eyebrows in question, willing Malakai to continue. But the Kaluduta answered her with a query and narrowed his eyes: "Have you heard from him?"

Arielle's heart raced as she blurted out, "No! Why would Abaddon talk to me?" She immediately regretted her words, realizing she had answered with what was effectively a lie. Her palms grew sweaty, and her throat tightened as she struggled with her deception.

But who else could that haunting voice belong to? Lael, now Abaddon, who had been her closest confidant and love, before he chose the darkness over the light.

Malakai gave her a long, hard look. “My kin, you are in the unique position of straddling the line between the light and the dark by your very nature. You are descended from the right hand of the Divine, yet now you walk the earth. You must tell us immediately if Abaddon tries to contact you. You were eternally bound when the damned one was known to us as Lael, before falling and making the transition to the servant of the Dark Forces. You had the strongest bond we Kaluduta can have as each other’s chosen. Now, as Abaddon, those whispers are deadly.”

Arielle swallowed hard, but a trace of anger tinged her response. “Yes, at the soonest opportunity. But you must understand, now that I am of the earth, I can no longer hold the memories of my time in Riyon close to me. The longer I spend here in this female form, the greater the distance from my life as a Kaluduta becomes.” She swallowed again and was well aware she sounded a little spoiled. “I am grateful for the Divine’s trust in me to bring the people of Amaris to unity. But it does not ease what some would say is a burden. The loss of my Divinity and the memories of that time are something that cause me pain and blessed relief.”

Malakai smiled with sympathy. “I appreciate your honesty, Arielle. I cannot imagine what carrying the burden of that sacrifice is like.” The messenger flexed those beautiful wings slightly with an unconscious movement, and a look of what Arielle could only identify as pity and relief passed across the divine being’s beautiful features.

Choosing not to acknowledge it, Arielle inclined her head as the Kaluduta shimmered into nonexistence.

Her mind was abuzz with worry. She always had that burden of purpose and duty, but now a shadow of doubt cast its ominous presence upon her. The voice she had heard was physically crawling under her skin. It had stirred something within her, a primal fear that shook her to the core.

She paced back and forth, contemplating her next move. *Should I confide in someone about the voice? Seek guidance from Tauheed?* Arielle's heart contracted. The Lael she knew no longer existed. And now as Abaddon, his whispers were insidious, luring even the most steadfast souls into darkness. *I cannot let myself fall prey to his machinations.*

As she turned toward the edge of the garden, her footsteps crunched on the freshly laid mulch, and Arielle noted that the sun was reaching toward the treetops, casting a warm golden glow over the city of Chinasa. She could hear the gentle rustle of leaves and the hum of insects, but her thoughts were consumed by the dark shadow looming in the distance—a threat that seemed to grow closer with each passing moment.

Chapter 2

Abaddon stood at the edge of the desolate landscape. The dense air, which had a sickly pallor, hung heavy with the acrid smell of sulfur as ashes fluttered down from above like delicate snowflakes. Jagged stones loomed ominously on the horizon, and the twisted, withered skeletons of trees dotted the landscape. Gray fronds of grass swayed mournfully in a breeze that offered no solace or relief. This realm was Naraka.

His gaze solemn, Abaddon turned and stared at the gaping maw that marked the entrance to Sephtis's palace, a dwelling reserved for the damned and the lost. The palace was for those who believed they could find a better life outside the loving embrace and protection of the Divine.

This was a palace of eternal death in a realm ruled by the master of deception. Though Sephtis promised fulfillment, those who fell into his clutches soon realized the bitter truth. Abaddon had been foolish enough to believe the lies, and by the time he'd discovered the true nature of his allegiance, it was too late. While he held a position of power and authority, unlike the unfortunate souls who suffered under Sephtis's rule, he was still bound to the darkness.

Abaddon had chosen to step away from the glory of Riyon and follow Sephtis, believing he would have more freedom. But the decision meant he had stepped away from the divine form he had been given. Now he now dwelled in the world of the eternally damned and tormented. Only when one fully embraced the darkness was it possible to comprehend that there was no way back to the light. It was a path of destruction, and the only way to relieve the pain and experience fleeting pleasure was to carry out Sephtis's bidding and bring him more followers.

And now Abaddon possessed a precious jewel to present to his master—Arielle, a fallen star, once a star the demon had held. As Arielle she was the ultimate prize—the Kaluduta who had plummeted from the heavens to Amaris at the request of the Divine.

There was a tightness in Abaddon's chest, for once Arielle had been his, when they had both walked in the gardens in the clouds. They had been entwined as Kaluduta, together for their immortality. But he had been wooed by the empty promises of his brother Sephtis and had forfeited Arielle's love, breaking her heart. What it would mean to him to possess her once again!

Abaddon could sense Arielle's anger and discontent as he had whispered in her ear and poured water on the seeds of dissatisfaction already sprouting within her soul. Arielle was indeed a prize that would surely earn Sephtis's favor.

Once the most beautiful of all the Kaluduta, Abaddon had shone in glory, some would say brighter than any of his kin. But his desires and ambitions had become twisted by his wish to consume power. The remnants of his previous self still lingered in his features, but he now had a haughty, corrupted beauty.

As Abaddon entered the palace, he raised his gaze to the flickering glow that danced upon the walls, casting sinister shadows. The flames from torches caught his razor-sharp cheekbones, his gleaming alabaster skin, and cold blue eyes hued with an ice-white fire.

Ahead, the throne of Sephtis loomed—a twisted structure forged from metal, wreathed in a halo of everchanging green and gold.

Sephtis embodied everything the Divine was not and would never be. Imprisoned in his own kingdom, he understood the delicate balance of free will and the necessity of darkness as a counterforce to light. Ruach and Resha provided the strength that spanned the universe. Disrupting that balance would tip everything toward chaos, and Abaddon knew this well. Sephtis was aware of it too, for he believed that only by convincing others through lies and manipulation could he hope to surpass the power of the Divine.

Abaddon turned his gaze toward the imposing throne, its form distorted and shrouded in darkness with the halo of emerald shadow. From its depths, Sephtis's chilling voice slid through the room like a viper, accompanied by the ominous glow of his eyes piercing through the gloom.

"Why are you here, Abaddon? To what do I owe this pleasure?"

The lord of the underworld enunciated the words, drawling with sarcasm. Each syllable sounded like nails scratching on metal.

"My Lord Sephtis." Abaddon's words quivered with a mixture of reverence and anticipation. "I've spoken to Arielle, and as you predicted, there exists a glimmer of hope that I can sway her to our cause. And with her by our side, we can conquer Amaris."

A deep, throaty chuckle rebounded from the shadowy throne, where Sephtis's figure and glowing eyes could barely be seen through the darkness emanating from it.

"Ah, just as the Divine foretold." Sephtis spoke with a hint of wicked delight. "One of His cherished children could stray from grace. The light always stands for truth, you see. Being banished and given dominion over darkness, I knew that the chance to seize power from the light would come to me."

A moment of anticipation hung in the air before Sephtis continued: "But there's one obstacle that could stand in our way—free will. We must make sure Arielle becomes distanced from the Divine, so she willingly turns to our side. We must show her the allure and advantages of walking with me. Go, my loyal servant, and see if you can shape destiny."

Chapter 3

Arielle was confused. She entered her room and closed the door, leaning against the cool wood and taking in long breaths. *Why am I overwhelmed?* Her heart hammered in her chest.

She had been running through how to manage this dreaded meeting, and the answer that kept coming to mind was she had to control these clan leaders herself.

This desire to rule Amaris is NOT the way forward!

But she couldn't stop thinking about how she deserved the power. It was niggling away at her, like an itch begging to be scratched.

The voice, which she now believed was Abaddon, had awoken something inside her when they'd last spoken, and she didn't know how to navigate it in her mind. Arielle was caught in a whirlwind over what was right and wrong.

She knew there should be no doubt in her mind that everything he said would take her down the wrong path. But Arielle longed to take control and make her own decisions for the good of this world for which she had sacrificed everything.

She walked to the chair and sat down, rubbing her wrists to ease her tension. Arielle weighed up everything she had given for the greater good of Amaris and its people.

"What have they given you, Arielle? What have you had in return? In their eyes, you are just a servant of the Divine. You have no real power."

She gasped as the icy chill came once again, the rasping whisper audible. The voice wound itself around her like a snake slowly drawing its coils tighter in a death embrace.

"All you are is a device for the Divine to communicate with these people. You gave up your wings! You gave up your life as a Kaluduta. They no longer see you as a Divine Messenger or a special protector. You are trying to guide people who really do not care about you at all, or anything you say."

Arielle recoiled at the words in her head as they penetrated her mind, like an insidious disease. *Why do I see the sense and truth in what he says? Could it be because if it is Abaddon, my former eternal companion, he has some inexplicable power over me now that I'm in human form?*

A column of mist began to take shape in front of her. As Abaddon stepped from the realm of Naraka into human form, Arielle's breath caught in her throat. Abaddon had a haughty, cold air. His presence was imposing. His face was hard yet impossibly beautiful. Her heart tore as memories of their love for each other came flooding back. Arielle clamped down on them. She must remember the day he'd been thrown from Riyon for being a traitor, for turning to the Dark. She must focus on when her heart had splintered into a thousand pieces at not only his betrayal of the Divine, but also of her and their eternal bond.

The aroma of death around him permeated Arielle's nostrils. And with that, Arielle sensed a yearning, greedy need.

"Arielle, I sense your struggle. The pain of rejection, losing control—it plagues your spirit."

She raised her eyebrows in surprise. The demon, relishing their shared connection, continued, "We are kin, you and I, bound by our Divinity and the love we once shared. Cast out from the realm we called home."

Closing the distance between them, Abaddon crouched down in front of her, his proximity chilling Arielle's skin. His long nails brushed her face gently, sending shivers down her spine, and his eyes burned into her. "Oh, my sweet love, I know all too well the ache of being forsaken by the Divine. When he banished you to Amaris, you lost the freedom to soar through the skies, to transcend boundaries. Do not deny the longing that dwells within you."

Arielle's throat bobbed. "The Divine didn't banish me; He requested I come here. To be the Divine's conduit between Himself and the people of Amaris was an honor." But she knew she sounded hollow and lacking in conviction.

Abaddon tilted his head to his side, and his eyes bored into her. She knew he sensed her doubt. "Is that what the Divine said it was? An honor? Do you truly believe it's an honor to be trapped here?'

Arielle tensed her shoulders. "I'm not trapped. I could go back to Riyon if I wanted to."

Abaddon's eyes narrowed with intensity. "Could you really? And be what? A social pariah? The Kaluduta with no wings." His words dripped with sarcasm.

Arielle dropped her gaze, and her conflicted heart wavered. Memories of a distant life tugging at her. Deep down, a part of her yearned for what she had lost, the power and freedom she'd once possessed. Yet she couldn't ignore the nagging voice warning her of the darkness that lurked in Abaddon's enticing words.

The conflicting powers of Ruach and Resha were pulling at her being, spiritually and physically. The twin life forces were coursing through every molecule in the air as she stood on the tightrope between the positive and negative. She tried to clear her mind and again questioned why she felt this way.

"Why are you speaking to me, Abaddon? Is it because your master thinks I can give him what he needs to achieve domination over the people of Amaris? Is it because you think I have forgiven you for what you did to us?"

Abaddon laid his icy lips on her cheek. His touch lit a fire in her that she wanted to quench to a smolder and stoke to an inferno in equal parts. She recognized this was not pure, not from a good place. This was not like her love for Tauheed, whom she couldn't even touch.

Abaddon drew back and stood up. He began to pace the room slowly, deliberately, his hands clasped behind his back. He paused and regarded Arielle, eyes as hard as flint. "I know I brought you grievous hurt, Arielle. That, I regret. But now I wish to make amends. And while I am not the Kaluduta I once was, now I can offer you so much more. You and I"—he stared at her intensely—"can enjoy so much more of each other outside the confines of the Divine."

Arielle gripped the sides of the chair as Abaddon's eyes raked over her, burning with a brightness that she could only call carnal. "I must say, the Divine did one thing right when he brought you to Amaris. Your human form is quite becoming of you. But then, you were always the only one I thought worthy of standing by my side, being bound to me as my eternal mate."

Arielle winced. Was she...embarrassed? Was that what they called this emotion? She tore her eyes away from his and stared at the floor. She could have been completely naked the way his gaze burned with lust.

"However, my desires do not matter here, although for us to be together again would be wonderful, would it not? I am here because Sephtis sees you, Arielle, as the perfect vessel. Do you not see that yourself? Do you not know the truth about your capacity for power?"

Abaddon clenched his fist, his tone carrying a sinister cadence. "That is what makes you the most beautiful of all creatures on Amaris, Arielle. Deep within you, the power of Resha and Ruach wrestle, threatening to tear you apart. Have you ever glimpsed the true might of Resha, the strength that surrendering to darkness can give you? Do you understand the incredible empowerment it holds?"

His eyes gleamed with insatiable greed. "You, dear Arielle, possess the direct bloodline of the Divine. As a Kaluduta, your bond runs deeper than any other creation to the forces governing Amaris. You have that yearning, that hunger for Resha. It courses through your veins."

A wave of exhaustion washed over Arielle, weariness seeping into her bones. The constant struggle, the waiting, and the endless disappointments had taken their toll. How much longer must she persist, following the Divine's guidance, only to face disappointment at every turn? Doubt crept in, eroding her resolve. How tempting it was to seek an alternate path.

Abaddon's smile widened, a gleaming crescent that revealed his delight in the intricate web of persuasion he skillfully weaved. "What do you get, you ask?" A glint of mischief sparkled in his eyes. "Why, my dear Arielle, you shall become the ruler of this world. My master desires your allegiance, and in return, he promises you control. He yearns to claim what the Divine has created."

His words dripped with derision. "The Divine will suffer the greatest anguish seeing his own creation turn away. It will break his heart," he mocked, feigning sympathy. "By causing this rift, Amaris will shift, and you shall be seen as their queen."

Arielle grappled inwardly with the taste of power, the allure that the Divine could never offer. The scars on her shoulders stood as a constant reminder of rejection. The unappreciative council leaders, her ceaseless struggle to mend and satisfy. She was tired, hurt, and angry. This was not how things were supposed to be.

She understood that the power of Resha would grant her unparalleled control. Finally, she could be the mistress of her own destiny. The noise in her head grew deafening as she tried to process everything, her eyes threatening to unleash a flood of tears.

"Abaddon, I need time to think." She mentally backed away from the flickering shadows of doubt that danced in her mind.

Arielle noted the sinister delight glowing in Abaddon's eyes. Was he savoring the turmoil she knew was etched across her face? The energy of her indecision was a taut wire ready to snap.

"As you wish, Arielle. The door stands open, awaiting you," Abaddon conceded, bowing his head. His form melted into the mist, leaving Arielle to stare at the empty air before her, mind swirling with uncertainty.

Chapter 4

Why did Tauheed have the unnerving sense that today would not go as planned? Maybe it was because when he'd opened his eyes this morning, the impending council gathering had filled him with a sickening dread that sent a shiver down to his bones.

Tauheed had sensed a discontent growing in Arielle in recent months, but he could not grasp what it was. Despite the warm smiles she offered to everyone around her, he could see the flicker of longing in Arielle's gaze, a silent testament to the sacrifices she had made for the people of Amaris she now served.

While Arielle's face would often light up with joy as she fulfilled her duties as a chosen one of the Divine, behind her smile, her eyes held a hint of sadness. He could see the strained edge to her demeanor whenever her brothers and sisters visited them in Chinasa, resplendent in their winged glory. There, for a moment, envy and longing were etched on Arielle's features before she composed herself.

Tauheed knew Arielle found dealing with bureaucratic problems tiresome. There were many internal conflicts and cases of bickering between the clans. She may have descended from the heavens, but she was still fallible. And he knew that the more time she spent in human form, the more she developed human foibles and traits.

His mind went back to the dream he had had a few nights before. A vision which saw Arielle as a catalyst that could throw the future of their world into jeopardy.

A dreadful fear was now sparked by that dream. Tauheed had woken in the middle of the night, dripping in sweat. In his vision, Arielle was incandescent with anger and visceral rage. Her hatred for the Divine electrified the surrounding air. An endless expanse of the people of Amaris, chained and bowed at her feet, stretched out before her as far as the eye could see.

Her eyes were devoid of love, a cold emptiness that chilled him to the bone. The Arielle he knew had vanished, replaced by a mere shadow of her former self. Before him lay the barren landscape of his once-beloved country. Behind her lay the lifeless, breathless bodies of the dragons and their riders, all defeated. Worst of all was the sight of her winged brothers, broken and scorched black by fire.

Tauheed had tried to shove down the vision, tried to forget it. But he knew it was a sign. He was full of dread as he recalled what was really a nightmare. Could it be true that Arielle was going to bring about the end of the world that she had sworn to protect and for which she had sacrificed so much?

Despite her knowledge as a Kaluduta being so evident, she seemed small and almost fragile in her human body compared with their majestic forms.

And while Arielle seemed happy enough with the burden the Divine had placed on her, Tauheed knew how much she missed Riyon, her home in the heavens.

Arielle was like a pet bird—one that now wanted to escape the confines of its gilded cage.

As the chief Divine Interpreter, Tauheed studied the planets, stars, and nature. He knew he was blessed to be able to channel the power of Ruach and have a closer relationship with the Divine than most. Was his connection to the power of their world why he sensed that a tipping point was near?

He was sensitive to the pressure of Resha, the darker side of that power, which appeared to be pushing the boundaries of equilibrium more than ever.

Tauheed ran his fingers through his dark hair. The study to enhance the power of a Divine Interpreter meant he had lived five years for every one of a normal person. He rubbed his unlined forehead, noting the smoothness of his skin. *One of the benefits of channeling the power of Ruach*, he told himself ruefully. It all but stopped the usual manifestations of age. Tauheed knew he exuded an air of ancient knowledge and understanding that belied his youthful appearance. He just wished he could trust in it.

Tauheed found himself standing in the grand palace library, a vast and dimly lit room that stretched on endlessly. Towering shelves lined the walls, overflowing with ancient scrolls and texts that held secrets of centuries past. The scent of musty parchment and aged ink filled the air, stories hidden among the pages recounting the era of Divine Interpreters and mysterious prophecies from just after the Creation, when the Kaluduta walked among the clans of Amaris. With a determined stride, Tauheed made his way toward the section dedicated to those revered figures from the beginning of their documented world, his heart fluttering with excitement and anticipation. As he ran his fingers over the spines of the sacred scrolls, their power and knowledge pulsed through his fingertips, beckoning him to unlock their secrets.

Something had been niggling at him, a thought he could not dismiss, and he knew in his heart this was where the answer was. This was what he needed to finalize the Lore Scriptures to ensure that the governance of Amaris would continue in peace.

Unrolling one of the ancient parchments, the Yasha Prophecy, he ran his finger down the page and read under his breath. *"When the great darkness falls, it will come by the hand of one once favored by the Divine. Only those like us, three in kind yet from a distant world, can stand against the endless night. Their blood, their beliefs—akin to ours. They come to save Amaris from the grip of shadow.*

"Through the union of ancient relics, forged from the dawn of time, shall we summon them and reignite the radiant flame. We will reclaim the light lost to darkness."

Tauheed's eyes traced the symbols scrawled across the parchment as he continued to read aloud: *"To bind the evil, we must craft a prison it cannot fathom—woven from blood unlike our own, and the lifeblood of Amaris. Only then will balance be restored."*

Tauheed's heart tightened with a potent mix of fear and uncertainty. Was it possible that Arielle, the woman he loved, could be the darkness, the grip of shadow, spoken of in the prophecy? She was favored by the Divine. Arielle was a part of Amaris, yet she seemed distant and disconnected from it. Could it truly be her?

Tauheed clenched his jaw. It wasn't just about deciphering the prophecy. His love for Arielle was like the sweetest blessing and the most horrendous curse. She was forbidden to love one of his kind, and he could not demonstrate the depth of his affection for her because of it.

It made his emotions for her all the more tumultuous, an all-consuming force because it could not be realized. At times, it overwhelmed him, like his heart would be ripped apart.

The Divine's rules and expectations were clear: Arielle had been chosen to be the custodian of Amaris, and her duty lay in dedicating herself fully to the clans and their people. There was no space for them to be together, no moments of stolen time to bask in their tenderness. Their love was a constant battle against fate and duty, but they clung to each other fiercely, hoping that their bond would withstand any obstacle thrown their way.

Tauheed's internal battle continued as he tried to make sense of the pieces of information he had gathered. He had always known Arielle to be a compassionate and selfless person, dedicating her life to serving the clans and protecting Amaris. But she had been so lost in her own thoughts lately, and the barriers growing between them were like walls of impenetrable granite. Tauheed couldn't help but wonder if she was keeping something from him.

He remembered one particular night as they strolled through the lush gardens, their fingers entwined, she'd abruptly halted and faced him. Tears had welled in her eyes as she'd confessed that she couldn't keep up the façade of happiness any longer. Tauheed had reached out to comfort her, but she'd quickly regained her composure and brushed it off as mere exhaustion from her demanding duties.

But now, with the possibility of her being connected to the darkness looming over their world, that moment stood out like a red flag. Tauheed shook his head again, refusing to believe that there was any truth to these suspicions.

The Divine Interpreter rolled up the parchment and pushed it back into bookshelves. He would have to put these thoughts to the back of his mind for now. There were more pressing things of which he needed to attend.

Chapter 5

Mariam, the powerful queen of the Adira, glided through her underwater palace with a furrowed brow. She swam past shimmering schools of fish and intricate coral structures, her mind consumed by troubling thoughts. For three consecutive nights, she had been plagued by the same nightmare—the sky was blackened by smoke, distant fires raged, and the ground was littered with death and destruction. In her dream, some unseen force had taken hold of the earth itself, paralyzing everything in its grasp. And each night, it only grew stronger.

The screams of dragons, soldiers, and innocents alike filled her ears as they fought against mysterious creatures from the dark. Amaris was being destroyed, and it seemed as if nothing could stop it. But Mariam couldn't figure out from where this darkness was coming.

She knew that there was only one creature who might help her understand the nightmare: Theodore. He had been born into the world when everything was created and had a wealth of knowledge. Mariam was intimidated at the thought of encountering him, knowing it would drain her of energy, but her concern outweighed her fear of exhaustion.

As her body glided effortlessly through the crystal-clear water, Mariam's mind drifted to Kaimana, her trusted captain who led the Adiran Army. Using the telepathic powers only the Adira possessed, she summoned him to meet her as she continued on her way to the underwater gardens.

Mariam nodded to the schools of fish that danced around her in greeting. They put on a mesmerizing display of colors, their scales reflecting every color of the spectrum under the gentle rays of sunlight filtering through the surface. It was a sight like no other, and Mariam couldn't help but marvel. She was awestruck by the beauty of this aquatic paradise sculpted by nature itself.

She came to a stop by one of the vibrant coral formations the garden was known for, each intricately shaped over centuries, and they too greeted her with their welcoming embrace. Kaimana swam into view, his fins cutting through the underwater current. He bowed, and Mariam smiled as he spoke with her, mind to mind: *Your Majesty, you called for me. How can I help?*

The queen's hair swirled around her like a turquoise halo as she smiled at the lead guard. *Kaimana, I need to see Theodore. But you know that meeting him may mean I will have to leave Maren for some time depending on the outcome of the encounter. I fear the world of those who walk on land is soon to bring about the downfall of our peaceful kingdom below the ocean.*

He grimaced at her in sympathy and held out an upturned palm in salute. *Yes, Your Majesty. I will care for Maren and any of the city's needs while you're away.*

Mariam smiled gratefully. *I know this journey will be difficult, but I have been plagued by terrible dreams of death and destruction. The Divine has not shown me the right path to follow if these terrible things happen. But I think that Theodore might give us some answers. I believe Amaris is facing a danger unlike anything we've ever seen before.*

I understand, Your Majesty. Kaimana bowed deeply. *I wish you safety and strength.*

Chapter 6

As Mariam descended into the depths of the ocean, the burden of her responsibilities as queen of the Adira pressed down on her. She had to find answers about the mysterious dreams plaguing her.

The underwater forest was an otherworldly sight, with coral trees reaching up toward the surface and strange glowing creatures swimming among them. But as she swam deeper, the light grew dim and Mariam's apprehension grew stronger. In this part of the ocean, even she sensed the unease.

Her shimmering mertail guided her through the thick branches until she reached Theodore's home—a complex of massive boulders intricately carved by centuries of weathering. The colors and textures were unlike anything else in the ocean, a testament to the power and age of this deep realm.

Mariam stopped in front of the entrance to Theodore's cavern, a giant hexagonal stone embedded in the ocean floor. Its surface was adorned with ancient symbols and markings from the old language of the Adira.

In the early years after the Dawning, her kind would often communicate with Theodore and his brethren, sea creatures which were said to possess knowledge of the oceans given to them by the

Divine Himself. They were seen as truth tellers, oracles to the Adira. But the caveat was that to commune with his kind was painful and draining, due to their powerful psychic abilities.

As time wore on, the Adira's connection with Theodore and his kind waned as her society progressed. Many believed there was no need to seek advice from mystics, especially when it was such a difficult process. Eventually the giant octopi sank into obscurity, and their existence became nothing more than a story to tell merchildren to keep them well behaved. Mermothers would teach the cautionary tale of the creature that could melt into your mind and discover if you were telling a lie. Only a privileged few in the royal house knew that Theodore still existed.

Steeling herself for what lay ahead, she approached the touchstone and prepared to enter Theodore's chamber. Scepter in hand, Mariam brought it down firmly in front of her on the stone. *Theodore, you of the ancient ones, the ones who were here at the beginning, Mariam, queen of the Adira, wishes to ask you a question.*

There was a deep rumbling sound in the distance, and the ocean floor shuddered. Mariam tensed her body to stop herself from falling.

From the mouth of the cavern, immense clouds of dust charged through eddies and undercurrents in the water. Mini whirlpools pushed around Mariam as she stood firm. Out of the cavern, a gigantic octopus, its tentacles hundreds of feet long, its head akin to the size of a cliff face, lumbered to a stop in front of the queen.

Theodore's huge golden eyes surveyed Mariam balefully as he spoke mind to mind: *Who summons Theodore? The queen of the*

Adira? Is that you? It has been many years since one of the ocean people sought me. What is your question?

Mariam winced as Theodore's mind probed her own. She reached for his consciousness—the octopus was metaphorically wrapping his tentacles around the different facets of her brain, wiggling into parts of her mind and delving and diving to connect with her. It was overwhelming and exhausting.

Theodore, you are in my mind and can see the horrific dreams I have been experiencing. What do they mean? What does it mean for Amaris?

Theodore snaked another of his eight arms toward her. He beckoned her to move closer with the tip of his tentacle. *Queen of the Adira, step forward and bond with me, and I will tell you what these terrible dreams are, these nightmares that plague you, how they will forecast your destiny.*

Mariam swam gently forward. She took a deep breath, and in a whirl of bubbles, she knelt and pressed her forehead into the ocean bed. Theodore's tentacle wound around her, a gigantic sucker touching her back.

Mariam's muscles clenched with fear and exhaustion. Her mind was flooded with terrifying images from her nightmares, causing her eyes to squeeze shut. Every ounce of energy was being drained from her body as Theodore delved into her essence, exploring the very depths of her being. It was a surreal and unsettling experience, one that lasted only seconds before Theodore withdrew his grasp. A sense of relief washed over Mariam as she gasped for air. Her body was in shock, as though she had just survived a near-death encounter.

Queen Mariam, your dreams are indeed troubling. And they are also a prophecy. What you foresee is a great evil that is going to plunge Amaris into war. A war that could see your world enslaved forever. It will affect those who walk on the earth and traverse the air. Your people, the Adira, are also vulnerable.

Mariam gasped. *But how can this be? How could the Divine let this happen to us?*

Theodore let out a cloud of bubbles from the slits under his eyes. *The Divine has given free will to all. And the great evil born to allow free will has found its way into your world. It wishes to bring about the downfall of the people of Amaris. If this comes to pass, your world will plunge into a darkness that will extend the dark dominion, Naraka, into your world and others.*

Fear clutched Mariam's heart. *How do we stop it? There must be a way.*

Theodore continued: *The Divine always leaves a pathway to the light for those in the darkness. You must find Tauheed, who will play an important part in the destiny of Amaris. Tauheed will bring three beings, the Yasha, from another world to save Amaris. However, the way for them to enter our world is not yet in existence.*

Mariam frowned. *How is Tauheed meant to help save us? And how are these beings, the Yasha, supposed to even come to Amaris if there is no way through from their realm?*

Theodore moved slowly away, back into the recesses of his gigantic cavern. *Mariam, the Divine has already put the power to do this at your disposal: Ruach.*

The octopus then moved another of his tentacles forward. Coiled within it was a piece of rock that glistened and shimmered. Theodore extended his tentacle and gently placed the glowing rock in front of Mariam on the ocean floor. *This is the most ancient of precious stones, the Jewel of Aikyam. It was born at the very core of Amaris. It has molecules and properties bound within it from other worlds created by the Divine. I was given the rock for safekeeping; such is its power.*

This precious stone will enable you to create the portal for the Yasha, the beings from the other realm, to transcend from their world to Amaris. For them to be summoned, the Jewel of Aikyam must be bound by the four elements of Amaris—earth, water, air and fire.

Tauheed is the key to creating the gate. The Jewel of Aikyam will open the lock to the portal you seek. It will enable energy powerful enough to open the gate from Amaris to their reality.

Theodore gave a rumbling sigh, inclined his head, and slithered back into the darkness of the cavern. As the turbulent waters settled, that profound sense of fear that had gripped Mariam's heart tightened. She knew that the future of her world now hung in the balance.

Chapter 7

Harda, the leader of the Caelum Bellator clan, sat in a reflective state, his sword resting on his lap, the metal glinting in the sunlight. He gently ran a cloth over the blade, polishing it to perfection, while casually leaning against a single dragon claw as its owner, Ananpal, dozed in the warm afternoon light.

Harda turned and gazed lovingly at the magnificent creature before him. Ananpal's scales were a dazzling display reflecting hues of amber and copper, a mesmerizing dance of colors. The beast exuded an aura of strength and grace, his powerful muscles rippling beneath a shimmering exterior. Harda smiled with affection. It was a sight to behold, and he thanked the Divine that they had bonded at the Choosing Ceremony all those years ago. The dragons were tense with anticipation, and their movements and actions signaled a sense of impending danger. Ananpal and his kin had been relentlessly hunting, sharpening their skills, and honing their battle tactics. Too many times, the air above the Koimeterion was thick with the scent of blood and fire as clashes between dragons became more frequent, each one of their bouts a fierce display of strength and dominance.

The dragons' agitation was having repercussions for their riders, such was their mental bond. Many were complaining of an inability to sleep.

Harda was also aware of the current frailty of the relationship between clans. As the people of Amaris grew in number, so did the need for resources. But they were not distributed evenly because of geography and the abilities the Divine gave to each clan.

It did not always come naturally to the different people of Amaris to share or be fair. But there had always been a mutual understanding between them.

The unrest he had been seeing among the dragons had been enough for him to send an envoy to the Council of the Clans. He knew they would see it as a snub, but his gut said that he should stay in Paracletes.

Harda was used to peace. There had been no battles between the clans for the past hundred years. The dragon riders lived longer than most—sustained by the life cycles of the beasts they rode.

He just couldn't shake off the sensation that something was coming, something big and dangerous. And he knew that when the dragons were on edge, it was time to be on high alert. But for what, he could not yet say. His mind was filled with different scenarios, each more treacherous than the last. But one thing was for sure: He and the Caelum Bellator would be ready for whatever came their way.

With a smooth, fluid motion learned from years of balancing in the saddle, Harda stood up from the ground and sheathed his sword. He gently nudged Ananpal with his foot, rousing the dragon from his slumber. The majestic creature's golden eyes snapped open, immediately scanning their surroundings with keen awareness before relaxing at the sight of his rider.

With a rumbling yawn, Ananpal unfurled his massive wings and shook off any remaining traces of sleep. As the dragon stretched and snapped his jaws shut, Harda affectionately laid a hand on the creature's giant cheek. The bond between them was strong, forged through countless battles and adventures together.

"How do you see the future of the clans of Amaris? Can we stay unified? Or is the desire for our kind to overpower each other just too much? Do you think we can ever live together in peace?"

The magnificent dragon turned his head, his scales glistening like molten gold. Ananpal's eyes, heavy-lidded, met Harda's gaze. He spoke telepathically to the dragon rider, filled with ancient wisdom: *Only time will reveal the true consequences. The Divine's gift of free will holds both good and grave dangers.*

Harda smiled at the beast, who had been part of his life since Harda was just twelve years old. He would never forget when they found each other and knitted themselves together in their consciousnesses forever. He was bound to everything Ananpal went through—his happiness, pain, sorrow, and love.

The dragon turned his mighty head and absentmindedly scratched his side flank with his muzzle. Harda walked toward the edge of the ridge, looking out over the valley. Used to great heights while flying, he was unfazed standing at the cliff's edge, surveying the dragon riders' citadel, Paracletes, and the lake of the Koimeterion at the center of the valley as it shimmered, cows grazing by its shore.

The ancient crater, the remnants of the volcano that had birthed Amaris, was home to the dragon riders. Around its steep sides were hundreds of caves just like his own. As Harda gazed upward, dragons wheeled on the air currents, enjoying the afternoon sunshine, and faint laughter came from dens near his own.

Ananpal gave a deep croon, and the dragon rider leader relished the intense rush of love that flooded through him.

Lexi and Axelia are approaching, the beast said in Harda's mind, and he stretched his mighty wings to their full capacity.

Shielding his eyes, Harda could see on the horizon the silhouette of a dragon heading toward them.

A magnificent silver-scaled beast swooped in with a graceful yet powerful glide to land on the edge of the rugged cliff. Her wings beat against the air, creating a low hum that thrummed through the valley. With a mighty harrumph, Axelia greeted Ananpal and lowered her head.

Meanwhile, Lexi removed her helmet and let out a sigh of relief as she shook out her long blond hair. Harda smiled at the sight of her in her leather flying gear, complete with various pockets that hid an arsenal of knives strapped to her body.

Harda sneaked a glance to Ananpal, thinking, *She really is very beautiful.*

Ananpal gave a low chuckle in Harda's mind. *Not as beautiful as her dragon.*

Harda stifled a laugh. *Well, you chose well for me then, my friend.*

With practiced ease, Lexi swung one leg over Axelia's back and gracefully dismounted in a fluid movement.

"Harda!" Lexi exclaimed, throwing her arms around him in a long embrace. He wrapped his arms around her gently in return, the heat from her body warming him. Harda closed his eyes and breathed in Lexi's familiar scent, a mix of smoke and spice, which comforted him.

As the two dragons intertwined their necks in a loving greeting, Harda leaned in and kissed Lexi deeply, her lips soft and warm against his. She melted into the kiss, and Harda was filled with a surge of love for his companion.

He pulled away and looked into her eyes with concern. "How has the day taken you?" he asked, his deep voice filled with genuine worry.

"The reconnaissance mission revealed what we have feared: Even more agitation and unrest among the dragon and their hunt is going farther afield." She grimaced. "They are now heading into Taura lands. Thank the Divine their kingdom is within the mountain, or their leader, Tamanka, would have something to say about it. I think given the agitation the dragons are experiencing, we should go to the Council of the Clans. We need to see if others have the same opinions we do."

Harda nodded. "The heavens have been saying as much as well. The recent eclipse can only be nature's way of preparing us. I had word from the Vanavasin while you were away. They say there are the rumblings of discontent in the forest. The Vanavashtha trees sense a shift in the balance of Ruach and Resha."

Lexi pursed her lips. "I never thought we would see that old teaching from the time of the Dawning come to pass in our lifetime. But then, every dragon leader who has passed down the shard from the very first dragon eggshell hatched on Amaris probably thought the same. Do you think it will be us who see what part the fragment has to play in protecting Amaris from an almighty evil?"

Harda ran his fingers through his coal dark hair, narrowing his eyes. "There is no doubt the powers of Ruach and Resha are being pulled out of alignment. If the Vanavasin are saying the dragon's egg shard must be used, then that is concerning indeed. It fits with the prophecy."

He looked out over the ridge as he recited the script every rider learned by heart before they were five years old: *"When the moon disappears in the darkness, the shell of the very first dragon egg will provide solace and saving, along with that from the dawn of the world and the blood of those from another."*

It had never really made sense to him.

He moved toward Lexi again and traced a finger down the side of her cheek, smiling at her with love. "You are by far the bravest and cleverest of all dragon riders, my beautiful one. That is why Ananpal and I fought so hard to be with you and Axelia. If anyone can fathom the meaning of the prophecy, you can."

Behind them, their mighty dragons were intertwined, nuzzling each other with affection and care. The vibrant colors of Ananpal's and Axelia's scales glistened in the sun, blending together as their wings overlapped, and the sound of their deep purrs was a soothing melody.

The tranquility of the moment was splintered by a deafening clap of thunder that shook the peaceful surroundings, causing both to jump in surprise. As Harda looked down at the lake of the Koimeterion, his eyes widened in awe as the calm surface of the lake transformed before them. As it began to churn and swirl, it was evident that a powerful force was pulling at its depths. The water bubbled and frothed with an intensity that could only be the result of Ruach.

Lexi's brow furrowed in concern, her features twisted with worry. "It must be something major if Queen Mariam is using her powers to enter the Koimeterion from the ocean."

Harda nodded solemnly, mirroring her apprehension. "I think we need to go and see what this is all about."

Chapter 8

Mariam emerged from the watery depths of the lake of the Koimeterion astride a magnificent giant fish in a cascade of spouting water. With a graceful somersault, the queen of the ocean people plunged into the clear aquamarine water and powered toward the shore.

By the time Axelia and Ananpal had descended gracefully to the shoreline of the lake, the queen of the Adira was wading out of the water. Shaking droplets from her hair, she had dried herself in moments, a remarkable ability the ocean people possessed when transitioning from the water to land. Harda suppressed a smile before turning to Lexi. “She always knows how to make an entrance.”

The gentle lull of the waves caressed the air. Harda couldn’t help but be captivated by the queen’s presence. There was an aura of ancient wisdom and power that emanated from her. As Mariam extended her hand palm up in a friendly gesture of respect, a sense of connection and reverence washed over him.

“To what do we owe the honor of your visit?” Lexi inquired as Harda took Mariam’s hand and pressed his palm on hers.

"Ah, Queen Mariam, your presence always sparks intrigue and wonder among us air dwellers. We are truly honored to have you grace us with your presence."

Mariam glanced between them. As she spoke, her melodic voice carrying a soothing tone that he had no doubt was harmonized with the rhythm of the ocean. "The honor is mine, young dragon riders. It is always good to venture from the depths of the ocean," the queen said, her voice carrying a hint of playfulness. "It never hurts to see what the land dwellers are up to."

Harda laughed, raising an eyebrow. "Well, it's not entirely accurate to call us mere land dwellers."

"Indeed!" Mariam flashed her pointed teeth at him. "While you are the rulers of the air, my kin and I are the rulers of the deep."

As the queen took a step back, her smile faded. She knitted her eyebrows together and her lips became a thin line. "However, I wish I could say that this visit was simply to extend my good wishes and respect. Alas, I have come because—"

"So you know it's there too," Harda interjected, his stomach knotted.

"Yes, if you are referring to the shift in the balance. You have also sensed the change in power?" Mariam sighed as the dragon riders nodded. "Then, although I had my suspicions, you have now confirmed what Theodore told me. You and your dragons know the scales have shifted; the life force of Amaris has become unsteady."

Harda grimaced as Mariam continued, "Then you also know we are all facing grave danger."

"If Theodore has spoken, then we have reason to worry." Lexi's face was grim.

Mariam gazed at the dragons, who were peacefully drinking from the lake. "The only solace we have is that I have been informed we possess the ability to stop this great evil, a malevolent power that predates the creation of Amaris itself. An evil that will strike at the very heart of our world, corrupting and using a vessel of the Divine."

Lexi gasped, and Mariam turned her gaze toward them both. "The identity of this vessel has not yet been revealed to me. However, I know of your reverence for prophecies, and I believe you have your own prophecy concerning this matter. I believe that we must unite the sacred objects from the people on Amaris, objects that represent the elements of our world: earth, air, water, and fire. This has been confirmed as the key to opening the path to save our world."

"Yes, we have our own version of the Yasha Prophecy," Lexi exclaimed, her eyes wide. "I never imagined that the nursery rhyme we learned as children would actually come true. We possess the sacred shard of the dragon egg. That would be our contribution as representative of the essence of air, with the dragon's command of it. But why not fire?" Her eyebrows were raised in a question.

"Some might think yours would be fire. But your people do not command fire—your dragons have the power to use it. However, you, as the Caelum Bellator, command the air."

Mariam reached into her clothing and drew out the Jewel of Aikyam; its depths seemed to swirl with the power of the ocean.

Harda took a step forward and narrowed his eyes as he looked at the object in the queen's palm. The stone glittered in the light, its center pulsing with sapphire blue. "I thought the jewel was merely a legend. It's something I never believed existed."

Mariam smiled. "This precious stone was present at the very birth of our world—my realm, where the jewel comes from, where I command the oceans."

Lexi's face lit up with recognition. "We have stories about the jewel in our teachings. But how do we accomplish such a task?"

Mariam's gaze turned toward the distant horizon. "One of us must make their way to Chinasa, as swiftly as possible. There, in the heart of the city, resides the one person who can aid us. And I think we may also find the element of earth that we seek." Her voice was laced with a sense of urgency.

Harda flexed his shoulders and exchanged a worried glance with Lexi. His determination was mirrored in her eyes, but fear also lurked there. He knew that time was of the essence, and they could not afford to waste a moment.

Chapter 9

Harda, Lexi, and Mariam sat up long into the night in deep discussion. Their conversation was fraught with tension, a mixture of hope and doubt that kept them entangled in one another's words. The queen of the Adira filled them in on everything Theodore had said.

She talked about the Yasha, the fabled saviors from another world, and how they would all have a part to play, a crucial role in saving Amaris.

When Mariam finally eased her stiff body out of the chair, the room was dark except for the faint glow of the moonlight shining through the entrance to the dragon's cave, highlighting Harda's and Lexi's strained expressions.

The candle had burned down to a guttering wick on the table, licking the edges of their empty plates with its watery light. It cast shadows on their faces as they contemplated their next move. The task ahead seemed almost insurmountable.

Lexi sighed, her fingers tracing the edge of the table, in deep thought. "We have to find the Yasha. But how can we reach across worlds? Can Tauheed really be a key? And what of Arielle? Where does she feature in all of this? She is the conduit of the Divine. Maybe she knows something?"

"The Divine has given us the tools to bridge the worlds," Harda replied, his lips set in a grim line. "Mariam, can you go to Chinasa? And Lexi and I must go to the Vanavasin. It can only be there, where the Vanavashtha trees first grew at the dawning of the world, that the gate can be formed. It has to be. The power of Ruach is stronger there than anywhere."

Mariam nodded. "I believe all will become clear when I get to Chinasa. But for now, we have to trust that we are being called to do this for a reason. We leave at first light. But now, let's get some sleep. We will need it."

Chapter 10

Harda stood next to Lexi on the high ridge of Paracletes, his eyes fixed on the dawning light. The sun kissed the snowcapped mountaintops, its rays transforming them into a fiery red. Axelia and Ananpal's breath curled in the cool morning air.

"It's hard to fathom," Lexi murmured, her voice tinged with both awe and apprehension. "To see such tranquility when we know that an unimaginable evil looms over us."

Harda gazed into the distance. His eyes narrowed. *How will the council view me sending my lieutenant, Deklan?* No doubt it would be seen as a slight by some of the other leaders. He had been planning to go to Chinasa himself in a few days. But now, with the weight of the impending threat pressing upon them all, he had to move forward with the strategy they had brought into play to safeguard Amaris. Too much hung in the balance.

Harda turned to the two women, who cradled bowls of steaming coffee. "Our world is truly magnificent. We have been granted diverse lands, peoples, and an environment that supports us. We must fight to protect it, to prevent division from tearing us apart."

Mariam nodded in agreement. "Beneath our skin, we share the same essence. It is this unity that must guide us forward—to protect the blessings we have been given, the very source of our existence. Amaris and one another."

Lexi smiled. "Did you know that eggs, despite their different outer appearances and colored shells, are all the same on the inside before they develop into the creature that hatches from them? Perhaps there lies a lesson in that."

Mariam flashed a small smile. "Our prophecies, as well as yours, indicate that we hold the key to overcoming this imminent evil. We must unite the people of Amaris."

Harda acknowledged the importance of Mariam's words. "We must also confer with Tauheed. Theodore told you we must get to him as soon as we can. He needs to be informed of his integral role in the events to come."

Mariam gave a resolute nod of her head. "I shall approach Tauheed and then bring him to the Vanavasin."

Harda chuckled softly. "Ah, the Clan Council. But you, Mariam, were not invited because your people are not of the land. I wonder, how will they take your appearance? Take no offense. Your domain beneath the waves is vast and presents enough challenges without involving yourself in our affairs. Nevertheless, we share a common origin. When the fate of the entire world is at stake, including the domain of the ocean, you hold a vested interest in the outcome."

Mariam's lips quirked. "Who's to say I will even attend the meeting itself? I have my spies! I will watch and wait. My main priority is Tauheed."

The queen approached the edge of the cliff. She gently placed her hand on Ananpal's side, and the mighty dragon responded with a resonant croon. "Such magnificent beasts," she whispered, her fingers gliding over the dragon's warm velvety scales. "It always astounds me how their strength and power coexist with such tenderness. Their appearance is deceiving, as if they were crafted from unyielding steel, impenetrable and cold. But when you touch them, when you truly know them, you realize their core is loyal, loving, and warm. Beneath their scales lies a love that rivals that of any creature in both our worlds."

"Appearances can be deceptive, my friend." Harda's chest lifted, chin held high. "We must never judge solely by what meets the eye. I too am grateful for the bond I share with Ananpal. The Divine has blessed me with his connection, and it fills me with gratitude every day."

His fingers tapped the sword at his side. "So, it is decided. You will embark on the journey to Chinasa, to seek Tauheed's counsel. Meanwhile, we will venture to the Vanavasin to discover if they hold any wisdom on uniting these sacred objects with the dragon's egg shard, all while trying to keep our nemesis, whoever they may be, oblivious to our intentions."

Facing one another, they showed their resolve with stacked palms. Harda's gaze shifted from one woman to the other, jaw set. "For the future of Amaris. It now rests in our hands."

Mariam and Lexi mirrored his sentiment, each word delivered with unshakable clarity and a sense of determination that left no room for doubt. "For the future of our people." The words reflected the commitment that bound their fates together, to safeguard Amaris from the encroaching darkness.

Chapter 11

Tauheed made a decision. After poring over the scrolls, it was time to confront his concerns head-on.

He and Arielle had an intimate connection. His heart yearned for her when they were apart. It jumped in her presence, and she filled his thoughts whenever he wasn't working. Even when he was.

They had cultivated a meaningful, rare, and beautiful relationship, even though they could not physically be together. But Tauheed had learned to be content with any fleeting touch. Arielle could send energy and light through his whole being by looking at him.

Tauheed had met her when he was a novice Divine Interpreter. Passionate about his faith and commitment to the Divine, he was initially in awe of Arielle. But when he was given the role of being the conduit between herself and the clans of Amaris, it meant they could break through any awkwardness and become close.

Their relationship quickly became more than just mentor and mentee. It became something deeper. Tauheed prayed daily that when she had achieved her purpose, the Divine would give His blessing for them to be together.

Tauheed knew Arielle found dealing with bureaucratic problems tiresome. There were many internal conflicts and cases of bickering between the clans. She may have descended from the heavens, but she was still fallible. And he knew that the more time she spent in human form, the more she developed human foibles and traits.

His mind went back to the dream he had had a few nights before, a vision that saw Arielle as a catalyst that could throw the future of their world into jeopardy.

He recalled the three beings who were indistinct, standing shoulder to shoulder with the people of Amaris, taking on the threat of the all-consuming dark power that was bent on holding their world in a viselike grip.

A dreadful fear was now sparked by that dream. Tauheed had woken in the middle of the night, dripping in sweat. In his vision, Arielle was incandescent with anger and visceral rage. Her hatred for the Divine electrified the surrounding air, crackling through every molecule of the atmosphere. An endless expanse of the people of Amaris, chained and bowed at her feet, stretched out before her as far as the eye could see.

Tauheed had tried to shove down the vision, tried to forget it. How could this be true? She had once been a Kaluduta, a direct descendant of the Divine. Her blood was pure, her heart weighed with truth and light. But he knew in his gut it was a sign. Tauheed's heart contracted at the recollection of the nightmare. Could it really be true that she was going to bring about the end of the world?

What were these flashes of unhappiness he had seen in Arielle of late? He knew he had to confront her. Was Arielle truly destined to bring about the world's end, despite her unwavering commitment and sacrifices to protect it? He had to know, and he had to see her.

Tauheed found Arielle in the garden, seated on the bench beneath the Jivanam tree, lost in her thoughts. Anxiety was etched on her face.

"What's troubling you? I sense a heaviness in your heart. It's the first time I've seen you despondent. Please, Arielle, confide in me."

She looked up, her eyes reflecting pain. "You know I hold deep love and respect for you, Tauheed. But there are things you can never understand." Her words carried a hint of frustration.

"You can never understand because you haven't given up what I had to sacrifice for the sake of our people. I gave up my Divinity. And what has the Divine given me in return? Nothing. He brought me to this world, to your world. And what do I have? Ungrateful people who constantly bicker. They don't care for me or appreciate my sacrifices. I am more than they can ever be. The blood of the Kaluduta still flows within me, even though I am in the form I am now."

Tauheed looked at her, his heart filled with concern and worry. "Where is all this coming from? I thought you loved our people. I thought you loved being here with us. We respect and appreciate everything you've done for us. You've brought us closer to the Divine."

"Do you truly understand, Tauheed?" Arielle rose to her feet, her words laced with bitterness. "Because I don't think you do. And I don't think you ever will. You can't see what I've given up because you're not me."

Tears welled up in her eyes, and she continued, anguish ringing through every word. "And your people, to my mind, are ungrateful.

They know nothing. The clans of Amaris are their own worst enemies. They make mistakes, and they make poor choices. I can see them making the right decisions only if I forced them to."

Arielle's eyes blazed with intensity, and Tauheed was horrified by her words. "Forced? Is that the path you advocate? Coercing others against their will? Suffering and manipulation are not the foundations of true love."

"Tauheed." Arielle sighed, her face filled with an unfamiliar pity. "When will you realize that true power comes from having control?"

Tauheed shook his head in disbelief. "I don't believe that's true. I don't believe we should pursue power at the expense of others. And I certainly don't believe it will bring you the happiness you seek."

Fear gripped Tauheed's heart, and he knew he had to share his doubts. He mustered the courage to speak, hands trembling. "I sought out the ancient texts, Arielle, and they speak of a being that will bring about the downfall of Amaris."

He saw an almost imperceptible shift in her gaze. *Does she have an inkling it might be her?*

"Not only that, the records advise of those from another world who will be summoned to help Amaris in its bid to evade being caught in the thrall of this creature—the Yasha Prophecy."

Arielle narrowed her eyes with suspicion. "What do you mean? I know of no such prophecy, and I am sure the Divine would have shared it with me."

When Tauheed spoke, he was barely audible, and he lowered his eyes, tracing the patterns on the wooden floor. His words caught in his throat. "I've had a vision, and it fills me with dread, Arielle. I want to believe it's baseless, but what you're saying makes me question it. Do you want to make the people of Amaris suffer just to gain power that you think was taken away from you unjustly? Please, Arielle, tell me it's not true."

Her eyes shone like flint, and she all but curled her lip into a snarl, akin to a trapped animal. "Tauheed, this conversation is over," Arielle declared, her hand slicing through the air, shutting him down with finality. "You and I, our relationship...well, now I don't know what it is. You clearly don't trust me."

There was a flicker of reproach and hurt in her eyes, as well as confusion. With a dismissive wave, she added, "I must prepare for the upcoming Clan Council meeting. I will see you there." She glared at Tauheed with a mixture of defiance and sadness.

He opened his mouth to speak, but the words died on his lips as she turned in a whirl of indignation and briskly walked back toward the stone archway leading into the palace.

Tauheed stood there, his heart aching with sorrow. *Did we just pass the point of no return?* There was no doubt their paths were diverging irreversibly, and he was powerless to stop it.

Chapter 12

The Council of the Clans of Amaris had assembled in the grandeur of the Great Hall in the Shekinah capital of Chinasa. The Great Hall had an aura of ancient wisdom, its walls adorned with intricate tapestries depicting the history of the land. Sunlight streamed through stained-glass windows, casting vibrant hues across the marble floors. The air hummed with anticipation as representatives from each clan took their places.

Arielle stepped cautiously into the grand hall, her eyes darting around the gathered crowd. Her heart was in turmoil, but she knew she had to push her emotions aside and focus on the task at hand. As she made her way through the sea of faces, her own was a mask of composure—a nod here, a smile there. But her heart hammered in her chest like a caged bird.

Arielle kept her gaze neutral.

The Vanavasin, with their ethereal grace and connection to nature, stood tall, their eyes gleaming with a profound understanding of the world around them. The Taura, stalwart and rugged, their weathered features gave evidence to the hardships they had endured in the mountains and their love for battle. The Elutheros emanated an air of rebellion with a languid air of self-assurance. The Rehmat stood serene and wise, their eyes shimmering with deep knowledge. And finally, the Hayim, steadfast, radiated a sense of unity and harmony.

Arielle's gaze settled on Deklan, the lieutenant dragon rider leaning casually against the ornate wall. A flicker of annoyance tugged at her thoughts. The Caelum Bellator, with their majestic beasts and unflappable confidence, often seemed to hold themselves above others. The aloofness they exhibited grated on Arielle's nerves, as if they believed their status granted them superiority. A pang of indignation, a desire to humble them and remind them of their place gripped her. How different would they be without their wings, without the very creatures that elevated them above the rest?

She was almost surprised she had never noticed this characteristic in them before. Yet another sign of the selfishness of the Amarisian people. Seeing that sense of self-importance on display, she couldn't deny the irritation it caused her now.

"You see their flaws, Arielle. Why do you still wish to champion them?" There was the voice again, winding its way lazily around her as if it were a tangible mist.

Suddenly unbidden, she was confronted with the image of her former mate, a memory from when they had both been in Riyon. He looked down at her, his gaze full of love, and then ownership. Arielle shook her head to clear it.

"Get out of my head, Abaddon!" she whispered angrily and hoped no one had heard her. The last thing she wanted to appear was out of control. *What message would it send if I stood here talking to myself? They would never respect me!*

Arielle took a deep breath. She had made it to her seat and gripped the edge of the obsidian table, its surface so polished that she could see her face in it. She knew that now was not the time for personal conflicts or grievances.

Focus! The fate of Amaris hung in the balance, and unity was essential. Regardless of the whirlwind of doubt she was experiencing, Arielle had a duty to fulfill, and her focus needed to be on the greater good.

She was determined to guide her people toward a future of peace and preservation in what she believed were the best terms.

Arielle tried to get a grip on the thoughts that swirled in a turbulent storm within her mind. As if Abaddon wasn't enough, the remnants of the heated argument with Tauheed reverberated through her.

Anger, a foreign emotion, had consumed Arielle like a raging fire, leaving her disoriented. A dormant volcano had suddenly erupted inside her, spewing out emotions she struggled to control.

After storming out of the garden, Arielle had sought solace in the sanctuary of her quarters. Standing before the mirror, she'd gazed into her own eyes, searching for any visible signs of the inner turmoil that plagued her. She had to remain composed. Did her reflection show her frustration and discontent? But the image before her had remained unchanged, revealing nothing as she'd grappled with the depths of her own emotions.

She was drowning in the swirling tempest of her own conflicting thoughts. *Perhaps surrendering to the current and releasing my grip on control might offer relief?* Arielle pushed away the thought, angry and confused in equal measure.

Every muscle was taut as a bowstring as Arielle watched the clan leaders in the room. She was so terrified that someone might sense the inner storm she was navigating. She released a slow breath—it was concealed from the outside world. The surrounding people were engrossed in their own conversations, unaware of the tempest that raged within her.

However, she became aware that one person continued to study her intently: Tauheed. His penetrating gaze bored into every fiber of her being, an unspoken inquiry that she deliberately ignored. It sparked longing, wrath, and fear. *Why is this happening? I have always cared deeply for Tauheed. I love him.*

She spoke the words in her mind as a talisman to herself—a confirmation. Arielle knew she was isolated. Her heart yearned for understanding and connection, yet her anger had become a formidable barrier, shielding her from the world.

She braced herself for the imminent council proceedings and cleared her throat. "I declare the meeting of the Clan Council open."

A gong sounded, infiltrating Arielle's bones and making her teeth chatter.

Tamanka, the leader of the Taura, the mountain people, stood, adorned in extravagant jewelry, and jingled his excessive gold chains between his hands, reveling in the ostentatious display of wealth. Known for their love of opulence, the Taura always sought to flaunt their riches. Knuckle dusters gleamed on Tamanka's hands, and ruby rings adorned his fingers. A glinting short sword hung at his side.

"Arielle, we have gathered to hear your wise words from the Divine," Tamanka proclaimed, eyes like slits, words dripping with condescension. “How do you propose we coexist in this world of ours? As custodians of the mountains, we have long managed the abundant treasures within the rocks of Elphis. But now, should we share this wealth with everyone? Have we not toiled for countless years to tame it ourselves?”

Arielle smoothed down her robes and narrowed her eyes, frustration dashing through her veins. The persistent resistance of these people ignited that deep annoyance within her, which simmered like a pot about to boil over. *It’s time to humble them, to make them realize that the gifts of the earth were not theirs alone.*

Arielle cringed inwardly. Now the voice was inside her head, like it was probing, raking its claws down her mind.

Shut up! she shouted her disapproval in her head as she raised a hand to her temple. *Why am I suddenly yearning for their obedience? Why do I deem them unworthy?*

Such thoughts did not align with the Divine’s desire for harmony and unity. The Divine sought the coexistence of all people, side by side. Arielle forced a smile to grace her lips. What was happening to her? The morning’s outburst now followed by this internal struggle—something had awoken within her.

“Tamanka, this meeting is long overdue,” Arielle began. The sweat beaded on her forehead, but to her ears, she was calm and resolute. “I have labored tirelessly to find a path forward, a way for us to unite. My proposition is simple: I, as the conduit and mouthpiece of the Divine, can offer guidance on how we may coexist in harmony. If you will listen and heed my counsel, together we can forge a future of peaceful cohabitation.”

To her own ears, it didn't sound like an attempt to control them—it sounded like a genuine act of assistance. In that moment, Arielle realized her journey held a purpose far greater than she had initially envisioned.

Louisa, the leader of the Rehmat, the spirit people, rose from her seat with a commanding presence. Clad in formidable battle armor, her figure tall and lean, she emanated an aura of strength. Her lilac hair cascaded in intricate braids, while her indigo eyes blazed.

"Why, Arielle, should you be the one to oversee us all in the name of the Divine?" Louisa balled her hands into fists, chin up, challenging Arielle's authority. "We understand the necessity of a conduit to represent the needs of the Divine because not all of us have the ability to communicate directly with Him or those from the realm of Riyon. And while the Divine Interpreters assist you—and we appreciate that because we cannot all harness the power of Ruach, and we need assistance to utilize its benefits—why must it be you to govern and guide us?"

The fury built within Arielle once more. The temptation of greed lurked in the depths of her being, but she swiftly suppressed it.

"It is for the greater good of Amaris, Louisa," Arielle responded, eyebrows knitting together as she crossed her arms tightly over her chest. "We must all come together as one, living in harmony. Can you not see that you too require guidance? Unity is essential. Though currently you might coexist in relative harmony, how long will it truly last? You need a leader who can nurture and guide you all."

Constans, the leader of the Vanavasin, the forest people, shook his head slowly. His dappled skin took on the hues of swaying leaves in the sunlight, tinged with deep reds that revealed his concern.

"Arielle, for countless ages, we have lived, albeit in a dysfunctional manner, side by side. Now you propose the need for someone to oversee us. Why have the Vanavashtha, who are deeply connected to the Divine in their own unique way, not shown us such a path? Our priests have sensed rumblings that foretell of an imminent threat to the tranquility of Amaris. Should we not be more worried about that?"

Arielle's heart skipped a beat. She understood the gravity of Constans's words, the subtle hints that something dark loomed over their world.

Arielle inhaled deeply, her chest rising as she steadied herself. Her gaze locked onto Louisa's, steadfast and intense. Each word deliberately enunciated with a quiet strength that filled the space between them, as much for herself as for her response to Louisa. "I may not have all the answers, but I implore you to trust in the guidance of the Divine. Together, we can face any impending peril and safeguard the harmony of Amaris. Let us unite, not out of obedience, but out of love for our shared world and its future."

As she uttered the words, Abaddon's breath was on her again, as if he were inches from her face. Heat bloomed on her neck as if he were caressing her as he had when they were mates. Arielle swallowed, forcing the mix of desire and disgust into her gut.

But as soon as she did so, from the pit of her stomach broiled seething anger. The insidious tendrils of Resha's dark energy reached for her, beckoning. Its sickly sweetness whispered in her mind, threatening to consume her. In a moment of horror, she halted herself.

"The Divine has made it clear we must be unified. It is my role to guide you on how to set aside your petty differences and arguments. And I must fulfill that role by any means," Arielle declared, lips in a thin line. She knew she was bending the truth, distorting the messages she had received from the Divine. Yet the whispers in her head and the undeniable thirst for leadership surged through her veins.

"Arielle, I fear this is not the right course," Tauheed interjected, his eyes filled with concern.

Through their bond, Arielle sensed a growing dread creeping into his heart.

"As you are all aware, esteemed leaders of the clans," Arielle retorted, her gaze piercing, "I stand as the chosen representative of the Divine." She locked eyes with each clan leader in turn, challenging them to defy her.

"It is not just my belief but also my knowledge that this is the path we must follow. Should you choose to disregard my proposal, the consequences for your people will rest solely on your shoulders." Her words hung in the air, an unspoken threat that was illustrated by the uneasy silence.

"Consider the implications of your actions if you dare defy the will of the Divine. Return to your lands and contemplate the repercussions of your decisions," Arielle cautioned.

With a swift, determined stride, she swept out of the chamber before anyone had a chance to respond. The air crackled around her, thick with tension and uncertainty.

Arielle leaned back against the cool stone wall of the corridor, listening to the murmurs of discontent, glad to be out of their sight—and their angry, confrontational glances.

But along the confusion was delight and thrill. *What is this unsettling power I have begun to wield?* She could almost taste elation in her mouth, bubbling in her veins, at the confused and frightened looks that had been on the council's collective faces as she had walked out of the room. *But what have I just done?*

Chapter 13

Arielle sat alone in her chamber, the pain in her heart burdensome. Her eyes were red and swollen from endless tears. Her thoughts were a relentless and unyielding tempest, while anger surged through her veins like white-hot lava. Yet, beneath the anger, tendrils of fear wrapped around her, threatening to suffocate her very being.

Her mind replayed the Council of the Clans and the bitter argument with Tauheed, and the taste of regret filled her mouth. Nausea washed over her, overwhelming her senses. How could she, a former Kaluduta, succumb to the allure of Resha—the darkness that stood in stark contrast to the benevolent power of Ruach? It defied all reason, and yet there it was. Arielle's mind and soul yearned for that sickly sweetness, knowing deep within her that it represented all that was opposed to goodness.

But there was more than just despair and temptation in her heart. Anger and rejection swelled within her, fueled by the realization that her efforts, her dreams for Amaris and its people, had amounted to nothing. Her dedication and sacrifices were meaningless, as if her every step had led to an abyss of futility. And all the while, that relentless voice chased around her mind, piercing her spirit with its taunting whispers.

As Arielle gazed out over the city and the rolling hills beyond, her heart held a mix of resignation and dread. "Divine," she called out, her body trembling, "if you truly love me, why did you abandon me? Why burden me with this when I cannot bear it? You promised me a better life, even if it meant forsaking my wings."

The words resounded in the chamber, each one carving another wound of failure. Anger surged forth once more, raging against those around her whom she perceived as self-serving and oblivious to the greater purpose. Arielle's knuckles turned white, the tension radiating through her body. She looked up at the sky, her eyes brimming with tears, as she pleaded with the Divine. "I cannot understand how these people can serve you with their free will. They need guidance, a lesson that your way alone cannot teach them."

Arielle rose from her chair, unable to contain her restlessness any longer. She paced the room, her nails digging into her palms, seeking solace in the physical pain that mirrored the turmoil within her. "You have forsaken me," she cried out with raw anguish. "You have taken away the very thing I hold most dear and left me stranded in this desolation."

As fury engulfed her, Arielle sensed the tainted edges of Resha, the dark power that beckoned her. It seemed to permeate the air, swirling around her like a palpable mist, mocking her with its alluring presence. The scent of Resha filled her senses, enticing and intoxicating. It promised a flavor so exquisite, surpassing any food she had ever tasted, and offered the satisfaction she had longed for. The potential of its power tantalized her, making her aware of the tangible possibilities it held. Yet Arielle knew that embracing Resha's allure was nothing but an illusion.

Resha's craving was never satisfied, even though it might seem like the most gratifying food. She knew the more you embraced its darkness, the more it consumed your true self. Shaking herself out of the trance, Arielle halted in the center of the room, a renewed determination taking hold.

Suddenly, a chill swept through the atmosphere. She knew it was Abaddon. Arielle's voice trembled. "What are you doing here?"

Abaddon smiled, a chilling expression haunting his eyes. "Arielle, you have just summoned me," he replied.

Indignant, she retorted, "I did no such thing!"

"But yes, you did," Abaddon insisted with a lazy smile playing on his lips. His gaze swept up and down Arielle, and she was suddenly vulnerable, naked. "Do you not realize that by opening your mind to Sephtis, he can seize you as his vessel? I am his conduit, his messenger. Your unrest and discontent with the Divine provide him with an opportunity to present an alternative reality to you. A reality where you can be in control. Isn't that what you desire?"

Arielle looked at Abaddon, her face a mask of confusion. He fixed her with an intense gaze, and she saw something in his eyes that she recognized deep within herself. And it horrified her. They had once loved each other so deeply. He had been her world.

"You're tired of answering to the Divine, and his rejection," Abaddon continued, circling around her with calculated steps. His eyes bored into hers. "You're tired of fulfilling his will, subjecting yourself to his whims, are you not? And these ungrateful people who cannot appreciate your efforts and sacrifices, you're tired of them too, aren't you?"

Anger welled up inside Arielle once more, her emotions threatening to become an uncontrollable torrent.

Abaddon now stood directly before her, the icy touch of his hand resting upon her shoulder, and his scent, a mixture of dark flowers and earth and musk, making her lightheaded. The scent that used to drive her mad with joy. But there was some kind of decay at the edges of it now.

"You know there is a better way, a way where you can be rewarded. Just imagine a world where all these *people*"—he spat the word with disdain—"and this world itself belongs to you. Imagine being in control."

There was a dreadful burning sensation in the place where her wings had once resided. Her shoulder blades served as a physical reminder of her mental anguish.

"Just envision a life where you no longer have to bow down to others," Abaddon continued, his tone persuasive and wheedling. "You won't have to consider their desires, only your own. Then you can attain the greatness you yearn for, the greatness you deserve."

Arielle stood torn, fully aware that the choice she was about to make would forever alter her life. The burden of the decision caused her to tremble, uncertainty mingling with determination in her heart.

Abaddon's hands drifted to Arielle's wrists, and he gripped them tightly, his hooked thumbnails piercing the delicate veins near the surface of her skin. It sent a sharp pain permeating through her body. Arielle's breath caught in her throat.

Abaddon's eyes blazed and locked with hers. He leaned forward, and their lips met. It was everything she wanted and everything she knew she shouldn't take. But with his kiss, his touch, her acceptance, came a lightness. The pain gave way to a rush of sweet relief, like a balm for her weary soul. Had she finally found what she had been searching for all along?

It was a power unlike anything she had ever known. It raced through her body like lightning, electrifying every molecule within her. She could sense her skin glowing with radiance, and her body trembled with newfound energy.

Abaddon pulled away slightly and spoke so quietly, it was like a whispered caress. "That is the power of Resha, Arielle." The temptation dripped like warm, sweet honey. "Embrace the strength of Sephtis. Taste the future he has in store for you. This is the moment you break free from the Divine's shackles and step into the boundless freedom of your new reality."

Her eyes fluttered, the power dashing through her. Abaddon took a step back and knelt before her in reverence. "Your old self is no more," he proclaimed, words hushed yet filled with conviction. "You are the fallen angel reborn. From this moment onward, you shall be known as Sathariel. This is but the beginning of your reign. Together, we shall make Amaris yours," Abaddon whispered with awe. "Your transformation is complete, Sathariel."

With every word Abaddon uttered, Sathariel's old self slipped away, replaced by a formidable presence that commanded respect and fear. She was no longer Arielle; she was Sathariel, destined for greatness.

Sathariel's heart swelled with newfound purpose, her mind ablaze with visions of the power she would wield.

As Abaddon spoke of her reign, Sathariel was filled with exhilaration. The world of Amaris would bend to her will, and she would forge her destiny amid the chaos she would unleash.

But, as the intoxicating power flowed through her, Sathariel's heart was torn with a deep sense of remorse. With a trembling smile, she whispered, "Amaris shall become mine, but at what cost? Those who dare oppose me shall do my bidding, yet I fear the path I have chosen."

"Together, we shall shape the very fabric of Amaris. Its lands, its people—all shall bow before your might," Abaddon declared. "This is only the first step toward the vast dominion that awaits you. Embrace your destiny as the fallen Kaluduta reborn."

Sathariel raised her head, her new title settling upon her shoulders. The fallen angel had risen, and her reign would reshape Amaris.

Abaddon rose and smirked with the thrill of his victory. "I must return to our master, Sephtis, Sathariel, but I will be back for you. Then you will learn exactly what plans he has and how we will shape your triumph." His eyes were greedy.

Sathariel swallowed, forcing any sense of worry or doubt at what she had done to the back of her mind. She needed to get to the garden. There she would be settled. There she would be connected. To what, she wasn't sure. But the fluttering in her chest was not just anxiety—it was also excitement. Now was not the time to question her decision.

She bared her teeth at Abaddon and straightened. "I will be waiting."

Chapter 14

A sudden chill crept over Tauheed's skin like a gust of icy wind was sweeping through the corridors of the citadel in Chinasa. But the late-afternoon air was still filled with warmth. He looked up at the sun and noticed that Pythagoras, the moon that had risen late in the evening, was now crossing its path.

"There is not supposed to be another eclipse," he muttered, his shoulders tense. A sense of foreboding settled in his heart, for he knew that according to the Elnathan Prophecy, an unscheduled eclipse was an ominous sign of impending doom.

His mind raced back to his recent conversation with Arielle. Could it be true? Could she have truly turned her back on the Divine? Tauheed's footsteps quickened as he hurried through the stone corridors of the citadel, fear clutching at his heart. He loved Arielle with all his being, and he understood the turmoil she was in, and her sacrifices for their world. But could she truly abandon all that was good and necessary for a need he could not comprehend?

Chapter 15

Sathariel gazed up at the canopy of leaves above her, sitting in solitude beneath the majestic Jivanam tree. She had severed her ties from the Divine, forsaking the possibility of forgiveness. But why was doubt still gnawing at her?

Had she made the right decision? Only time held the answer, and she pondered if her bold act would unleash repercussions beyond her imagination.

Beneath the sprawling branches, bathed in the dappled sunlight casting intricate shadows upon the blooming rose beds, Sathariel studied the tree's majestic form. Running her hand along its ancient bark, there was the tangible cadence of Ruach, the positive life force of the realm, vibrating through her fingertips. It tingled with a peculiar new sensation, a side effect of embracing Resha, she presumed. Although mildly discomforting, it did not cause her pain. It was no doubt light separated from darkness as she had forsaken Ruach, no longer solely bound to its goodness.

Lifting her hand away from the tree, she witnessed a startling transformation. The bark reacted violently, as if touched by acid, with a perfect handprint seared upon its trunk. Within the confines of the handprint, the bark withered, turning black. A strange satisfaction washed over Sathariel. She watched with a twisted pleasure, an alien sensation but one she also enjoyed, as her power slowly devoured the life force within the tree.

A whooshing sound and blinding light shattered her solitary reverie. It took a moment for her eyes to adjust. The Kaluduta Malakai was standing before her, face etched with sadness. "What have you done, Arielle?" The Divine Messenger's palms were outstretched, eyes wet with tears.

Anger flowed within Arielle, fueled by the pain of her losses and the perceived injustice inflicted upon her.

She raised her eyes, stony like flint, to meet Malakai's, the lines of the Kaluduta's face tracing a portrait of sorrow.

His dismay only stoked the fury burning within Sathariel, hot as the sun. She narrowed her eyes to slits, and gave Malakai an accusatory glare. "Why should the mortals choose their own destinies, while we, the celestial beings, are denied that privilege?"

Memories of her wings being stripped away, her confinement to Amaris, and her constant rejection from its people flooded her mind. Yet she also tasted the seductive allure of Resha's power, its sweetness on her tongue.

Malakai's expression was grim. "Arielle, is this your final decision?"

The absence of Divine intervention, the absence of the Divine, only strengthened her conviction. "I am Sathariel now," she declared defiantly. "Where is the Divine? Does He love me so little that He sends you?"

Malakai's expression softened to one of pity. "Arielle, don't you see? Your choice has led you into darkness. Your soul is becoming corrupted, and you will become a creature of the shadows. The Divine's heart is heavy with this betrayal."

A deep sickness welled up within her, but a renewed surge of anger quickly swept it away. "And what of the Divine's teachings? Of forgiveness? Of second chances?" she retorted bitterly.

"Your existence is unique," Malakai responded, a hint of desperation lacing the celestial being's tone. "You were made from the very essence of Ruach, the embodiment of goodness. You've turned your back on your true nature to embrace the darkness, to distance yourself from the Divine's love."

Sathariel sneered, relishing the twisted sense of justice. She placed her hand again on the tree beside her, eyes full of dark pride. "Then let this be my realm, my palace of death."

Malakai looked at her with tears, a deep sadness reflected in those piercing eyes. "I mourn for the eternal struggle that awaits you, Sathariel. The Divine's gates are closed to you for now, and your pursuit of power will be met with resistance."

The Kaluduta bowed solemnly and disappeared, leaving Sathariel alone, a painful heaviness settling in her chest.

Sinking to her knees, she choked back sobs, a deep sense of loss washing over her. Arielle was convinced the path she had chosen was now irreversible—the possibility of redemption had severed her ties from the Divine. She closed her eyes and uttered, "Sephtis, it is done. I am coming to you."

Chapter 16

Standing in the center of a formidable circle of stone giants, Hana, the revered elder of the Vanavasin, bowed her head. She was deep within the Mountains of Elphis, far from the city of the Taura where Tamanka held court.

Hana smoothed down her simple silken shift and fell to her knees, then pressed her forehead to the cool floor of the chamber where she had her audience. The flagstones rumbled with appreciation from the impassive giants around her, whose granite facial features shifted and moved like liquid running through limestone.

Such was the might of the Hephaes that they held dominion over the very essence of rocks and minerals. The stone giants wielded the power to shape them effortlessly.

Hana's skin, which reflected the hues of autumnal leaves, emitted an eerie glow in the presence of the veins of molten lava running through the chamber's walls, and the crystalline gemstones and streams of precious metals that adorned the cavern, twinkled like a thousand bright watchful eyes.

To the untrained ear, the sound was merely the grinding of rock against rock. But to those who understood, it was a language as ancient as time itself. These rebounding rumbles were the memory of Amaris taking shape, the symphony of creation woven by the Hephaes when the world was birthed. They had aided the Divine in fashioning the majestic mountains, hills, and sprawling forests, while providing a steadfast foundation for the Vanavashtha trees to flourish.

Hana sat back on her heels and placed her hands in her lap, interlacing delicate long fingers.

Lids lowered in reverence, she focused on the colossal rocky creature in front of her, its eyes glowing like molten iron. "Mighty Hephaes, I have journeyed from the Forest of Myrkvior to seek your counsel. The Vanavashtha have warned me of Sephtis seeking to exploit a vessel of light to seize control of Amaris. The delicate balance of Ruach and Resha, our life force, is teetering on the edge of oblivion."

The stone giants resounded in unison, grinding and crunching each enunciation. "We are well aware of the prophecy, just as you are. We know Mariam possesses the Jewel of Aikyam and has spoken with the leaders of the dragon riders. But what do the Vanavashtha say about the arrival of the Yasha, those from a realm beyond, who will be our saviors?"

"Tauheed holds the key to forging a gateway, but he has yet to discover his true purpose." Hana's eyes were still. "We are locked in a race against time." The Hephaes rumbled as Hana continued her grave revelation. "Only Tauheed can summon the three Yasha, but we must bring them into our realm before it is corrupted beyond redemption."

“Does Tauheed perceive the peril that Arielle poses to our world?” inquired the stone giants together, concern etched upon their stony features.

Hana’s eyes widened in disbelief. “Arielle is the threat? She whom the Divine sent from the heavenly realm to bring peace?”

They rumbled in unison, and the giant nearest to her rearranged its features, baring gigantic flagstone-size grinders.

Hana shuddered to think what damage those teeth could cause. “I suspect not yet, for love is half blinding him to any changes within her.”

Another Hephaes made a snorting sound, its breath like cool wind. “I believe he must sense the shift.”

Hana shook her head slowly. She then cocked it to one side in puzzlement as she mulled over their words. “‘But how can Arielle, who is a bastion of all that is good, be corrupted?”

The Hephaes nearest to her gazed at Hana balefully. “We who are forged from the fires of the earth see all worlds and all things. Our dominion extends through the asphalt and the lava into the realms your kind cannot see or know. Arielle is being turned by a darker evil from before the dawn of this world, one that is using her own kind to snatch her from under the very nose of the Divine.”

Hana grimaced, and a knot formed in her stomach. “Are you talking about Sephtis? But I thought he had been banished eons ago to the domain of Naraka.”

“Yes, child of the forest, you are right, but the unrest and distrust that is gaining momentum among the people of Amaris has enabled him to gain strength. So much that he has now been able to send an emissary to Arielle to try to turn her.”

One of the other stone giants lumbered toward a towering pillar of rock at the chamber's rear. Extending a massive hand, it touched its fingers to the structure, which liquefied, turning to a stable yet rippling substance. The stone giant passed its fingers through it and grasped something in its palm.

"To vanquish Arielle's darkness, she must be contained within the Fylakistone, a creation that is born of the sacred rock of Sambandh," the Hephaes revealed. "The Divine gave the Rehmat the rock for protection. Arielle shares a profound connection with this rock, as it hails from Riyon, the celestial realm where the Kaluduta reside."

Hana's expression was grave. "And we must bind the Jewel of Aikyam, the shard of the dragon's egg, and other essences of Amaris together, forging the Thura Gate," she affirmed.

The Hephaes nodded to its companion, who extended its hand toward her. "You will also need the essence of the mountain itself." Within the giant's palm, drawn from the very fabric of the mountain, was a glinting, twinkling rock.

"This is the Misham. It is one of the first materials to be mined from the Mountains of Elphis."

Hana carefully took the stone and placed it in her pouch.

"To make the Thura Gate you seek, you will also need the fruit from the Jivanam tree, which Arielle has touched. It is born from the Vanavashtha tree, that which is part of the fabric of Amaris at the Creation. But now she has infected it with darkness. The Misham and the fruit must be bound within the gateway."

"And not only that," another of the rumbling giants said, "the Fylakistone must be split asunder from the rock of Sambandh, which can reduce Arielle's ability to draw on Resha. Then you must use it to imprison her."

"Hana, priestess of the Vanavasin, the time has come for the blending of powers," the Hephaes said, in a grinding chorus. "The essence of the mountains rests within your hands. Its connection to Amaris is profound, as it embodies the strength and resilience of the land itself."

Hana's grip tightened on the pouch, her resolve solidifying. "I shall not waver. I shall honor the ancient bond of Amaris and fulfill my role in this monumental task."

The Hephaes nodded, their presences shimmering with approval.

Hana looked down, eyes searching the floor as she reached for an answer she wasn't sure she had. She rubbed her cheek and looked up at the stone giant, whose granite features were impassive.

One of the Hephaes held up a stony hand. "To overcome Arielle, the blood of the three Yasha must be intertwined with that which originates from the realm of Amaris. In this profound fusion, she will be bound by the very essence of both her own existence and the worlds she seeks to control."

Hana's gaze became unfocused as she searched for answers in the depths of her thoughts. Then a smile of realization dawned on her face. "The Yasha embody a unique connection between realms, bridging the boundaries of this world and another. Their blood, infused with extraordinary power, will serve as a catalyst to finalize the creation of the Fylakistone."

The Hephaes nodded in unison, rumbling as one. "'The essence of Amaris, the life force flowing through its lands and its people, must intertwine with their essence. Through this union, the Fylakistone shall embody its destiny, becoming a formidable artifact capable of containing the darkness that consumes Arielle."

Hana clenched her fists. "We must forge the bond that defies the boundaries of worlds. Only then can we hope to restrain Arielle and restore balance to Amaris."

"And only with the knowledge that now resides within you can Tauheed manifest this union," the Hephaes rumbled.

With their task completed, the giants receded, melding seamlessly into the very walls of the cavern. Hana stood alone, and urgency gripped her. She knew she had to return to the Forest of Myrkvior immediately.

Chapter 17

The air whirled around Sathariel in a maelstrom. She tasted metal, dirt, and death, and a smell acrid and rotting filled her nostrils. As she shut her eyes, the presence of Abaddon was once again with her.

Recalling the moment she had descended from Riyon to Amaris, Sathariel knew she was moving into the realm of Naraka. As the winds around her subsided, Arielle regarded the expanse of the long cavern that enveloped her. High, vaulted ceilings stretched overhead, seemingly reaching toward the heavens, while walls hewn from glistening black rock enclosed her within their embrace. The polished surface of the walls reflected the dim, dark emerald light, casting fragmented and distorted images of her own reflection.

As her eyes adjusted to the semi-darkness, Sathariel's attention was drawn to the center of the cavern. There, amid the shadows, stood the ominous silhouette of a throne. It seemed to materialize from an intricate web of sharp rock formations, a masterpiece crafted by a malevolent hand. The seatback was spun in a display of power, its stone structure woven into cruel and jagged edges. The hard facets were so sharp, they appeared capable of easily piercing skin and bone.

Every detail of the throne emanated an aura of danger and dominance, an emblem of the darkness within this realm. Sathariel couldn't help but shudder as she recognized the symbolism, a stark reminder of the cruelty and power she had embraced.

The figure on the throne remained shrouded in darkness, but his presence was overpowering. As Sephtis spoke, every word dripped with an ancient, primal force that made Sathariel's skin crawl. A mixture of fear and revulsion bubbled in her gut, as well as a deep understanding of the power that stood before her.

"Finally, Sathariel, I meet you as I always intended you to be. No longer in the thrall of the Divine." Each syllable was cut with hatred and darkness.

Sathariel's body was torn—the opposing force of Resha was reaching out, trying to rip through her soul, a force that both attracted and disgusted her. The being before her spoke with an arrogance that hinted at unimaginable abilities, that had claimed a domain separate from the Divine.

Sephtis rose from his throne, a commanding presence as he descended the steps, his form illuminated by the flickering green flames that lined the cavern. He appeared both youthful and ancient, his features chiseled, cruel, and ethereal. Piercing blue eyes penetrated her soul, while his jet-black hair contrasted against flawless pale skin.

As she gazed upon him, Sathariel realized the depths of his knowledge and the absence of love within. It was as if he had been stripped of any capacity for compassion, leaving only a cold, hard beauty that defied understanding.

"You forget, my child." Sephtis's tone was sardonic. "I can hear your thoughts. However, I take no offense at your accurate assessment of my nature."

The ruler of Naraka smiled, but it did not reach those glowing eyes. "You and I share similarities. I have experienced the rejection of the Divine. You were asked to take up the task of protecting the people of Amaris. But did you have a choice? Was it a poisoned cup you were given? Did you ever have the option to say no? I was cast out for daring to believe that my creations could surpass the Divine's. And now we are the same. You too have been rejected after choosing a new path. Is that not what we strive for? To create and improve, to surpass our own limitations?"

Sathariel listened, her mind grappling with Sephtis's words.

The underworld king bared his teeth at her. "I present a new path, and with it, I give you the power of rework. With this gift, you have the capacity to mold Amaris to fit my vision. I have no intention of limiting myself to just Amaris. No, our influence will stretch across innumerable realms. Free will...it is a farce, a folly of the Divine. Look at the havoc it wreaks. Look at the mess these clans create with their choices. Under your guidance, there is no need to suffer or question. It is a different sort of freedom, you might say."

A sly smile played on the ruler of Naraka's lips. The air grew thick with anticipation as Sathariel awaited the unveiling of these newfound powers.

With a wave of his hand, Sephtis summoned forth creatures from the shadows. They slithered and crawled toward Sathariel, a macabre dance of grotesque forms. Their features were both mesmerizing and unsettling—sharp claws, gnarled teeth, and piercing eyes that glowed in the dim light of the room.

A shiver ran down Sathariel's spine as the creatures surrounded her, their movements synchronized as if following some unseen leader.

"These, my child, are my personal servants," Sephtis declared with satisfaction. "They shall be by your side, aiding you in your endeavors. With their assistance, you will establish your presence in the capital of the Elutheros, and there you shall reign, your power growing with every soul that succumbs to your will."

A mixture of awe and abject disgust filled Arielle as the creatures encircled her, their allegiance sworn to Sephtis. Now she was bound to serve him for eternity. The taste of power mingled with the bitter knowledge that she had willingly traded her freedom for this dark path.

Sathariel could not help but wonder what awaited her in this twisted existence she had willingly embraced. The journey into darkness had just begun, and she couldn't fathom the depths of the challenges and sacrifices she would face in the name of her newfound allegiance.

"But first, before they can be at your side, you must return to whence you came, to the garden, and sever your ties with Tauheed. For he must learn that he is nothing to you now."

Sephtis turned his back on her and began to retreat into the shadows of his throne.

In the recesses of Arielle's heart, something was shattering into a million pieces. Was that her love for Tauheed being snuffed out? Being forced out of her being, so nothing kind or good was left?

The lord of Naraka turned to her once more. "There is no room for love on this path you now tread, Sathariel. And once you have done what I have commanded you to do, I will gift you something very special that will enable you to seize the world of Amaris in your grip." Sephtis vanished into the darkness.

Abaddon stepped forward out of the shadows, a wicked smile playing on his lips as he addressed Sathariel. "Now it is time for you to return to say goodbye to Tauheed, that lackey of yours, for good. He was never enough for you, and an insult to what we once shared. Return and free yourself from him, Sathariel."

The winds began to gather, and she was being transported back to the garden once more. Sephtis's dark influence was tugging at her soul.

Chapter 18

As Tauheed entered the garden, a wave of unease washed over him as he took in the darkened bark of the Jivanam tree. It was marked with sinister black rivulets, like veins filled with death. And there, in the shadows, stood Arielle, her back turned, head bowed.

She slowly turned to face him, and Tauheed gave another sharp intake of breath. Her eyes blazed with a fiery intensity, a reflection of the power she had embraced. Her skin seemed almost translucent, as if a strange glow emanated from within her. There was a jolt in Tauheed's chest as Arielle's gaze met his own—a grasping, clawing sensation, as though she were attempting to drain his very life force.

"Arielle?" Tauheed's voice quivered, barely more than a whisper. "Arielle, please tell me—"

"What is there to tell?" she interrupted, crossing her arms and lifting her chin. "That I have made the choice to seize control of my life at last?"

His heart sank, a sharp pain piercing his chest. Was this heartbreak? He could see the love they had once shared crumbling before his eyes. The Arielle he had known and cared for was no more. This being who stood before him was lost, consumed by the darkness.

"Tauheed, whatever bond existed between us is now severed," she declared triumphantly. Her beauty, always captivating, now seemed magnified, but there was a coldness to it, an edge that unsettled him. Tauheed found himself torn between attraction and repulsion as he looked at her.

Arielle raised her palms, and with dread, Tauheed saw the fire of Resha blazing in her eyes like a wild inferno. He shook his head, a mixture of sadness and concern etched on his face. "Arielle, I believe you have made a grave mistake."

"There is no mistake," she retorted with conviction. "My only mistake was waiting for so long, sacrificing myself for your people." She hissed out the last word with contempt. "Now, I will claim what is rightfully mine—this world. The shackles of my misguided loyalty to the Divine no longer bind me. Now, I can fulfill my true potential."

Tauheed took a hesitant step toward her, pleading. "Arielle, you must understand, this path you've chosen is empty. It will not lead to fulfillment or satisfaction. Can't you see the darkness that awaits you?"

"Arielle is gone," she sneered, her eyes flashing with anger. "I am Sathariel now, a new name symbolizing my rebirth. You will never understand, for you remain enthralled by the Divine."

Her face softened, words taking on a seductive tone, as if she were trying to convince him. "I offer you a choice, Tauheed. Stand with me; embrace the power of Resha. You will realize that it can grant you the freedom the Divine never will."

Tauheed stood his ground, trying to quell the fear that threatened to overwhelm him. “You know I can’t do that. I love you, but I can’t forsake all that is good.”

For a fleeting moment, a shadow of sadness crossed Sathariel’s face, but it quickly hardened into resolve. Tauheed stared at her, sorrow bubbled up inside him like a river ready to break its banks. He had to let go of Arielle, whom he once loved. She was no longer before him. “Sathariel”—he choked on the word—“any pleasure you believe you are offering to those who follow you is empty and shallow. It might satisfy you for a moment, but it is not grounded in goodness.”

“Very well,” Sathariel snarled at him with venom. “That was your one and only chance. Tauheed, be warned. You had the opportunity to join me, and now you are my enemy. And when the time comes, I will make you bow to me by force, and it will bring you no pleasure.”

With that, she closed her eyes, her palms resting on her chest. A mist began to envelop her, obscuring her physical form.

Just before she vanished, Sathariel opened her eyes one final time, and Tauheed recoiled, as he saw the fire burning within her as she locked her gaze with his.

Chapter 19

Sathariel was once again back in the throne room of Sephtis. She straightened her shoulders as the lord of Naraka approached her, gliding across the polished stone floor without making even a hint of a sound.

Sephtis regarded her, a hint of a smile playing on his lips. But his eyes were cold and all-consuming. He clapped his hands together. "Come to me, Abaddon. I have a special gift for you."

A pillar of shimmering turquoise smoke began to rise, swirling and coalescing into a form. Sathariel's eyes widened as the shape of Abaddon materialized before them, stepping out of the smoky veil.

"Almighty, what is your pleasure?" Abaddon's tone was laced with obedience and loyalty.

Sephtis circled the fallen Kaluduta slowly, examining him from every angle. His expression was inscrutable. "Yes, Abaddon, you will do very well. Loyalty deserves its rewards, and you have been a faithful servant. When I was cast out, you stood by my side, one of the few who turned away from the light and embraced the dark with me."

Sephtis turned to face Sathariel. A smirk played on his lips. "And now, with his reward, you will get one of your own."

"Would you like your wings back, Abaddon?"

Sathariel gasped, her eyes widening in disbelief. The thought of Abaddon regaining his wings filled her with a mix of wonder and jealousy. They were brethren, both fallen, both stripped of their wings. There was a pang of longing for what had been taken from her.

"The rest of our kind," Sephtis spat, "remained blissfully ignorant as I was rejected by the light and banished from the heavenly realm. Abaddon chose to follow me as I was forced to turn my back on the Divine. All for having the audacity to believe I had more power than it was deemed I deserved."

Sephtis moved silently toward Abaddon and placed a hand on his shoulder. "His wings, like yours, were cruelly ripped away. He, like you, should never have known the pain of losing them."

Abaddon knelt before Sephtis, eyes glistening. "Almighty master, to fly once more is all I desire."

Sephtis placed his hands on Abaddon's shoulders, his touch radiating dark energy. "And so it shall be," he proclaimed.

At first, nothing seemed to happen, and Sathariel wondered if it was all a cruel trick. But as Abaddon locked eyes with Sephtis, his expression shifted from adoration to agony. A guttural cry escaped his lips as his body convulsed, contorting in pain. Sathariel watched, her heart aching, as enormous leathery wings sprouted from his shoulder blades, each tipped with cruel, hooked claws.

Abaddon's skin transformed, turning scaly and rough. His once familiar face melted away, dissolving into grotesque features. His screams transformed into a snarl, and his eyes vanished, replaced by burning black holes that emanated an icy white light.

Sathariel couldn't tear her gaze away, even as pity and fear welled within her. Abaddon was now a true child of darkness, her kin in this twisted realm.

Sephtis stepped back to admire his creation. "Behold, Sathariel, your first Malevolent," he announced, gesturing toward Abaddon. "He shall aid you in your quest to overcome Amaris."

Abaddon, now fully transformed, knelt before Sathariel. "I am here to serve you," he rasped. "My powers will complement yours, and together, we will conquer. I can amplify the Resha that flows to you, granting you even greater strength. But know this, Sathariel: My hunger for life force is insatiable and unending. To sustain me, you must feed me with the life force of others so that we may continue to dominate and overpower the people of Amaris."

"Sathariel, you are my trusted servant," Sephtis uttered authoritatively. "It falls upon you to ensure that the prophecy remains unfulfilled. Seize Heliopolis and twist the Elutheros to your bidding. In their submission lies the key to Amaris and the fulfillment of your dark ambitions."

The Narakan lord's face twisted. "With Heliopolis under your control, Sathariel, you may yet prevent the arrival of the Yasha, those who have been prophesied to save Amaris." Sephtis sneered as he continued: "Their hopes of salvation shall crumble in the face of your cunning. Inflict chaos upon Tauheed's journey, and obstruct the Yasha's every move."

Sathariel nodded, and she swallowed down her hunger, her need to succeed, even though it was a daunting prospect. "I will not falter."

Sephtis bared his teeth with malice, eyes ablaze. He turned toward his throne and glanced back at Sathariel. “Now, it is about time you got to work.”

Chapter 20

Tauheed's tears flowed as he crumbled to his knees. Sorrow engulfed him completely—for himself, for the twisted form of Sathariel, and for Amaris. Despair threatened to consume him as he questioned how he could possibly halt her destructive path. He had delved into the ancient prophecies, seeking answers, but the events unfolding seemed to defy all reason.

"Oh, Divine, please do not forsake us," Tauheed pleaded, choking with anguish. "I understand that you had to release her, but do not allow her to seize our world. Have we strayed so far? Have our efforts been so feeble? Have we failed you so greatly?"

In the depths of his despair, Tauheed had plummeted into a profound and dark chasm. It was as if smooth walls enclosed him, making it seemingly impossible to scale their heights. Was this the true embodiment of despair?

His eyes shifted to the sky, where the clouds danced. It was a beautiful day, bathed in soft hues of apricot as dusk began to paint the horizon. But within Tauheed's heart, there was no trace of beauty or tranquility. Grief and melancholy stained his soul.

"How can I stop her, Divine?" Tauheed trembled as he turned his gaze to the majestic Jivanam tree, using the back of his hand to wipe away the tear stains from his cheeks. "Show me the way."

He released a guttural cry that rent the air around him. His isolation was absolute—devoid of any signs or answers he desperately sought.

A hushed silence enveloped him, broken only by the continuous bubbling and trickling of the nearby fountain. In this moment, Tauheed realized the burden of the terrible evil and imminent danger upon his shoulders. He alone carried the knowledge of the impending peril.

Summoning his inner strength, Tauheed straightened his posture and reached out to touch the rough bark of the tree. A gentle calm washed over him, and he stood there, savoring his connection to nature's embrace.

"Pull yourself together," Tauheed chided himself, inhaling four slow, deep breaths to regain composure. He knew he needed to set achievable goals, to take small steps forward. Each stride would inevitably lead him closer to a solution, wouldn't it?

First and foremost, he realized the leaders of the clans had to comprehend the imminent threat they faced. Would it come down to a battle? Tauheed fervently hoped for an alternative to stop Sathariel without resorting to bloodshed. And what of the Elnathan Prophecy?

The resounding rush of water abruptly disrupted Tauheed's train of thought. He turned, eyes widening as the fountain unleashed a torrent, surging and roiling with an extraordinary force that surpassed its stone confines. It was as if the very essence of the ocean were attempting to burst through the stonework.

He shielded himself as waves of water crashed upon him, tasting the salt on his lips. And then, from the heart of the geyser, a figure emerged—a woman adorned in iridescent rainbow scales. Gracefully somersaulting through the air, she landed before him.

Shaking off the excess water, the shimmering woman ran her fingers through her hair, seemingly unaffected by the fact she had been drenched just moments before. She exuded nonchalance, as though she had casually strolled into the garden during a leisurely afternoon walk.

"Tauheed? It is Tauheed, isn't it?" The woman's voice carried a note of certainty despite the question.

The Divine Interpreter, dumbfounded, managed a nod in response.

"I am Mariam, queen of the Adira, the ocean people," she introduced herself. "Typically, we do not venture onto land," Her nose wrinkled in distaste. "But when the Divine compels us, we must. I find these"—she gestured disdainfully toward her slender legs—"so cumbersome and awkward. I truly admire the Divine, but I cannot fathom what He was thinking when He devised them."

Tauheed gave a faint smile at her candid remark.

"I am aware that we face a grave danger, an unspeakable evil threatening our freedom," Mariam continued urgently, her lips set in a thin line. "And you have a pivotal role to play. You must aid us in bringing the Yasha to Amaris so that we may fulfill the prophecy."

A spark of hope bloomed in Tauheed's chest, and his heart swelled. He was not alone. His mind eased. "I know the evil of which you speak," he confessed. "It is Arielle, or rather, the being she has become, Sathariel." The words caught in his throat, and he whispered them with a tinge of grief. "She has succumbed to darkness and now walks at Sephtis's side."

"The Kaluduta? She who is now a woman, who was once the Divine's confidant?" Mariam's eyes widened in disbelief. "She has turned to the darkness? We had our suspicions, but I never thought it would happen."

Queen Mariam paced back and forth, her face etched with worry. "This is far more terrible than I could have imagined. Her newfound powers will surpass our understanding if she has forsaken the light. As a being with a closer connection to the Divine than any of us on Amaris, she possesses the potential to twist and corrupt everything that was bestowed upon her in goodness."

Numbly, Tauheed nodded in agreement. "Indeed, you are right. The thought of what she is capable of horrifies me."

"Tauheed, we must swiftly reach the Vanavasin," Mariam declared, expression resolute. "You must summon the Yasha and forge a gate between their world and ours. Only you possess this ability."

"Why only me?" Tauheed interjected. Frustration laced his words, and his shoulders were tense. "I pored over the ancient texts and prophecies. I cannot fathom the method or comprehend what needs to be done."

"You possess a pure heart, Tauheed," Mariam responded, smiling with kindness. "Your role is a load that not everyone could carry, but you are a faithful and loyal servant of the Divine. He walks beside you in the darkest moments, carrying you forward. You are a Divine Interpreter, intimately connected to Arielle, or should I say Sathariel, and the ancient flow that is imbued into every living entity on Amaris—the essence safeguarded by the Jivanam tree. Even though we presently find ourselves on opposing sides," Mariam sighed, leaning forward to trace her elegant fingers along the spreading blackened bark, "Arielle still resides within Sathariel. Though forgotten, the bond of love is not easily broken."

Mariam glanced at the discolored surface of the tree; her brow furrowed with worry.

"Hmm," she mused, "I can see she has already begun to tip the balance of Ruach and Resha. But has she done enough?"

The queen grimaced, her face dark. "Sathariel has poisoned it. I don't know how much damage she has already done."

She continued to study the tree, peering up into the leaves, and then smiled with relief. "It is not too late, Tauheed; see here." Mariam pointed up into the branches, and there, nestled among the foliage, was a golden fruit.

"This is still pure—the pure essence of the land of Amaris. I bring with me the essence of the ocean. The dragon riders have the essence of the air, and the mountain people—the Taura—bring with them the essence of the earth. It isn't too late."

Tauheed's eyes widened in awe as he beheld the golden fruit. A flicker of hope ignited within him, dispelling the shadows that threatened to consume him. "Together," he whispered, "we can create the Thura Gate and bring forth the Yasha to save us."

Mariam nodded, her eyes gleaming with confidence. "Yes, Tauheed. We must gather the essences and unite them by using the gateway. It is through our combined strength and enduring faith that we can overcome the darkness that looms over Amaris."

With caution, Tauheed plucked the golden fruit from its branch. Mariam gestured toward the remnants of the fountain, where water had gathered in a deep pool. Beckoning him to follow, she extended her hand. “Anywhere there is water on Amaris, I can travel. We must make our way to the Vanavasin without delay. We must halt Sathariel before it is too late.”

Tauheed clutched the golden fruit tightly and placed his hand in Mariam’s. Together, they stepped into the fountain, its surface rippling as they disappeared beneath.

He gasped for breath as the water swallowed him whole, engulfing him in its watery depths. The pressure bore down on the Divine Interpreter from all sides as if it sought to squeeze out his life. But amid the suffocating embrace, Mariam held his hand tightly, providing comfort.

Struggling against the impending burst of his lungs, the panic rose within Tauheed, bubbling faster than the surrounding air bubbles. The queen of the ocean glanced at him, her wide eyes urging trust, and in one fluid motion, she whipped him around to face her. Her index finger, adorned with a long, glittering nail, danced behind his ears with a swift, practiced motion.

Panic surged through Tauheed, his mind consumed by fear, far beyond the confines of his comfort zone. The primal instincts within him screamed in a frenzy of fight-or-flight response. And in his mind, he shouted that breathing underwater was impossible, a mad notion. His lips involuntarily tightened, and his throat constricted, blocking any escape for air.

But Tauheed knew he had no choice but to surrender to the watery depths. The pain in his chest constricted like a vise, threatening to crush his very being. Mariam nodded, signaling for him to open his mouth, and he heard her within his mind, soothing yet firm: *Let the water flow over your lungs. I promise, you will be able to breathe.*

Fear clutched at Tauheed's heart as his lungs ached, bursting beyond limit. The only thing to do was let the water in. Every nerve screamed no. Mariam nodded at him again, eyes shining as she licked her teeth and opened her mouth wide. With a trembling resolve, he parted his lips, allowing the water to cascade over his tongue and down his throat, flooding into his chest. A strange sensation washed over him as his lungs, so accustomed to oxygen-laden air, grappled with confusion. Was he in the first stages of drowning? Then, a fluttering sensation behind his ears, and the water seemed to retreat from his chest as if being slowly drawn out.

The pressure within his lungs subsided, and Mariam's smile reflected relief and triumph. *I have granted you gills, Tauheed. They will be temporary,* she said in his mind, tucking behind her ear a halo-like cascade of hair, which floated like a crown. Tauheed raised his hand, and under his fingers were fluttering gills, tiny chains of bubbles dancing in and out of the delicate flaps of flesh.

Now, for the time being, you are one of the Adira, Mariam proclaimed. *Your gills will serve you well on our journey to the Vanavasin.*

Tauheed nodded, gratitude washing over him as the watery tunnel ahead widened, revealing an expansive underwater world. Mariam still clutched his hand, her shimmering tail propelling them forward with remarkable power. And in an instant, they were expelled into a vast expanse of water.

Tauheed marveled at the newfound clarity of his vision as he acclimated to the use of his gills. The underwater world unfolded before his eyes, shimmering in shades of green and brown. Mariam halted their movement, and together, they floated in the depths for a few precious moments.

We have arrived at the great Lake of Hisoki, Mariam declared, with pride and caution. *Our path lies across these waters, toward the mouth of the river that leads to the Forest of Myrkvior, where the Vanavasin dwell. We need only to make our way across to the river mouth that feeds the lake and swim up the waters of their capital.*

She paused momentarily, her gaze fixed on Tauheed, her eyes filled with caution and reassurance. *However, you must be aware there are creatures I have little or no command over here. This is the deepest lake on Amaris, and there are said to be monsters dwelling in its depths. I do not yet know the breadth of Sathariel's powers.*

Tauheed's heart raced with a mix of excitement and trepidation. He turned to Mariam, searching for guidance amid the unknown. She met his gaze, a mischievous smile playing on her lips. *Don't worry,* she said, filling his mind with assurance. *We will have other ways at our disposal of overcoming anything that tries to stop us.*

Curiosity sparked within Tauheed as he watched Mariam reach into a pouch slung around her hips. She retrieved a horn, its polished surface gleaming even underwater. Raising it to her lips, she blew into it, and a long keening sound crackled through the water. *I am summoning some friends of the Adira,* she explained, her eyes glimmering with anticipation. *They should make our journey much faster.*

As Tauheed squinted through the murkiness of the waters, he saw three graceful creatures approaching them. Their smooth, mottled skin shimmered in shades of blue and green, reflecting the underwater light. Tauheed's eyes widened with recognition—he knew them as the Kano, one of the most intelligent water animals on Amaris. As their long fins propelled them through the water, their birdlike beaks clacked and smiled at him. The Kano swam up to Mariam, their movements synchronized in a show of respect. Tauheed was amazed by their grace and intelligence. Mariam nodded in acceptance of their greeting, her hand resting gently on the fin of the largest Kano. Tauheed nodded back, acknowledging the creatures' presence.

The Kano will take us to the mouth of the river and watch out for any potential threats, Mariam explained. She gestured for Tauheed to hold on to one of the Kano's dorsal fins while she did the same. *Hold on tight,* she advised, her eyes glinting with excitement.

With a sharp nod from Mariam, the creatures responded with a series of audible clicks. Tauheed tightened his grip on the Kano's fin as it took off with remarkable speed, slicing through the water with astonishing agility. A rush of adrenaline surged through Tauheed's veins as they navigated the currents, far swifter than he had imagined. The underwater world unfolded before him, a mesmerizing tapestry of waving fronds and glimmering fish.

As they soared above the undulating sea forest, Tauheed was stunned by the vibrant colors and intricate movements of the marine life below. Rays of sunlight pierced through the depths, painting the underwater canopy in shades of aquamarine and fuchsia. The water surged and swirled around them, carrying them closer to their destination. He glimpsed schools of radiant fish darting through the currents, their scales gleaming in iridescent blue and green shades. It was a world unseen, hidden from the surface, one that left Tauheed with nothing less than awe and wonder.

Suddenly, a gigantic manta ray emerged from the kelp forest, its wings beating with slow grace. Tauheed's eyes widened in astonishment as they glided down, only to be greeted by a majestic herd of sea cows. Overwhelmed by this hidden realm's sheer beauty and diversity, Tauheed turned to Mariam, his mind brimming with thoughts.

I never realized there was an entire world down here, he silently communicated to her. *We are so ignorant of the beauty of our planet. On the ground, we think we know it all, and yet there is so much that is hidden from us.*

Mariam's laughter carried through the water with a hint of mirth and understanding. *My kingdom is so much vaster than yours, Tauheed,* she replied, her smile warm and kind. *There are countless things we do not understand or know about in the creation of our world. That is the beauty of it. We always have room to discover, explore, and learn more. We must embrace the unknown and not be fearful.*

Tauheed nodded in agreement, their journey continuing through the vibrant underwater landscape. Mariam's gesture drew his attention to a distant cliff face rising dramatically from the lake's floor. He could discern a narrow chasm splitting it in two. *There is our destination,* she declared. *That will lead us to the Vanavasin.*

The Kano intensified their speed as they approached the chasm. Suddenly, an earth-shattering roar rocked upward from the forest of plants in the depths of the lake beneath them. The Kano clicked an alarm, and Mariam pulled up, her expression clouded with concern. *It is as I feared,* she admitted with a grimace. *The Iniko serpent. I have heard tales of this creature.*

A rumbling emerged from the depths, and a massive creature burst forth from the underwater forest, its fiery red scales glistening. The Iniko serpent advanced toward them with astonishing speed, rows of sharp teeth bared in a menacing display. Tauheed's eyes widened as he saw a black collar around its neck, a thick treacle-like substance that was clearly causing the creature immense pain.

Sathariel is trying to stop us from reaching the Vanavasin, Mariam explained. *Your bond with her must be strong if she senses where you are.* She surveyed their surroundings, searching for a solution amid the swirling waters. *However, we have the might of the ocean.*

Mariam released her hold on the Kano and raised the horn to her lips once again. This time, a gut-wrenching wail erupted from it, causing Tauheed to instinctively cover his ears. One of the Kano swooped in for an attack, but the Iniko serpent effortlessly flicked it away with its tail, emitting another roar of defiance.

By the Divine, we need backup! Mariam exclaimed, blowing the horn once more. The serpent began to encircle them, driven by a relentless determination to impede their progress. *It doesn't want to kill us; it's trying to stop us. Sathariel needs what we have.*

A rumbling noise caught Tauheed's attention from behind. He turned, and the water currents gathered strength around him. Mariam had manipulated the currents, and he could see what was akin to a vortex of water spinning toward the Iniko.

It let out a third roar as it was caught in the fierce eddies that held the Iniko tight. Mariam uttered an incantation: *Ptach bli lefgoa,* and flicked her wrist in an opening motion. The creature moaned, and the collar began to dissipate as the vortex that held him became one with the water.

Tauheed's gaze lingered on the serpent, its once vicious collar now dissolved, revealing the raw wounds it had endured. Mariam's eyes reflected a mix of disgust and pity. *That poor creature. Sathariel used it as a pawn in her schemes, and now she has abandoned it to its fate. I have asked the Kano to bring one of my healers to soothe the Iniko's wounds. It is not to blame for the suffering it endured. But we must go from here now because we do not want to be pulled down into the remnants of the vortex.*

With immense effort, Tauheed and Mariam grasped a Kano's dorsal fin. The creatures moved them forward, the combined force launching the pair out of the spinning waters with breathtaking speed. They hurtled toward the chasm.

When they came to a sudden halt, Tauheed realized that the surface was tantalizingly close, a mere ten feet above them. Rays of sunlight filtered through the watery ceiling.

Mariam turned and extended her hand in a gesture of gratitude to the Kano, who responded with respectful bows before swimming back toward the lake.

Mariam lifted the horn to her lips once more and gazed back into the lake from where they had come. The currents in front coalesced into a shimmering wall of water to create a barrier. Tauheed turned and now an aquatic passage was forming in the eddies for them to follow.

Mariam gestured for them to swim forward. *The barrier behind us will hold for only so long,* she cautioned with urgency. *It is a precaution in case Sathariel sends us any more of her nefarious surprises. We must follow to passage to the Vanavasin.* Tauheed's fingers intertwined with Mariam's, and a surge of energy vibrated between them. As they soared through the aquatic passage, a kaleidoscope of colors and sensations overwhelmed Tauheed's senses. They were one step closer to their destination.

Chapter 21

Lexi and Harda flew through the vast expanse of the skies, their dragons' powerful wings beating in perfect harmony. The wind rushed past them, carrying with it a sense of exhilaration and freedom. As they maneuvered through the air, their eyes met, and grins spread across their faces, their unspoken bond palpable.

There is nothing more magnificent than flying together with you. Lexi conveyed her thoughts to Harda, their connection deeper than mere words, through the mental bond they shared as mates. When they rode their dragons side by side, they became one entity, minds intertwined, their thoughts merging effortlessly.

Harda's eyes sparkled, but his lips were grim. *I just wish our circumstances were different, without this danger and uncertainty.*

The Forest of the Vanavasin loomed ahead, a lush green oasis rising defiantly from the desolate landscape. It stood like an impenetrable wall, reaching toward the heavens. The Vanavashtha, guardians of the Forest of Myrkvior, had woven a protective force field around their domain, shielding the inhabitants from harm. The majestic trees' protection stretched for miles. Legends whispered that those lacking purity of heart would forever wander the depths, unable to find the path to the city of the Vanavasin. It was a place of enchantment where only the deserving would be welcomed.

The dragons approached the forest's perimeter without hesitation, their bond with their riders guiding them forward. Lexi shifted her position on Axelia's back, cradling the delicate dragon egg within a leather purse for safekeeping. The surface of the egg was fragile, as if it could shatter into a thousand pieces, yet its strength was unmatched, akin to the legendary avinash—the mightiest metal on Amaris.

Suddenly, the dragons began to choke and cough, their flight faltering. Lexi's heart raced with concern as distress radiated from Axelia. She gently caressed the dragon's neck, eyes searching and urgent. *Tell me, dear one, what ails you?*

I...cannot breathe, Axelia gasped, fear in every word. *The air is poisoned.*

Lexi's eyes widened with worry. *Can you make it to the edge of the forest? There, within the safety of the Vanavashtha, you may find respite.*

Axelia shook her head weakly. *It...it's too far. We must land.* With great effort, the dragons descended rapidly, their landing abrupt and unsteady. They skidded to a stop, struggling to draw in each breath.

Lexi's heart was tight with alarm as she leapt from her dragon's back.

She glanced at Harda, who had landed next to her. He was rubbing his neck and coughing.

Lexi clutched at her throat. "Whatever affected the dragons must have invaded our lungs as well. What could have caused this?"

She knew they were completely vulnerable. The dragons, while complete in their strength in the skies, could unleash their fiery breath at a moment's notice while airborne. But while on the ground, they could not wield that power.

A chill cut through the air. "I am the cause."

Sathariel, the self-styled queen of darkness, materialized before them in a swirl of shadow and smoke. The air around her crackled with malevolent energy, and her presence alone sucked the warmth from the air around them. She was a sight to behold, clad in iridescent dark green armor that seemed to shift and change with every movement, and her long crimson hair was intertwined with streaks of gold that glinted in the dim light.

Harda's eyes widened in shock at the sight of her, disbelief palpable as he spoke her name. "Arielle?"

But Sathariel's expression remained as cold and impenetrable as granite as she gazed upon them. "Arielle is dead," she declared. "I am Sathariel, and soon you shall bow before me as your queen."

Her eyes fixated on Lexi and the chest strapped to her, which contained the shard of the dragon's egg. A wicked smile played upon her lips as she took a step closer. "I believe you possess something I desire," she said with menace. "Hand it over, and I might spare your lives."

Lexi's grip on the chest tightened, and she stepped back. Her eyes blazed, her jaw set. "The shard is not yours for the taking," she stated firmly. "And I will protect it with my life."

Sathariel's expression darkened, and she let out a low chuckle. "You are a foolish girl," she hissed, taking another step closer.

Lexi's face contorted as she stared directly at Sathariel. "Do you truly believe I would surrender the shard so easily? You underestimate my resolve," she cried, eyes flashing. "By the Divine, I will not let you take this egg from me, nor will I allow you to claim dominion over Amaris."

A cold smile curled upon Sathariel's lips as she met Lexi's enduring gaze. "Careful what you wish for, dear Lexi. You may soon find that you have no choice in the matter."

With a swift motion, Sathariel began reciting a summoning incantation: *"Adfer quod procul est ad latus meum statim."*

Abaddon, her Malevolent, materialized at her side. Involuntary shivers ran down Lexi's spine. Death permeated the air like a tangible presence.

"Now, my dear dragon riders," Sathariel purred, eyes like flint, "you will find yourself preoccupied while I claim what rightfully belongs to me."

"By the Divine, you will have to slay us all if you seek to take it." Harda drew a long knife hidden within his boot. Lexi unsheathed a sword from her back. It gleamed in the light, and the blade hummed.

Sathariel's eyes narrowed, a predatory gleam in her gaze. "Ah, but you see, I am aware of the bond between you and your dragons. As they suffer, so shall you, unable to breathe and tormented by pain."

The air crackled around Lexi. The sting of dark power, more painful than a scorpion, slid across her skin. She watched helplessly as Ananpal cried out in agony. Harda clutched his chest and buckled to his knees, gasping for air.

"See how I can harness the essence of darkness, Lexi?" Sathariel cackled. "It is piercing the heart of your mate, splintering into every fiber of his being as we speak."

Sathariel turned to face her, and gestured to the Malevolent lurking nearby. "Now, witness as your beloved dragons become sustenance for my Malevolent. Their life force shall be its feast. Now Abaddon is so much easier to control. Once my lover, now he is my pet." She almost crooned the words. "Now take your fill!" Her voice dropped to a low, calculated growl.

The Malevolent let out a guttural snarl, launching itself onto the Ananpal's back, its claw-like fingers digging into his hide. The wails of pain from Ananpal and Harda were unbearable. Tears welled up in Lexi's eyes, but her resolve remained unbroken.

"Why don't you surrender the egg to me?" Sathariel taunted, anger flashing in her eyes.

Harda strained with anguish, every muscle in his neck taut. He turned to Lexi and shook his head with every ounce of strength he could muster. Lexi pressed her lips together, her eyes burning bright. "Never."

An enraged fire burned within Sathariel's eyes. "I cannot take the egg shard by force, but perhaps I can sway you to my way of thinking," she sneered. Clapping her hands together, she began reciting another incantation, accompanied by intricate hand gestures—which Lexi knew, with a sinking heart, was a binding goitera.

In an instant, bonds appeared in the air, coiling around Lexi and Axelia, constricting tightly around their necks and bodies. Lexi's movement was restricted, her body held rigid by the bonds.

She knew that Sathariel had tapped into the power of Resha, embracing the darkness and channeling its evil. Just before she succumbed to unconsciousness, Lexi whispered a desperate plea, barely audible. “Divine, you must save us.”

Chapter 22

Tauheed stood amid the towering Vanavashtha trees, their majestic branches reaching toward the heavens, seemingly touching the sky. The air was thick with the scents of flowers and earth; the rustling leaves emitted a gentle, soothing sound. In the clearing's heart stood the Vanavasin temple, a white structure adorned with columns, open on all sides to embrace the surrounding beauty.

A sense of calm washed over Tauheed as he gazed at the temple, its pristine white walls blending seamlessly with the pale blue sky.

Dressed in flowing robes of purest white, Hana, the Vanavashtha priestess, awaited Tauheed within the structure. Her long hair shimmered with the fiery hues of autumn, and her skin seemed to mirror the vibrant greens of the forest canopy above.

She gestured to the whispering trees around her with her palms outstretched in greeting. "The Vanavashtha are weary." She spoke with solemnity. "They struggle to stay alive and thrive as they battle the poison Sathariel has unleashed upon our world. With each abuse of Resha, she assaults the very core of Amaris."

As Tauheed stepped forward, he swallowed hard, but determination burned bright in his core. "Hana, you are aware that we need the shard of the dragon's egg to fulfill the prophecy and bring the Yasha to Amaris. But Sathariel has captured Lexi. We must retrieve the shard."

Hana's gaze met Tauheed's, her eyes brimming with wisdom. "Tauheed, as you know, each capital of the clans on Amaris has a sapling, which connects the Vanavashtha. This is how we possess an all-seeing knowledge of events unfolding everywhere in our world."

Tauheed nodded, absorbing Hana's words. The priestess continued, concern etched on her features. "Even the mountain dwellers, secluded within their lofty peaks, possess a Jivanam sapling. It is one of these very saplings that Sathariel poisoned within the grounds of the Divine Interpreters' palace. She remains unaware of the far-reaching consequences of her actions."

Hana's gaze shifted, her focus determined. "The Vanavashtha have received word from the Jivanam tree in the garden of the palace in Heliopolis. The city is under threat of falling under Sathariel's control, and even now, she gathers her Dark Forces to take it by any means necessary."

A hushed gasp escaped the Vanavasin standing behind Tauheed, realization sinking in. Hana pressed on, steady. "Yet, through the power of Ruach, we can empower you to utilize the sapling within the capital of Heliopolis as a pathway to reach Lexi, Axelia, and the dragon's egg. Sathariel has been unable to claim the dragon shard for herself, for she can neither touch nor destroy it. As the guardian, only Lexi holds the key to release the shard from its protective chest. Sathariel cannot harm her while she is bound to the shard."

The priestess, adorned in a flowing white gown and a crown of twisted branches, turned to face Tauheed. Her eyes, a deep amber, were warm and welcoming yet held a hint of sorrow. She reached out a slender hand, beckoning Tauheed to follow her.

Curiosity and apprehension mingled within Tauheed as he stepped forward, his footsteps hushed by the thick carpet of moss that covered the sacred forest floor. In the center of the temple stood a plinth, upon which rested a wooden chest—and within it a stone, the very same one bestowed upon Hana by the Hephaes.

As Tauheed drew nearer, there was an unmistakable energy emanating from the stone, as though it were imbued with a life of its own. It was a reminder of the united forces that stood against Sathariel's darkness—a reminder that he was not alone in his quest.

The priestess placed a hand on Tauheed's shoulder, their eyes locking with a fierce intensity. "This stone holds great power," she said, words low yet commanding. "But it is up to you to harness it. Only then can you defeat the darkness that threatens our land."

"The Aiyakamstone—the shard of the dragon egg—and the fruit from the Jivanam sapling must be combined with the Mishamstone," Hana explained. "Then, and only then, shall we possess the elements of water, air, earth, and stone from Amaris, allowing us to forge the Thura Gate. It is through this gate that you can bring forth the three Yasha. But first, you must free Lexi and Axelia from Sathariel's clutches."

With a gentle gesture, Mariam handed the Mishamstone to Tauheed. He winced at the mention of Sathariel's name. Memories of their past, of happier times, of their love flooded into his mind.

Hana placed a comforting hand on his shoulder. "I know your anguish, but Arielle, the being you once knew and loved, is no more. Sathariel seeks only harm for the people of Amaris, and she harbors the darkest intentions toward you. You stand as the barrier between her and domination."

Troubled, Hana paused, her eyes clouded with concern. "Before you leave Heliopolis, you must also destroy the Jivanam tree. By doing so, we sever Sathariel's connection to the Vanavashtha and the other capitals. Only dragon fire can ensure the tree's permanent demise."

Taking hold of a rolled script beside the stone, Hana presented it to Tauheed. "Here is the incantation you need to release Lexi and Axelia from the bonds of Resha. By breaking those chains, you shall restore their freedom and grant them the strength to face the challenges ahead. There is no doubt that by the time you arrive in Heliopolis, Sathariel will have made the Elutheros capital her own."

She then revealed another roll of script, this one containing a shielding incantation. "Once you take to the air, recite this incantation to safeguard your escape from Heliopolis before Sathariel can mobilize her forces. No doubt she has been gifted terrible creations by Sephtis. Our protection can shield you for only a limited time."

Hana's words hit hard and resonated deeply. Resolve roiled in Tauheed.

"However, there is a crucial piece of information of which you must be made aware," Hana continued, her expression grave. "Once the Thura Gate is created, any sapling on Amaris will become a portal from the Yasha world to ours. That is why it is imperative to destroy the Jivanam tree. Sathariel might seize this opportunity for her own ends if the sapling exists. We must imprison her before she can destroy both our world and another."

"With the Fylakistone, created from the rock of Sambandh, gifted to the Rehmat, the spirit people, we shall fashion a prison for Sathariel," Hana explained, eyes shining, her tone ringing with determination. "This stone is a combination of earth and spirit, an embodiment of ancient forces, meant to safeguard Amaris from her evil."

Conviction laced her words as she continued, "The Fylakistone, born of Sambandh's essence, shall bind Sathariel and prevent her from wreaking havoc upon our realms. It is the ultimate weapon of containment, a culmination of powers aligned against her. We must succeed in our quest to unite these forces, for it is our duty to protect Amaris and all its inhabitants from Sathariel's grasp."

Chapter 23

Sathariel sat tall on her midnight-black steed, the cool night breeze ruffling her hair. She surveyed the sprawling cityscape of Heliopolis from her vantage point. An intoxicating blend of power and anticipation pulsated in her veins. Rows of gleaming soldiers and her seven Malevolents' monstrous forms hissed restlessly before her, illuminated by the dying light. Their hunger was as tangible as the chill in the air.

Sathariel spurred her horse forward with an unflinching resolve. "March forth and feast, my devoted servants. Bend the willing to our cause; mark them as our own. I command you to find the king and queen. I want to find them humbled and shackled, awaiting my arrival in the heart of their castle."

The Malevolents turned, their eyes glowing eerily in the semi-darkness. A chorus of deep, gravelly voices united: "As you wish, our queen."

Heliopolis, the capital city of the Elutheros, a beacon of prosperity and peace, was caught entirely off guard by the brutal onslaught. The city, unprepared for the unexpected assault, crumbled under the Malevolents' fierce attack, unable to assemble a meaningful resistance.

As Sathariel passed through the entrance to the city, now little more than smoldering rubble, she slowed her steed to a trot. The once-bustling streets lay eerily silent, except for the occasional whimper of despair. The cobbled paths were strewn with the lifeless bodies of brave warriors and innocent civilians alike, a morbid testament to the savagery of her army.

Terrified citizens, their eyes wide with fear, had been herded into the central courtyard of the palace. Their hands were bound tightly behind their backs, knees scraping the cold stone as they were forced to bow in submission. The spectacle of despair was a grim tableau, stark against the city's once-vibrant backdrop. But to Sathariel, it was the sweet taste of victory and the first step toward her reign over Amaris.

"So, you have chosen to bend to my will instead of facing certain death. A wise decision," Sathariel declared, dismounting gracefully from her horse and approaching the group. "But first, the king and queen. Where are they?"

A man and a woman cautiously stood up. The faces of King Damianos and Queen Gerlinde were etched with defiance.

"I want you to witness how easily the people of Amaris yield to another's power," Sathariel sneered. "All it takes is a display of force." She motioned toward the dragon Axelia, who was still bound by her enchantment. Lexi was tied to her back, listless and weak after enduring the assault of Resha.

Speaking an incantation, Sathariel conjured more chains that ensnared Axelia and Lexi, limiting their movement to just a few feet from a stone pillar. She then turned her attention back to the king, queen, and their trembling subjects. “Consider yourselves fortunate that I spared your lives, for now.”

The king locked eyes with Sathariel, his defiance unyielding. “I will never bow to you, and neither will my wife. We will never submit willingly.”

Sathariel’s face twisted into a cold, calculating expression as she spoke. Her eyes burned with an icy intensity. “In that case,” she said sharply, “I must demonstrate the consequences of opposing me.” With a sharp flick of her wrist, she summoned the Malevolents; the dark, sinister creatures swallowed the light around them.

Two stepped forward, hissing in delight. They loomed over the king and queen, their massive forms casting shadows on the ground. The couple huddled together in fear, their regal garments now tattered and torn. As Sathariel watched with cruel satisfaction, the creatures enveloped the king and queen in their cloaks. Shuddering screams pierced through the air before falling silent. In just a few moments, it was over.

As the Malevolents drew back, all that remained of the king and queen were two emaciated corpses; their once-vibrant bodies were now mere husks. It was a haunting reminder of the merciless fate that awaited anyone who dared to stand against her.

“So, which of you would like to face your fate?” Sathariel’s rallying cry rang out with a chilling edge, her gaze piercing the crowd. “Or would you rather come to me willingly?”

A tremor ran through the onlookers, their faces etched with terror. Yet, from the midst of the fearful silence, a lone figure stepped forward, determined. “If it pleases you, Queen, then I will fight for you,” the brave soul declared.

Sathariel nodded, acknowledging his choice. "A wise decision, given the circumstances." Pointing toward the ground directly in front of her, she commanded, "Come to me and kneel." The man approached, his body shaking with trepidation, and sank to one knee before her. Sathariel gently cupped his face in her hands, with an almost tender touch. "We must make you stronger," she whispered seductively. "The power of Resha running through you, molding you into the perfect soldier for my cause."

The man's eyes widened as her hands pressed against his cheeks, and an anguished choking sound escaped his lips. His features contorted, contending with an otherworldly force that consumed him. Sathariel released her grip, stepping back to observe the transformation unfolding before her eyes. The man writhed on the ground, his body convulsing in agony.

"Do not fear," Sathariel declared, her tone cool and detached. "The discomfort will soon pass, replaced by newfound strength and purpose. Embrace the power I have bestowed upon you, for you shall become a vital part of my Legion."

The man's agonized cries subsided, his breathing labored. Slowly, he rose to his feet, turning to face the astonished crowd in the courtyard. Gasps of disbelief and disgust rippled through the onlookers as they beheld his monstrous countenance. Snarling and struggling to maintain a semblance of human speech, he declared, "Yes, I am ready to fight for you, Queen Sathariel."

A cruel smile played upon Sathariel's lips as she nodded in approval. "Very well. Your first task awaits you." She gestured toward a sobbing woman, whose tears stained her cheeks. "Bring her to me, so she can join you at my side. You will fight together in my army." The transformed man seized the woman roughly by the arm, dragging her forward. The woman's cries mingled with the sounds of chaos and despair.

Chapter 24

From her vantage point, Lexi, who was bound to her saddle, could do nothing but watch in horror. Hot tears streamed down her face as she witnessed the unfolding tragedy—she was helpless. Her heart ached for the innocents who were falling victim to Sathariel's merciless grip.

But amid her despair, a glimmer of hope ignited within Lexi. She clung to the belief that Tauheed and Mariam would not falter in their mission to rally the forces of good. Lexi prayed for their swift arrival, for their intervention to stem the tide of darkness that threatened to engulf them all.

Lexi stared down at the chaos unfolding below, and her heart sank like a stone. But, though she may be bound for now, her spirit remained unyielding. She vowed to resist, to fight for freedom, and to save those she held dear from the clutches of Sathariel.

Chapter 25

Tauheed stood at the base of one of the towering Vanavashtha trees, his heart pounding in his chest. Slow and even breaths filled his lungs as he braced himself for what lay ahead. He knew he had no choice but to confront Sathariel, the one he had once loved. The darkness creeping through the tree's trunk in front of him served as a haunting reminder, a visual representation of the poison slowly corrupting their world. And Sathariel was the one who had caused it.

Hana stepped forward and placed a comforting hand on Tauheed's shoulder in reassurance as she instructed him. "Place your hand upon the trunk, Tauheed. Breathe slowly; find a state of calm within yourself. As I recite the incantation, push your palm into the Vanavashtha's trunk. Keep pushing until the tree yields beneath your fingers, then begin to walk forward."

Tauheed's incredulous expression mirrored his disbelief. "Into the tree?"

Hana's smiled kindly as she nodded. "Yes, into the tree itself. As you venture deeper, the sound of my words will fade away, and you will open your eyes to a new realm. The Vanavashtha's network will guide your journey, allowing you to traverse distances as if you had not moved at all."

Hana's eyes were serious as she continued: "Seek the changing colors, the transition from autumn to winter. That will signify the gateway, the entrance to the Jivanam tree within the courtyard of the Elutheros capital, where Lexi and Axelia are imprisoned. Act swiftly, for you must seize this opportunity as night turns to dawn."

Tauheed took a deep breath, his hands trembling as he placed his palms gently on the tree trunk. Suddenly, a chorus of sound flooded his mind, overwhelming him for a moment with a surge of incredible knowledge. Past, present, and future merged, the collective essence of Amaris coursing through him. It was heat, light, sunrise, and sunset. He sensed the power of growth, the density of the earth and the changing seasons. When the intensity subsided, Tauheed was consumed with a newfound understanding of the very fabric of his world. Of Amaris.

"That is the power of the Vanavashtha," Hana said as Tauheed released his palm from the bark. "They possess the ability to see and know all. Embrace this connection, Tauheed, and let it guide you on your path."

She pressed a folded piece of paper into his palm. "You will need to recite this to free Lexi and Axelia."

Tauheed stuffed it into his pocket, and Hana gestured for him to press his palm into the tree's bark again.

Hana began to speak an incantation, her words soaring around him like butterflies:

> *"Ptach bli lefgoa, etz ha'chaim hu haderech sheli.*
> *Over bein ha'anafim, brachvi ha'olam ani*
> *Be'ketzav ha'etz ani mekadim, brachvi ha'zman ani ne'elam."*

At first, the trunk was solid, its warmth comforting beneath his fingertips. But as he persisted, the bark grew spongy, yielding to his touch until it gave way entirely, covering his hand in a sticky, viscous substance. Hana paused momentarily, signaling him to step forward.

Eyes closed, Tauheed began to walk, and the warmth enveloped his arm, spreading across his body. He knew he had entered the tree, his senses attuned to the surreal experience. Hana's voice grew fainter, eventually fading into silence. When Tauheed opened his eyes, he found himself in a tunnel that had walls pulsating with vibrant color and light. Streams and rivers seemed to flow within the rock, roots and soil, full of life and energy.

Amazement welled within Tauheed as he observed the streams, witnessing images of butterflies and creatures of the seasons within their currents. It was a symphony of Amaris's beauty, encapsulated in these rivers of energy. Adjusting to the peculiar sensation, he broke into a quick walk, marveling at the breathtaking colors surrounding him.

The orange hues gradually transformed with each step, darkening into shades of blue and silver. Tauheed squinted ahead, his gaze fixed on a tunnel section radiating ice-white light. An indentation resembling a doorway came into view, its rippling colors distinct from the surroundings. Understanding dawned upon him, and he extended his hand and shut his eyes as he proceeded through the gateway.

Once again, Tauheed was surrounded by the thick, warm liquid of the Vanavashtha's subterranean network. He pushed through the matter, and his hand met cool air. Tauheed blinked, and as his eyes adjusted to the evening light, he saw that he had arrived in the grounds of the Elutheran palace. The moon lit up the garden, casting an ethereal glow over the shadowy forms of Lexi and Axelia, both bound by the chains of Resha. They looked frail and weakened yet still defiant in their captivity.

Tauheed's heart clenched at the sight of them. He knew he had to act quickly, before it was too late. With a determined set to his jaw, he strode toward them.

"Lexi, it is Tauheed. I have come to rescue both of you," he whispered.

Pale and exhausted, the dragon rider looked up with a start. She trembled, a glimmer of hope shining through her weariness. "How can you possibly free us? We are trapped in Resha's grip, and Axelia has little life force left. It is a miracle she's still alive."

Tauheed's set his lips in a grim line. His reassurance was resolute. "Through the Divine's gift, I have been given the means to liberate you. As the bonds of Resha fall away, you will be nourished by the power of Ruach, granting us the strength to escape."

Lexi nodded weakly. "What do you need from me?"

Gathering his resolve, Tauheed summoned a smile. "I need you to convey to Axelia that I mean her no harm, that she will be restored to full strength. But before we depart, we must destroy the Jivanam tree. It is imperative, despite Axelia's weakened state. If we fail to act, Sathariel will unleash even greater havoc upon Amaris."

Tauheed approached the dragon, the negative energy and despair surrounding Axelia so strong, it left an acrid taste in his mouth. It emanated like invisible smoke from the chains of Resha. He placed one of his hands upon the coils, and a surge of darkness intertwined with sickly sweetness consumed him. Steeling himself, he retrieved the script Hana had given him from his pocket, his eyes scanning the words.

With determination burning within him, Tauheed began to chant the incantation aloud:

> *"Mushrarar mi'shrashraot hara, koach hachaim shelcha yashuv eleicha.*
> *Beshem ha'or ve'ha'chaim, ani mevakesh shechorercha.*
> *Kishrei hachoshech yitfotzetz, vehachaim yachzeru el nativcha.*
> *Be'koach ha'ahava veharachamim, hamusarim munachatim."*

Tauheed gently placed both of his hands on the thickly wound chains around the dragon's body. As he spoke the words, his hands emitted a soft glow. The sensation was like he was attempting to melt an enormous block of ice. The Resha resisted, emanating darkness that unsettled him, the chains composed of negativity, loss, and despair.

His hands trembled as he reached out to touch the cold metal. It caused pain in Tauheed's fingertips, such was the power of the imprisonment. Resha's presence, potent and dark, the chains like a thick fog that threatened to suffocate him.

Taking a deep breath, he closed his eyes and began to pull on Ruach. He focused on channeling his energy, intertwining it with the force of goodness. Tauheed pictured Ruach as a bright light that could pierce through the darkness of the Resha chains.

A soft glow began to permeate the chains from his fingertips, the light growing stronger. Each touch melted away a layer of the chains. The Resha resisted, emanating waves of negativity, loss, and despair that threatened to overwhelm his efforts.

Tauheed's heart raced, his body trembling as he pushed through the darkness, refusing to let it consume him. The dragon's power, her primal energy, was tangible like syrup in the air, and he knew that he was getting closer to freeing Axelia from her chains.

With each repetition of the incantation, something shifted, and the radiance from Tauheed's hands began to sink into the chains. Sweat streamed down his face as he pushed back the tide of evil that was Resha, using the force of Ruach. The links crackled and sputtered while the power of light consumed its dark counterpart.

Looking up, he saw Lexi creating space between the loosening chains. She rose to her feet with great effort, and the coils dissipated like smoke, leaving her gasping in wonder.

With a final burst of strength, Tauheed broke through the last layer, Resha's darkness evaporating like a stormy cloud. The dragon's body uncoiled, her massive wings spreading, and Axelia's eyes glowed in thanks.

He looked up and saw the tears running down Lexi's face—a silent thanks for his efforts.

Tauheed fell to his knees, exhausted but relieved. The dragon, now free, looked down at him with eyes of gratitude and understanding. And in that moment, Tauheed knew that he had done something truly extraordinary.

Lexi stiffly eased herself from her position of imprisonment and turned and placed her hand on Axelia's neck. The majestic beast rose to her feet, and Tauheed could sense her life force returning, the heat rekindling within her flesh as the fires ignited in her belly once more. Lexi scrambled onto the saddle on Axelia's back. Axelia had only one chain remaining around her front leg. Tauheed, exhausted from using Ruach to overcome Resha, was intensely nauseous. The strain of breaking the bonds of such profound evil threatened to overwhelm him. With one final effort, he watched the chain binding Axelia's leg dissolve into nothingness.

Falling to his knees, Tauheed retched, expelling a bubbling dark black liquid. With each heave, his mind and body were lighter. Coughing and wiping his mouth, he glanced at Lexi, who observed him with concern. "They didn't prepare me for this part," he gasped, leaning over to vomit again.

"It must be the darkness," Lexi remarked, forehead wrinkled with concern. "Better out than in!"

Tauheed gestured toward the tree, composing himself as he labored for breath. "The tree, you must destroy the tree!"

Lexi nodded, then laid her hand on Axelia's neck. "My love, I know you have been through so much. But I need you to summon the energy to get off the ground and breathe fire. Can you do that?

Axelia turned her mighty head, and with a push, expanded her wings and flew into the air, grunting deeply. The dragon pivoted to face the sapling, then unleashed a roar that engulfed the tree in white-hot flames.

Tauheed, clamping his hands over his ears, heard the screams—the cries of the Vanavashtha as they experienced the pain of one of their own being incinerated.

Her body spent, Axelia came back down to the earth and lay on the ground, her breath coming in short bursts of exhaustion.

Lexi leaned down and extended her hand to Tauheed. "The Legion must have heard us by now. Using a dragon is hardly inconspicuous!"

In the distance, Tauheed could now hear a commotion and the heavy footfalls of Sathariel's soldiers approaching.

Then the air filled with another kind of scream—one that scraped down his soul. Tauheed hauled himself up into the saddle beside Lexi. He turned as soldiers thundered toward them from the main castle, but they were unlike any man. These beasts had twisted and grotesque faces. The soldiers lumbered toward them, bodies and limbs warped into something beyond his comprehension. Part human, part animal, part demon—their appearance betrayed their corruption. As Axelia prepared to ascend into the sky, tears welled up in Tauheed's eyes, and he muttered, "Oh, Arielle, what have you done?"

Lexi cast him a hard look. "Arielle is gone, Tauheed. Show Sathariel no mercy, for she has shown none to any of these poor beings who were once people. She is, I believe, beyond redemption."

Lexi spoke in soft tones to Axelia. "You can do this, I know you have the strength. We are almost free. Take us home."

The dragon took in a deep breath, pulling from inner reserves of strength that Tauheed prayed to the Divine would be enough. Axelia's muscles tensed and bunched, and with a roar, she soared up into the night sky. Tauheed had barely a moment to wipe the tears from his eyes before a hissing, screaming monster approached them, bearing down to the right. Axelia's head darted back and forth as she tried to fend off the creature. "What is that thing?" Tauheed gasped.

"A Malevolent—a creature of pure evil that devours souls for lunch. There's no time to explain. Tauheed, Axelia is running low on strength. You have to do something!"

He needed no further encouragement. "Tell her to ascend as high as she can, then dive, and pull up to the right!" Tauheed shouted into Lexi's ear. He began to pull on the force of Ruach, and his fingertips tingled.

She nodded, and the dragon began to climb. The Malevolent hissed and spat with venom as it pursued them. Below, more of the evil creatures emerged from the castle.

Tauheed channeled Ruach and shouted the enchantment at the top of his lungs: *"Vinctus et retentus esto intra fines huius loci. Vinctus eris terrae donec exoriatur aurora."*

The air around them rippled and shimmered. "Dive now!" he commanded.

"Hold on!" Axelia plunged toward the castle, while the Malevolents, momentarily disoriented, regrouped and advanced toward the dragon, seething with fury.

Roaring, Axelia veered to the right and soared upward, drowning out Tauheed's shouts as he continued to bellow the spell. Risking a glance downward, Tauheed witnessed a shimmering dome forming around the castle and its grounds. The Malevolents shrieked in rage, realizing they were about to be trapped. Soldiers fired arrows, but they fizzled into nothingness upon striking the nascent barrier.

Yet the danger was not over. Screeching with anger, a lone Malevolent pursued them from behind, clawing at the air.

"Quickly, my Axelia! Fly as fast as you can!" Lexi urged desperately, her eyes wide.

The dragon tensed her muscles and exerted a tremendous effort, beating her wings even harder as she sliced through the frigid night air. Above them, the dome was sealing shut. "There! Head for that opening!" Tauheed's breath was fast, and he pointed at the sliver still left to complete the dome as the edges crackled toward each other at breakneck speed.

Axelia, understanding, propelled herself toward the sky with every ounce of strength, the Malevolent snapping and screeching at her heels.

As Axelia ascended, Tauheed's ears popped, and his head spun from the altitude. The dragon exerted one final push and, shifting to a sideways position, passed through the gap, her wingtips grazing the edges of the closing dome, which fizzed shut behind her. Inside, the Malevolent screamed, a gut-wrenching sound, and it clawed at the dome's interior, now trapped beneath the protective barrier.

"How long will it hold?" Lexi asked, breathless.

"Long enough for us to distance ourselves," Tauheed grimaced.

Lexi placed her hand on her dragon's neck. "You were remarkable, my beautiful Axelia. I just need you to endure a little longer. Fly us to the Vanavasin, and then you can rest. Can you do that?"

The dragon turned her head, her eyes glowing in the dim light, and intensified the beating of her wings.

Chapter 26

Bloodcurdling screams rebounded through the ancient stone corridors of the castle, sending chills down the spines of those unfortunate enough to hear them. The grand throne room trembled under Sathariel's wrath as she stormed from one end to the other, a tempest of rage and frustration. The air crackled with her power as she blasted a hole in the stone wall to vent her destructive fury.

Sathariel's eyes flashed, and she spun on the cowering guards and Malevolents who stood silently. "How could you let this happen? How could you have failed me?" Her words were a potent blend of anger and disappointment, each word dripping with venom.

In blind anger, Sathariel demolished everything in her path. Glassware shattered into a million glimmering shards, delicate ornaments were reduced to mere fragments, and plates splintered under the force of her furious onslaught. Nothing was safe from her wrath.

As the chaos raged around her, Sathariel's eyes locked onto a figure chained in the corner of the room. It was Viera, the Divine Interpreter of the Elutheros, a symbol of hope and resistance. Her defiant gaze met Sathariel's fiery stare.

"I do not serve you," Viera declared, unyielding fire in her eyes. "I will not embrace the corrupting power of Resha. No matter how tightly you bind me, I shall never bow to your wicked bidding."

Sathariel's snarl revealed her frustration, her teeth bared like a predator ready to strike. "If you won't willingly tell me what I need to know, then I shall extract it from your mind by force," she threatened.

Closing the distance between them, Sathariel seized Viera's delicate chin in her iron grip, forcing the Divine Interpreter to meet her intense gaze. With a cruel touch, she placed her other hand gently upon Viera's temple, a twisted mockery of tenderness.

Tears welled in Viera's eyes, a testament to the torment she endured.

"Ah, poor child," Sathariel hissed. "Does my invasion into your mind hurt?"

Viera pressed her lips together in a thin line and clenched her jaw. Tears dripped down her cheeks and blood ran from her nose as she remained stoically silent.

"It's like an assault on your soul," Sathariel said with a smirk.

As abruptly as she had started, she withdrew her hand, leaving Viera gasping for breath as she sank to her knees. The tyrant queen began to pace the room again, her mind racing with newfound knowledge. The fragments of understanding began to align in her thoughts.

"The barrier that the Divine Interpreter created to hold us used a binding incantation," Sathariel murmured to herself, in a low growl of contemplation. "One that taps into the raw power of Ruach, so it is tangible and manipulable. But it cannot be traversed or undone."

Turning back to face Viera, Sathariel's eyes burned with a mix of anger and curiosity. "Yet, my intuition tells me that this field will gradually dissipate back into the very fabric of nature. Without someone to maintain it, Ruach cannot defy the will of the world. This field, as unnatural as it is, cannot persist beyond the course of the day."

Sathariel paused, a realization dawning upon her. "It has been bound by the rising of the sun, so it stands to reason that by the time the moon rises, the sun's grip on this shield will weaken," she mused aloud.

Closing the distance once again, Sathariel approached Viera with a predatory grace. She leaned closer to Viera's face. "And tell me, why did they destroy that tree? You should know, shouldn't you? You were originally Vanavasin, a priestess before you became a Divine Interpreter. I know that only the priestesses of the Vanavashtha can make that transition, aside from those who are born into it, like Tauheed."

A steely resolve settled upon Viera's features, her expression inscrutable. "You know I will never reveal their secrets. I will not give you the means to cause more harm to our world than you already have."

Sathariel's eyes narrowed, her patience waning. "Then perhaps I shall have to remove that disobedient tongue of yours since you refuse to loosen it for me," she intoned with sadistic delight.

Restless in her thoughts, Sathariel resumed her pacing, her mind racing through the fragmented memories. Suddenly, she stopped, her gaze fixated upon Viera.

"Yes, I remember now," she whispered. "I remember when I touched that tree, the Vanavashtha's sacred tree. I remember how the darkness tainted its branches, how its essence withered under the weight of Resha. That tree is a direct conduit to the Vanavashtha and all the other Jivanam saplings."

Viera remained steadfast, her expression unyielding. Sathariel turned and halted directly in front of the Divine Interpreter, her gaze boring into Viera's soul. "That tree must be the gateway they need to create for the Yasha to come into our world. For the Thura pathway, the connection between worlds requires the essence of all parts of Amaris. The Vanavashtha, the heart and soul of this land, are intrinsically linked to the Divine."

Now she realized the scope of their plan. "The Vanavashtha are connected to everything—through them, I can connect to the gateway and pass through it, can I not?"

Viera flinched, wrists jangling in the cuffs crafted from Resha, which prevented the Divine Interpreter from channeling Ruach. "You cannot hide it from me," the queen hissed with triumph. "You cannot prevent me from uncovering the truth."

With a swift motion, Sathariel reached out, placing her hand against the side of Viera's head once again. She applied pressure, pinching the interpreter's jaw between her fingers, an act of control.

Viera gasped as Sathariel shot spears of pain through her skull. Viera's eyes widened in distress. Sathariel pried open the Divine

Interpreter's mind, digging deeper into the recesses of her memories and secrets.

Releasing her grip on Viera's face, Sathariel turned her attention to the windows. "This shield, it is nothing more than a momentary inconvenience, a temporary obstacle in my grand design," she muttered to herself with disdain.

"If I have grasped their plan correctly," she continued, "once they open one gateway, every Jivanam tree on Amaris becomes a conduit to other worlds."

Sathariel grinned wickedly. "Why should I limit myself to conquering just this world? Why settle for less when I can have more?"

Viera laughed bitterly, a hollow sound that cut through the throne room. "Do you not think they have prepared for such a scenario? Do you think they don't have a plan? You won't be able to reach the Jivanam tree of the Taura or the Caelum Bellator. Only the founding clans possess saplings, which means—"

Sathariel interrupted her. "I know what it means. The Rehmat, the spirit people, and the Hayim, the plains people, are the only two other clans with saplings. The spirit people already have defenses, thanks to their connection to the Divine Interpreters and their ability to channel Ruach. But the plains people, their Jivanam tree may not be so well-guarded."

Clapping her hands together, Sathariel summoned two of her Legion soldiers into the throne room, accompanied by two Malevolents. "Once this shield is gone, we shall head straight to Qualea. It seems Sephtis has more to offer than just the gift of

Amaris. The prophecy holds no concern for me now. I shall claim another world as my own."

Chapter 27

Tauheed approached the Vanavasin temple, the towering trees whispering their secrets in the gentle evening breeze. Beside him, the priestess, Hana, held a branch from the Jivanam tree that bloomed within the citadel garden of Myrkvior.

The moonlight glittered through the canopy of ancient trees as Tauheed stepped into the hushed glade. Across the clearing, he caught sight of Lexi. Her pale countenance glowed in the eerie light, a stark contrast to her dark, worried eyes. She looked as though she had regained some vigor after the harrowing imprisonment at Sathariel's clutches, but her spirit still bore the shadows of that ordeal.

"Have you spoken to Harda?" Quiet worry stirred within him.

Lexi shook her head, green eyes flashing with anguish. "No, not yet. One of the Vanavasin healers met with us after we left you and set to work immediately. Axelia sensed that Ananpal was still recuperating after the Malevolents' attack. They sucked out much of his life essence. I can sense them in the citadel, so while I am worried, at least I know they are nearby." Lexi set her mouth in a determined line. "They *will* be here."

Tauheed offered a gentle nod and placed a comforting hand on her arm. "They will join us soon. I'm certain of it."

He turned his gaze to the stone pedestal at the center of the glade, where an open chest rested. Each line of gold embedded on its surface and interior danced and weaved in the sunlight, like silken threads across the wood. The pattern was so richly embedded, it was almost alive, and it appeared to pulse with the breath of some ancient power. Its contents, the shard of dragon egg, the luminous Mishamstone, and the Jivanam fruit from the garden of Chinasa palace were potent tokens of a prophecy unfolding. Mariam stepped forward and placed the Jewel of Aikyam inside with a soft click, and it settled gently into the chest's hallowed cavity with the other sacred objects.

A sudden shadow danced over them, drawing their eyes skyward. The sight of Ananpal descending toward the clearing brought a grin of relief to Tauheed's face.

Lexi's gasp was a whisper in the wind as she sprinted toward the landing dragon. With grace belying their size, Ananpal and Axelia entwined their necks and touched the tips of their wings in greeting.

As Lexi reached the dragon's side, Harda slid down Ananpal's broad shoulders and caught her in a lover's embrace. "I feared I'd never see you again," her mate confessed, his concern raw as he buried his face in her hair, inhaling its scent.

Tears glistened on Lexi's cheeks as she tried to contain her joy and relief. "I believed in you, Harda. But the fear was so real...I thought—"

Harda pulled back and looked into her eyes, a fierce determination in his gaze. "Don't even say it, Lexi. For you, for

Amaris, I would have given everything. But we are here, and now, together, we will destroy Sathariel and her wretched reign."

Their fingers entwined, Harda led Lexi toward the gathered circle by the plinth to join Hana, Tauheed, and Mariam.

As one, with conviction resonating in their united cry, they began the sacred chant:

"The essences of all, their destiny entwined,
Earth, air, water, and steadfast rock,
Bound together, a key to unlock.
United they stand, in harmony they merge,
Creating a gate, a pathway to surge.
Transverse time and ethereal space,
To join realms as one, in an embrace."

As their words faded, Hana turned to Tauheed, eyes solemn. "We must speak the words and you must channel the power of Ruach. Together, we shall create the Thura Gate."

She nodded to three hummingbirds that were hovering nearby. "Once opened, we will send the hummingbirds through as our emissaries."

Tauheed nodded, his heart pounding with a mix of excitement and trepidation. Hana placed her hand on the edge of the plinth, beckoning Tauheed to do the same. The priestess began to sing, and the Divine Interpreter joined her.

"Where worlds collide and destinies align,
The essences entwined, a celestial sign.
So let the elements converge and blend,
As one united force, their strengths extend.

In realms unknown, the barriers unbind,
The essences of all, forever intertwined."

As her voice waned, she nodded to Tauheed, signaling for him to continue. As he sang the words, they materialized in the air, swirling around him in a mesmerizing dance of light. Encouraged by Hana, he continued reciting the incantation; the power of Ruach swelled within him. The words circled faster and faster in the air, creating a luminous vortex of energy.

On the third recitation, Tauheed stepped back, awestruck by the spectacle before him. The spinning walls of light began to solidify, taking form and substance as the arch of the gate. Hana motioned for the three hummingbirds to approach.

"It is time for you to fulfill the prophecy and bring us our saviors," she whispered to the vibrant birds. "May the Divine guide and protect you on your journey."

The hummingbirds nodded, and with a swift burst of motion, they soared into the whirling walls of the Thura Gate, their colorful forms blending seamlessly into the radiant light.

Hana turned to Tauheed, eyes bright. "Now, we wait and trust in the Divine to bring the Yasha to us."

Chapter 28

Fatiha gazed out across the dawn landscape as the sun's rays kissed the hills with the first caress of light. In the distance, a steady drumbeat rose over the cacophony of more than two hundred thousand people, drifting toward her in the early morning air from Glastonbury Festival.

Fatiha smiled. She had been right there with them, dancing with wild abandon in the din until a few hours ago. Now, as she absorbed the peace of Glastonbury Tor, she took a slow, deep breath and pulled in the coolness around her. *It's so good to be away from the craziness of the festival and be alone with my thoughts.*

The journey to Glastonbury was supposed to have been a shared adventure, an exhilarating escapade with her now ex-boyfriend, Theo. But her world had shattered and her plans had become void when she stumbled into his room to surprise him with tickets to the festival ahead of their trip.

Fatiha's stomach knotted as she attempted to blank out what she had seen: Theo caught red-handed and red-faced, grappling with sheets as he tried and failed to hide the fact he was most definitely in the midst of getting very intimately acquainted with her best friend.

Acid roiled in Fatiha's stomach as she remembered with too much clarity that once she had recovered from the shock, she realized they were enjoying her discomfort. Her now ex-boyfriend had laughed at Fatiha's stupidity for not realizing sooner he was cheating on her, and she was most definitely now surplus to both of their requirements.

And all the while, the girl she had once trusted with her deepest secrets sat there, the white sheets gathered loosely around her nakedness, with a smirk playing on her lips.

She mused that perhaps, in time, she might have found the strength to forgive them both for that.

But then Theo had mocked her trust even more. In a bid to keep it quiet that he had cheated—he had his reputation to preserve, after all, as the golden boy at school—had shared the intimate photos Fatiha had sent him to their mutual friends, flaunting her vulnerability. The pain was sharp, almost tangible, and a profound wave of shame and loneliness threatened to consume Fatiha.

She had taken those intimate photographs for him months after they had got together, and they had told each other they were in love. Back then, the concept of their breakup had been alien, an impossibility that seemed distant. They had been head over heels, whispering sweet nothings and dreaming of embarking on thrilling adventures together once their exams were over.

Yet the most bitter betrayal was that the entire time Theo had been holding her in his arms, he had been seeing her best friend. Each word of love, each promise for the future was now a poisoned arrow piercing her heart.

Choosing to venture to Glastonbury on her own had been a decision that drew every ounce of her courage. Her mother had fretted, but Fatiha was resolute. She was determined to stand tall and be strong. She would show Theo that his deception, his utter betrayal, would not shatter her. She was not a victim of his deceit but a survivor, ready to face the world on her terms.

Fatiha lay down on the fragrant grass and looked up at the sky, slowly turning from an inky dark blue to golden yellow and tangerine. It was said Glastonbury Tor was on the site of powerful ley lines and linked to King Arthur.

The view was spectacular, and Fatiha was comforted by its beauty, although she was away from all those festivalgoers. All those thousands and thousands of people. Here she could commune with nature and connect to the earth. Deepak Chopra said if you touched a tree or placed bare feet in the grass, it helped you reconnect to the power that ran through everything on earth. Pushing her palms and bare feet down into the soft green fronds, Fatiha could well believe that as calmness washed over her.

She willed positivity to run through her veins. *This is going to be a new beginning for me. Tonight, I'm going to see my favorite band, and who knows, I might meet somebody new.*

Fatiha's thoughts meandered, and she imagined the countless pilgrimages that had converged at the doorstep of the Tor over the centuries. She took in the expanse of landscape stretching out beneath her. A pang of longing jabbed at her heart. *It would have been wonderful to share this serenity with Theo.*

She forcefully pushed away the thought like an annoying fly, refusing to let it eclipse her moment of tranquility. She whispered,

"What hurts you only makes you stronger." Each word held a resolve, a quiet fierceness.

As the vista of the Somerset countryside shimmered below, birdsong filled the air—the dawn chorus. Shutting her eyes, Fatiha listened to the sounds of nature. A whirring noise distracted her reverie. A tiny bird with iridescent plumage shimmering in the morning light floated in front of her. Fatiha narrowed her eyes and surprisedly realized she was looking at a hummingbird. The tiny creature whirred back from her a few feet and hovered, looking at her quizzically.

Fatiha had heard that, according to Native American folklore, hummingbirds could transcend time and space. They were the only creatures on the planet that could do so. *Where did this bird come from? You certainly don't see them in the English countryside.*

Fatiha pulled herself to her feet and walked toward the bird, which darted away. It hovered a few feet ahead of her, then wheeled again. Before she knew it, the little bird had led her to the entrance of the monument, St. Michael's Tower. It was clear to Fatiha that the hummingbird, with its colors like flame and narrow gold-edged wings, was trying to get her to go inside. When Fatiha approached, it flitted into the opening, its wings a blur of color. The noise coming from the distant festival seemed to fade as her ear tuned in to the immediate sounds of chirping birds, buzzing insects, and the breeze rustling in the trees.

Guided by the hummingbird's iridescent form, Fatiha ventured into the shadowed heart of the tower. As her eyes sought to adapt to the contrasting gloom, she blinked, and her gaze rose heavenward.

She was met with a spectacle of the sky awash with hues of pink and orange.

A sudden, disorienting force yanked Fatiha off balance. Glancing down in bewilderment, she discovered the source of the peculiar sensation—an indentation in the stone floor beneath her. Confusion washed over her as she tried to decipher the origin of the magnetic pull.

She discerned that the indentation carved into the cold stone was no arbitrary design but a deliberate one—a circle enclosing a triangle. As she studied the symbols, they lit up with a luminous glow.

Heart racing, Fatiha's gaze snapped up, and she squinted incredulously at the hummingbird, which appeared to speak: "Fatiha, Amaris is waiting for you."

Too stunned to question the surreal reality of words coming out of the beak of a hummingbird, Fatiha could only blink in disbelief, her mind whirling as if it couldn't catch up with what was happening. A bird—tiny, delicate, impossibly swift—was actually talking. Words. Complete sentences. Her thoughts scattered like leaves in a gust of wind, and she barely had a heartbeat to collect herself, too amazed to even wonder how such a thing could be possible. *A talking hummingbird? Surely I must be dreaming.*

A stretching sensation began to surge through Fatiha, like her body was being reshaped into strands of stringy cheese. *Is this what happens when you are pulled in every conceivable direction at exactly the same time?* A gasp escaped her, not from pain but pure shock.

In one moment, Fatiha stood with her eyes squeezed shut, and before she could even inhale a breath, she simply ceased to exist.

Every inch of Fatiha's body was being compressed into a minuscule space, as if her bones were shattering and her skin was being sucked through a narrow hole. The sensation was overwhelming, like an invisible force pulling her through a tiny tunnel, until she emerged on the other side. The comparison to a camel passing through the eye of a needle flashed in her mind, emphasizing the enormity of what she was experiencing. She was hurtling at lightning speed, everything around her whizzing by in a chaotic blur that made her head spin. It was like she was caught in a cyclone, unable to control her own movements as she traveled through this impossible space.

Fatiha's body tensed and she braced herself for the wave of pain that must surely be coming. But instead, a warm and gentle embrace enveloped her. She opened her eyes to find herself inside a large bubble, floating through the vastness of space. The stars and planets soared past her, painting streaks of light and color across the dark expanse. Despite the fear that still lingered within her, there was a strange sense of security within the bubble, as if it would guide her safely to her destination, wherever that may be.

She ran her hand along the side of what she could describe only as her craft through the cosmos. A shimmering substance coated her fingers. She rolled it between her fingers and thumb and made it into a small ball. The circular object pulsed with light. Fatiha shoved it into her pocket.

Time became an enigma to Fatiha. Had she been traveling for hours or mere seconds? She didn't know. A mounting pressure started to build around her, causing the vivid colors of her surroundings to dim. Gradually, it seemed as if all the lights in the universe were extinguished, save for a single, faint thread that pulled her bubble forward. Fatiha's gaze fixated on the thread, and to her astonishment, she noticed movement along its length—a tiny, whirring object drawing nearer. It took shape before her eyes: a hummingbird, but this one appeared to move in slow motion, its wings beating with visible strain against the currents of space and time.

Fatiha's mind was reeling, her thoughts swirling like a chaotic storm. She shut her eyes tightly again, trying to find some sense of control amid the overwhelming sensations. Suddenly, a loud pop pierced through her consciousness, and a kaleidoscope of vibrant colors burst behind her eyelids. Slowly, her senses settled and she became aware that she was lying on solid ground, the coolness of the earth seeping through her clothes and into her skin. The air around her was still tinged with the remnants of that powerful burst, leaving an electrifying energy in its wake.

Chapter 29

"Come on, keep up! We're almost there!"

Cosmo gave a long sigh. He was sure his father had told him five times they were almost there. And they weren't. Cosmo glanced up at his father's face and tried to hide a smile. His dad's cheeks were pink with excitement.

Shielding his eyes from the bright sunlight, Cosmo followed his father's lead and gazed at the breathtaking sight before them. The majestic Borobudur Temple stood tall against the backdrop of the azure-blue sky, glinting and twinkling as the sun reached its zenith. The largest Buddhist temple in the world, it was a maze of sprawling compounds. *Have I climbed every single ladder in this place and examined all of historic carvings in this entire complex in minuscule detail over the past few days? It damn well feels like it!*

His father took a deep breath, his eyes filled with wonder as he surveyed their surroundings. "Can you believe this, Cosmo? Isn't it the most incredible thing you've ever seen?"

Cosmo offered his dad a weak smile, trying his best to muster enthusiasm. "Yeah, Dad, it's pretty amazing."

This was their third day at the temple. Cosmo's father, a renowned archaeologist, had longed to visit this sacred place, which mirrored the Buddhist concept of the universe in its design. They had explored every nook and cranny of the ancient pilgrimage site, believed to symbolize the path to enlightenment.

Not much farther now, then I can sit down! Just keep thinking about how happy this makes Dad. Cosmo summoned his resolve for the last stretch to the summit of the monastery. It was impossible to deny the enchanting aura of the place; he sensed the profound spirituality that permeated its very foundations. He marveled at the monks who had constructed this feat of architecture in the eighth and ninth centuries. There were supposed to be places in the world where the veil between dimensions was thin, where you might be able to step into another reality. Cosmo believed this sacred spot was undoubtedly one of them.

He gazed toward the distant horizon, the dense jungle rolling like a green ocean.

Are they as tired as me? Cosmo rolled his shoulders and leaned over to rub his aching thighs. He was sure that no one else who had visited the temple had found it as tough as him to conquer the ladders of Borobudur.

The deep gong of a bell snapped Cosmo out of his thoughts and into a mental maelstrom. The sound was triggering, sending him headlong into a memory he continually had to stuff down.

He was back, the ground shaking violently and the buildings around him and his mother crumbling to the ground. As the church bell had struck midday, Cosmo's mother had grabbed his hand tightly, trying to shield him from the rocking chaos that gripped every object in their house. But then a massive crack split the ground beneath their feet, and before either of them could react, they were swallowed by the earth. Debris crashed around them as they fell into darkness, Cosmo's scream mingling with his mother's until they hit the ground with a sickening thud. The impact abruptly cut off their cries.

As he lay there in the silence that followed, all he could hear was the bell still, by some miracle, counting the hour of the day. Cosmo's mind raced with guilt and sorrow. His mother's lifeless body lay beside him, her hand still clutching his own. Somehow he could have prevented this tragedy. He should have been the one to protect her.

For three agonizing days, Cosmo was trapped in the rubble of what had once been their home. The darkness pressed in on him, broken only by fleeting glimpses of daylight filtering through the cracks above. He rationed what little food and water he could find as the roof of debris shifted above him.

His cries were finally heard and his father was there, ashen and wild-eyed as they pulled Cosmo's chalk-white body from the beams and rocks. Cosmo knew neither he nor his dad should have the desperate pain of responsibility for his mother's death.

But they both took on the burden of guilt like a comforting blanket. Unable to bear the thought of facing more heartache, Cosmo retreated into the digital realm of gaming, where the challenges were predictable and the outcomes within his control.

In the glow of his computer screen, he sought solace from the pain that threatened to consume him. The virtual worlds he explored offered a temporary escape from reality, a fleeting reprieve from crushing grief.

But even that couldn't stop Cosmo's panic attacks growing more frequent, each one more suffocating than the last. The memories of those three days trapped under the rubble haunted him, replaying in his mind like a never-ending nightmare. Sleep also became a distant luxury; every time he closed his eyes, he was transported back to that moment when he lost his mother.

His friends noticed the change in him, the way he became more withdrawn and lost in his own thoughts. They tried to reach out, to bring him back from the darkness that threatened to consume him. But Cosmo couldn't find the words to explain the turmoil raging inside him. How could he make them understand the guilt that cast a stain on his soul?

In those virtual worlds, he could be anyone but himself, losing himself in quests and battles that held no real consequence.

As the peals of the bell died away, Cosmo forced himself to breathe in and out, slowly, and steadily, holding for four counts. *Inhale and exhale, inhale and exhale.* He held it to him as a mantra, and the fight-or-flight panic that had been building in his nervous system started to wane.

As he blinked and came back to reality, Cosmo's eyes fell on one of the imposing bell-shaped structures. Now was the moment to investigate what was inside the sacred space. Maybe he would see something that no one other than the monks had looked at for centuries.

Cosmo stepped out of the sunlight and into the cool air of the entrance. The air was thick with tiny filaments. His hand brushed the rough, ancient surface, the sensation of time itself locked in the crevices of the stone. Slivers of sunlight slipped through the diamond-shaped gaps in the walls, casting strange, shimmering patterns that danced around the dim space, like whispers of forgotten stories. Dust particles floated lazily in the shafts of light, and the air tasted faintly of incense and rain. The silence was thick, almost tangible, and yet, there was a hum, a low vibration. *It's like the walls are alive—waiting, watching.*

Cosmo noticed a tiny hummingbird perched nearby. It took off in a blur of color and flew in circles, moving forward and backward, guiding him. He hoisted himself up the curvatures of the structure and slipped through a diamond-shaped opening.

With a leap, Cosmo stood within, marveling at the dome towering above him. Though the air carried a musty scent, the grandeur of the space remained intact. Leaning against the cool stone wall, he savored the peaceful moment. An incessant stream of worries often consumed Cosmo's mind like white noise that would never quiet. He had fretted over his father's well-being since his mother had died, and anxiety over the future plagued his thoughts. Global warming, wars, and the world's uncertainties weighed upon his shoulders. What if another pandemic struck? What would become of them then? Sometimes, he yearned to cover his ears, to drown out the cacophony and release his frustrations in a scream that could silence it all.

The hummingbird, its wings shimmering green and red, hovered in front of Cosmo's face with a soft whirring sound. "Come on, we don't have any time to lose," it urged.

Cosmo's heart raced as he struggled to process the words. "Are you really speaking to me?" His eyes widened in wonder.

The bird replied with a mischievous twinkle in its eye: "I don't see anyone else here."

Cosmo's mind reeled at the impossible conversation he was having with this tiny creature.

He pinched himself, half expecting to wake up from a strange dream. But the pinch resulted only in a sharp pain, confirming that he was indeed awake.

"But...birds can't talk!" His mind raced with questions as he tried to make sense of everything.

"Who says? Who makes the rules that birds can't talk?" the hummingbird countered. "Perhaps they cannot speak where we are right now, but what if there are places where they can? Just as the monks believe these temple spheres exist simultaneously in different realities, maybe I exist in two different places as well. In one of those places, I can talk. And right now, you are witnessing me in both existences."

A wave of overwhelming emotions engulfed Cosmo—disbelief and amusement—propelling a laugh to erupt from his throat. His lips quirked. "Am I really conversing with a talking hummingbird that defies the laws of physics? This is beyond anything I could have imagined."

The tiny bird fluttered and buzzed around Cosmo's head, its wings a blur of motion. "Do you want to save the world?" it chirped.

Cosmo raised his eyebrows. "Well, my feathered friend, are we talking about this world or the one you believe you're a part of?"

"What are your thoughts on transcendental travel? The kind that defies the boundaries of space and time," the hummingbird continued.

Now this was something Cosmo did know about—his father's teachings from those complex science books. "Hmm, yes, it's familiar, but it's not something I've pondered much." His response was guarded. *Where was this going?*

He shook his head violently. *This isn't real. It can't be. I've inhaled some kind of weird fungus in here and I'm hallucinating.*

The hummingbird's response was cryptic. "Yasha, I am sorry to inform you, there is not much of a choice in the matter. But I wanted to offer you the option to decline."

Before Cosmo could even respond, another loud, reverberating gong rang out, shaking the ground beneath him. The sound grew louder and louder, filling his head with an overwhelming clamor. Acid rose in his mouth, the familiar squeeze in his chest as the panic began to grip him. Salt and smoke filled his nostrils as his body shuddered. He clapped his hands over his ears, desperate for the noise to cease. "Make it stop! Please, make it stop!" he pleaded, assaulted by the relentless gong.

Unable to bear it any longer, Cosmo dropped to his knees, shielding his head with his arms, and tried to block out the cacophony. An immense force gripped his body, yanking and pulling him as if he were caught in a colossal whirlwind. Squeezing his eyes shut, he sensed a blinding, radiant light piercing through his eyelids. And then...everything went silent.

Chapter 30

Jiyanu's eyes began to glaze over as he stared at the countless rows of stoic soldiers. Each one stood tall and unwavering, creating an army that stretched as far as his eyes could see. He knew it should thrill him to be at the tomb of Qin Shi Huangdi, the legendary first emperor of China. People from all corners of the globe traveled to witness the marvel of these terracotta warriors. But truth be told, Jiyanu was disinterested.

He grimaced and let his attention drift. Jiyanu did not enjoy history, and he dreaded the inevitable project or essay that awaited him once the Xi'an trip concluded.

As he glanced down at his phone, idly scrolling through social media, a nasally voice brought him back to reality. "Hey, Jiyanu, don't wander off from the group. Focus more on your studies instead of being glued to that phone," his teacher admonished, standing in front of him with hands on hips.

Jiyanu looked up at his teacher, a hint of sarcasm in his words. "Yes, sir. I'm paying utmost attention to these amazing statues surrounding us."

The teacher wagged a finger at him.

Despite his preference for the latest trending videos and lack of interest in anything to do with the past, Jiyanu had to admit that the army standing silently and stretching into the distance was an awe-inspiring sight. The meticulous craftsmanship of the warriors, each one carved with intricate detail, was truly impressive. All he had accomplished in his years on this planet was a hefty following on TikTok.

His teacher droned on the edges of his consciousness. “Approximately two thousand warriors have been excavated since the site’s discovery in 1974. But it’s believed the mausoleum houses around eight thousand statues. Many of them remain covered for preservation, shielded from the air that might hasten their deterioration. Did you know that the emperor burned most books in the country in 213 BCE, except those on certain topics, and murdered around four hundred and sixty Confucian scholars?”

Yada, yada, yada. But there was a grandiosity to the emperor’s vision. To create an entire city and army to accompany him in the afterlife, there was no doubt he had held firm beliefs about his importance.

Or perhaps he had possessed knowledge about the afterlife that eluded others? *He definitely hated school as much as me if he burned all those books and killed those scholars.* Jiyanu chortled at his own joke.

He glanced at his classmates, engrossed in their fascination with the warriors. He shifted uncomfortably.

I don’t fit in. But on social media, I can escape judgment and even become the judge myself, safely hidden because no one truly knows me.

Straying from the group, Jiyanu walked along a pathway, hoping to get a closer look at a statue. He preferred his own company most of the time. He ventured into a part of the exhibit closed off to the public, where the soldiers were still being excavated. The realization that nobody was watching caused excitement to prick at Jiyanu's skin. He ducked under the rope cordoning off the forbidden area. Jiyanu ignored the prominent sign in vibrant red Chinese writing that declared NOT OPEN TO THE PUBLIC, along with translations in multiple languages. Being told not to go somewhere only fueled Jiyanu's desire to explore.

The thrill of exploring forbidden territory rushed through his veins. A mischievous plan formed in his mind. *I can finally get a real look at these warriors, and if I capture it on video and share it online, everyone will be amazed. I'll gain so many followers!*

The other kids at the orphanage couldn't comprehend his struggles. They didn't understand what it was like to see your mother killed by your father.

They whispered behind his back, calling him "the boy with the haunted eyes." But he didn't care about their ridicule. He had learned to block out the noise around him, focusing instead on his own internal world.

Memories of that fateful night flooded back to Jiyanu. The sound of shattering glass, his mother's scream, the metallic tang of blood in the air. But amid the chaos and terror, there was one moment that stood out in his mind: the moment when his father's eyes met his own. In that brief exchange, Jiyanu saw no remorse, no love—only a cold emptiness that chilled him to the core. And it was that emptiness that drove him now, pushing him to survive and overcome every obstacle in his path.

He had been in and out of foster care, in and out of homes, a pawn in a system that didn't seem to know what to do with him. He just couldn't choke down the anger that on some days overwhelmed him so much, he had to just *do* something to let it out.

Sometimes he took it out on objects around him—smashing them up in a tirade. Sometimes he would be mean—verbally or physically—to anyone too close to him physically.

But on social media, that's where no one knew who he truly was or what he had been through. He could be anyone he wanted to be.

His obsession had started as he scrolled through his news feed. There was a pang of envy in Jiyanu's chest as he saw curated lives displayed in perfect squares. He couldn't help but wonder what it would be like to have a life as picture-perfect. The more he thought about it, the more he realized he could create a new persona online, one that was free from his past and insecurities.

While Jiyanu craved solitude in real life, he longed for validation and recognition. It was a way to escape the gnawing loneliness that haunted his nights, a means to be accepted and liked. And yes, there was judgment and nastiness, but they were judging a version of himself he had created. And that made it easier.

The day he had put his heart in a little box and thrown away the key had made it much easier to cope with being dead inside.

For Jiyanu, often each of those days blurred into the next, a monotonous routine that shielded him from the pain of his past. But deep down, he knew that locking away his heart was not a permanent solution.

Jiyanu jumped down into the partially excavated pit, eye level with one soldier who looked at him with an inscrutable expression.

Jiyanu reached out a hand to touch the terracotta statue, knowing that he probably shouldn't. There was that shiver of excitement again.

"Why are you looking at me like that? Are you going to disintegrate?" With an admonishing look, he waggled a finger at the clay man.

Jiyanu maneuvered his phone into the other hand so that he could film. He didn't dare go live. *What if I get found out? Who knows what might happen then?* Yes, he liked to push boundaries, but being arrested was not an experience he wanted to go through.

Jiyanu gently touched the statue's surface, lightly brushing against the terracotta material. To his surprise, his fingers seemed to sink into the solid form, as if dipping into a bowl of thick treacle. He couldn't help but gasp at this unexpected sensation, his mind racing with questions and wonder. *What kind of illusion is this?*

Jiyanu's hand and arm continued to fade into the warrior's chest, like a ghostly apparition merging with solid flesh. His eyes were wide with wonder and confusion as he slowly withdrew his hand, gazing at it in disbelief. To his amazement, all of his fingers were intact and unharmed, despite seemingly being devoured by the warrior's body.

With a shaky hand, Jiyanu reached toward the statue and placed his palm on its chest again. His hand disappeared into the clay. He gasped again and pulled it out, heart racing with excitement. Fumbling for his phone, he hit record and exclaimed to the thick air around him, "This is insane! Everyone needs to see this! This video is going to blow up!"

A strong force suddenly grabbed his wrist and squeezed like a metal vise. His bones ground against each other as he struggled to break free, but the grip only tightened. With a loud clattering noise, his phone fell from his grasp and crashed onto the ground.

Panic rose up in him like a tide as he pulled with all his might. But it was no use—one of his arms was now entirely trapped in the statue's unyielding grasp. A shock of pain shot through his body as he was lifted off the ground by his trapped limb, held captive by the merciless terracotta figure.

His muscles strained as he attempted to push his body away from the imposing warrior, but it was no use. Jiyanu made the mistake of trying to purchase leverage by pushing his body away from the statue with his other hand. The unseen force grabbed hold of his fingers, and his other hand sank into the smooth surface, sending shivers down his spine.

Jiyanu's arms were now sunk into the clay up to his shoulders, as he was pulled closer to the statue in a deathly embrace of terrifying strength.

Desperately, Jiyanu tried to free himself, using all his might to pull his arms out of the statue's unyielding grasp. But suddenly, a surge of power jolted through him and his feet slid along the floor. The statue jerked his body into itself, swallowing up Jiyanu. His frantic cries were cut off by a sudden choke as he vanished into thin air.

Chapter 31

Fatiha could see the shades of vibrant colors through her eyelids. Blinking her eyes open, she looked up to find a man and a woman peering down at her. Fear mingled with awe as she studied their faces. They appeared different from anyone she had ever encountered. The man regarded Fatiha with curiosity and elation. The woman, whose skin seemed to ripple with the hues of autumn leaves, extended a hand to help her up.

"Welcome to Amaris." Hana smiled as Fatiha stood to her feet. "I'm Hana, and this is Tauheed, the Divine Interpreter. I apologize if the journey was unsettling. Creating the Thura Gate was an unprecedented event. Did you experience any pain or fear during the transit? Are you...intact?"

Fatiha decided the best way to approach this situation, given the fact she had just traveled through space and time, was to be polite, not show fear, and to ignore what her mind was currently screaming at her: *WTF is happening right now?* She gingerly squeezed her limbs, stood up, and patted herself down. She seemed unharmed and plastered a smile on her face, which did not give any indication of the fact she was quite scared. *Best not to antagonize anyone until I have worked out exactly what is happening here.*

"Yes, I think I'm all in one piece. No broken bones, it seems."

"You must be wondering where you are," Tauheed said, his gaze filled with gentle understanding.

Fatiha tried not to laugh at what she thought was a stupid question. *That's stating the obvious!*

"Well, yes," Fatiha responded. She was standing in a forest like nothing she had ever seen. Towering trees reached toward the heavens, and an indistinct symphony of sounds—birdsong or perhaps animal calls—filled the air.

Fatiha marveled at her surroundings. "Yes, about that," she began, filled with curiosity. "Where exactly am I?"

As Fatiha took in her new environment, a sense of calm washed over her. Her lizard brain, usually prone to meltdowns, remained composed. She thanked her daily meditation practice, which had been working wonders to regulate her emotions.

Tauheed offered her a kind smile. Fatiha would have placed him a few years older than her, but his dark green eyes belonged to someone in the same age range as her father. He was clean-cut and handsome, with tan skin and dark hair that fell to his shoulder in soft waves.

"You are in the world of Amaris," he revealed. With a grand gesture toward the majestic trees that loomed overhead, their branches stretching toward the heavens, he continued, "To be more precise, you are in the Forest of Myrkvior, in the Sacred Clearing of the Vanavashtha. We summoned you through a Thura Gate, a mystical portal we created to bring you from your world to ours. Now, where were you in your own world when this extraordinary event occurred?"

Fatiha's brain whirled in disbelief. *I'm in another world and came through a mystical portal. Seriously, what is happening right now? And are they really going to know what I am talking about if I tell them where I was? Mind you, Glastonbury is supposed to be a bit mystical. To hell with it; I'm just going to tell them.* "I was standing at Glastonbury Tor, a place rumored to possess spiritual power. Perhaps that's why you were able to bring me here?"

Tauheed contemplated her words. "Hmm, that might very well be," he mused. "With the guidance of the Divine, we hope to learn how to control the Thura Gates, determining when and where we can use them. However, we are still in the experimental phase. Regardless, we are incredibly relieved that you arrived unharmed."

Hana nodded in agreement. "While we may not comprehend the methods or meanings behind every decision made by the Divine, we are overjoyed to have you here," she expressed warmly. "However, my concern lies in the fact that you are the sole person from your world to make it to us. There should be two others like you."

Tauheed furrowed his brow, casting a questioning gaze between Fatiha and the priestess. "Did you encounter anyone else...?" he inquired and trailed off, clearly searching for her name.

Fatiha burst into laughter, momentarily forgetting the gravity of the situation. "My name's Fatiha. And in answer to me seeing anyone else—are you kidding me? Are you telling me this has happened to other people as well? To be honest, I didn't have time to notice because everything was a blur, and I could barely keep myself from spewing everywhere!" she exclaimed, using vivid gestures to illustrate her point.

Confusion clouded the faces of Tauheed and Hana as they exchanged puzzled glances. Fatiha, realizing their lack of understanding, clarified by mimicking the action of throwing up. "You know, vomit, be sick."

Understanding dawned on them, and Tauheed nodded empathetically. "Ah, that would have been rather unpleasant. We will have to find a solution for that."

Hana, dressed in long flowing robes that undulated with shades of emerald and green, walked toward one of the colossal Vanavashtha trees in front of them and gently placed her hand on its ancient trunk. She closed her eyes and appeared to be engaged in a silent conversation.

Fatiha watched with incredulity. "Is that woman talking to the tree?"

Tauheed nodded with a reassuring smile. "Indeed, Hana is a priestess. She possesses the rare gift of communicating with the Vanavashtha. They are the oldest living creations of Amaris, intricately connected to every aspect of our world. I understand that all of this must be incredibly confusing for you."

Fatiha nodded, and Tauheed clearly took it as sign to continue. "I will explain everything to you soon and clarify why you are here. But first, we must find the whereabouts of the other Yasha. They are the others of your kind who are destined to aid us in saving our world, as foretold in the prophecy."

Fatiha looked from one to the other of these very strange people. She pointed to her feet. "Okay, implementing a suspension of disbelief right now, if you need me to help you to fulfill a prophecy and save you all, I could probably do with some shoes."

Before Tauheed could answer, Hana shut her eyes for a moment and then opened them, her expression a mix of fear and concern. "The others have arrived," she said urgently.

"Where?" Tauheed wrung his hands. "Why aren't they here at the Thura Gate with us?"

"In creating this portal, we activated the other Jivanam saplings as transcendental conduits," Hana explained. "As we feared, some of the remaining sapling tree sites across the realms have become active gateways. To add to this, for some reason, the entry points to Amaris have not been right at the Thura Gates. One of the Yasha has arrived some way from the sapling itself. "The Vanavashtha have revealed that one of them is safe—he has arrived in Salama with the Rehmat, the spirit people, who will keep him protected. There is no way Sathariel can reach him. The Jivanam tree at Chinasa where Sathariel first spread Resha is too corrupted to act as a portal."

She rubbed her face and crinkled her brows in worry. "But the other Yasha has been sent to Qualea, the Hayim capital, and will have to journey to the city. Thankfully, the hummingbird will be a guide," Hana continued grimly.

Tauheed appeared troubled. "Let us hope the Yasha is not harmed in any way. They could be vulnerable to Sathariel's grasp. They will have no idea their Jivanam tree has become a portal."

"Then we must reach him before she does," Tauheed declared, his tone resolute. "We cannot allow him to fall into her clutches. She will now no doubt know that their unity is crucial for us to imprison her."

Fatiha watched them both and realized that whatever was happening, it was clearly serious.

Hana nodded in agreement with Tauheed. "We must hasten our journey back to the Vanavasin capital. Once there, we can convene with the Taura and the Vanavasin leaders. The sooner we unite the Yasha, the better our chances of thwarting Sathariel."

He beckoned to one of the hummingbirds. "Make haste to Qualea and explain to Charaka, their leader, what is happening. They must prepare themselves."

"I'm on it," the little bird tweeted, and it whizzed into the air in a blur.

Fatiha blinked in amazement.

Tauheed called out, "Harda, Lexi, come here."

Fatiha turned behind her for the first time to see who he was waving at and did a double take. Two tall, fit, and extremely beautiful people strode toward them. They looked like they had stepped out of an action movie.

The man had piercing amber eyes, his muscular frame wrapped in midnight-black riding leathers with subtle silver threading that caught the light.

The woman's platinum-blond hair was pulled back in tightly wound plaits that complemented her leather armor with platinum buckles.

But it was the two gigantic dragons who lounged behind them that really made her want to pinch herself. Eyes lidded in relaxation, the beasts rustled their wings as their scales refracted the light in myriad patterns. Their translucent wing membranes were so thin that sunlight passed through them, projecting rainbow kaleidoscopes on the ground below.

One of the dragons opened an eye wider and stared right at Fatiha. The beast's pupils contracted into vertical slits as the creature focused, irises changing from gold to crimson. Ancient battle scars crisscrossed their hides, some sealed with what looked like molten silver or gold.

Fatiha raised her eyebrows and tried not to let her jaw fall open in amazement. *How can this be possible? Dragons? This day is getting crazier.*

The woman smiled and thrust out a hand in greeting as her face lit up with a warm smile.

"Lexi, at your service. Don't mind them," she said, nonchalantly waving her other hand toward the dragons. "They just ate two cows a few hours ago; they are too sleepy to do anything."

The man next to her gave a deep laugh as he placed a hand on Lexi's shoulder. "Ananpal and Axelia are both very impressed with your ability to fly through time and space. It's not something even they can do."

Fatiha gave a shy smile. "Thank you, I think? Can you tell me why I am here?" *That would be very helpful.* It was then she noticed the other person in the clearing, standing near the dragons.

A woman moved toward them, gliding over the ground as fluid as water. There was translucent webbing between her elongated fingers, and her skin shifted in tones of aquamarine. She appeared to be clothed in an outfit composed of fish scales in shades of mother-of-pearl.

"Queen Mariam," Tauheed called out, and the woman smiled warmly, exposing pointed brilliant-white teeth.

Tauheed gave Fatiha a brief outline of why she had been brought the Amaris. With each sentence, the pressure in her chest grew. *Is this for real? How am I supposed to do this? Evil queens? Magical forces? This has to be a dream.* But a sharp pinch indicated she was apparently very much awake. Fatiha bit her cheeks, trying not to feel overwhelmed.

She was brought back from her ruminations by Queen Mariam. "I think the best thing is for Harda to take the queen of the Adira to Salama. Lexi, you can stay with us. We need to go to the Taura and see if they will join forces against Sathariel."

The dragon rider nodded in approval, and the woman with clothing made of scales smiled, her skin changing to a deeper blue. "Absolutely, Tauheed. But I think this one needs some food and a more detailed explanation of exactly what is going on."

Fatiha looked from Tauheed to the priestess, brimming with curiosity. "Yes. Can somebody please tell me because it's not every day you fly through the galaxy and end up in a forest with dragons and talking trees and hummingbirds!"

The hummingbird she had encountered on her journey fluttered before her, as if it knew it was being talked about, its wings a blur of motion.

"I can explain everything as we walk," Tauheed said.

Fatiha tried to take a moment to process all these strange occurrences in what was shaping up to be a very bewildering day. She realized that she would have to go with the flow to avoid a panic attack. It would not be a good look, she surmised.

“All right,” she agreed, summoning her suspension of disbelief. “Fill me in as we head to...Myrkvior, was it? Considering the circumstances, I don’t seem to have much choice in the matter other than to go with you. But I’m not sure if I’m going to be able to help you. Being a superhero and saving worlds are not things I’ve been working toward as a career path. That’s a pretty tall order.”

Hana and Tauheed exchanged glances and gave a small nod of approval. The Divine Interpreter then turned back to Fatiha. “I believe you are going to be just fine in assisting us with our task, Yasha,” he said, a spark of hope shining in his eyes.

Chapter 32

One minute, Jiyanu was thinking about how filming his hand pushing into a statue was going to blow up his TikTok. Then the next, he was being swallowed by said statue, agonizing pain piercing every part of his body as he was sucked into the clay.

He saw a flash of blinding light through his eyelids, which were squeezed shut as he was suffocated and choked by the statue itself, which, to his mind, was trying to eat him.

Then it vanished, and Jiyanu opened his eyes and spluttered. He was floating and bobbing through the darkness of the universe, suspended in a bubble, transcending the space-time continuum. Jiyanu couldn't even begin to wrap his mind around that. The planets and stars flashed past him as he traveled so fast that it must have been more than the speed of sound, or even light.

Now he was having the most incredible adventure of his life. "Wait until I get back to the orphanage and tell them all about this!" he exclaimed out loud with excitement.

Jiyanu was completely immersed in the present moment, relishing the joy of something truly extraordinary shaking up his otherwise mundane existence. He had decided to let go of fear and simply embrace whatever was happening to him.

As he rode through the vast expanse of the universe in his tiny transcendental sphere, colors and shapes merged into a mesmerizing blur. As Jiyanu placed his hands against the sides of his strange craft, the walls began to shudder. *Is this thing going to break up?*

His lungs started to burn, and a strange squeezing sensation enveloped him. The sphere gradually filled with a peculiar pink mist. Jiyanu started coughing. His lungs were now filling up with the substance that was an acrid taste on his tongue. He squeezed his eyes shut, hugging his knees to his chest. Suddenly, an almighty popping sound split the air.

"Help me!" Jiyanu cried out as he tumbled endlessly, falling over and over. Then, with a resounding thump, his body collided with the ground.

Opening his eyes, Jiyanu gazed up at the sight of roots emerging from the earth above him. Light streamed through the gaps in the soil, accompanied by a faint draft of air caressing his face. He wiped his mouth as a bit of soil made its way inside.

Sitting upright, Jiyanu took a moment to assess his surroundings. As he surveyed the scene, he noticed roots and chunks of rock embedded in the soil along the edges of the large hole he found himself in. It seemed possible to scale the wall and climb up through a larger gap about six feet above him. Jiyanu stood up and made his way to the side of the hole. He grasped one of the sturdier-looking roots and began pulling himself upward, determined to reach the patch of light.

After a few minutes of strenuous effort, Jiyanu found himself suspended from the ceiling of the hole. Hanging like a nimble monkey from the branch of a tree, he mustered one final push, shimmying along the large root until he managed to push his face and one arm through to the ground above. With a series of twists and wriggles, he hauled the rest of his body through the gap.

Huffing and puffing, Jiyanu emerged into the warm afternoon sunlight. Dusting himself off, he stood upright, facing the majestic tree trunk. As he caught his breath, he had the chilling sensation he wasn't alone. Slowly turning away, he stared directly into the fierce countenance of a warrior.

With intricately braided violet hair and armor accentuating every muscle, the warrior wielded a spear as if poised for battle. Her eyes sparkled with an alertness that Jiyanu believed not even ten cups of coffee could match. Standing beside her was another woman, dressed in more-serene attire. Her lilac braids cascaded loosely down her back, and she wore a flowing robe of shimmering gold.

"Welcome, Yasha." The warrior spoke first, her fierce appearance in stark contrast to her soft-spoken words. "You are truly a gift to behold. Welcome to Amaris, and Salama, the capital of the Rehmat, the spirit people."

"A gift to behold?" Jiyanu questioned, bewildered. "Does that mean you knew I was coming?"

"We have been waiting for you and the other Yasha from your world," replied the woman with the golden robe, her smile radiating warmth. She gestured toward her formidable companion. "This is Louisa, the leader of the Rehmat, and I am Moirah. We are here to ensure your safety and answer all your questions."

Jiyanu nodded, finding himself at a rare loss for words. Usually, he was the quick-witted one, ready with a clever retort or a humorous quip. But now, he was simply dumbfounded.

"Jiyanu, er, pleased to meet you." He was embarrassed at how meek he sounded.

Turning his attention back to the tree behind him, adorned with blossoming flowers, Jiyanu couldn't help but notice a creeping darkness near its base. Louisa motioned with her spear, indicating they should proceed toward a large wooden archway in the garden's corner, leading to a courtyard. Jiyanu had no intention of arguing with an Amazonian-style warrior wielding an enormous weapon. She was undoubtedly the one calling the shots.

As Jiyanu stepped into the courtyard, his gaze immediately fell upon the most exquisite rock he had ever seen. The stone, about six feet tall, seemed to vibrate and breathe like a living entity, seamlessly blending into the surrounding grass and earth. Its multifaceted surface reflected the colors of the surroundings in myriad ways. Flanking the rock were two more fearsome women warriors, their appearance and attire as formidable as Louisa's.

Jiyanu gaped in awe. "That rock looks like it's alive!"

Louisa nodded in agreement. "You are beholding the rock of Sambandh, an integral part of the very fabric of Amaris, gifted to us by the Divine. It was created during the time of Creation. We guard it, along with the Jivanam tree of the Vanavashtha, through powerful incantations."

Suddenly, a screeching noise boomed above them. Jiyanu shielded his eyes from the sun's glare and saw a breathtaking sight: a dragon soaring through the sky.

“If I see nothing else in this place, that dragon alone is enough for me. In real life! Wow!” Jiyanu exclaimed, his eyes wide with wonder. He watched in amazement as the majestic beast gracefully landed on the battlements of a nearby sand-colored building. Two individuals descended from the dragon’s side.

“It’s Harda, the leader of the dragon riders, and Queen Mariam,” Louisa informed Moirah. “They must bring news from the Vanavasin. We should meet them inside the citadel.”

Jiyanu followed Moirah and Louisa into the cool interior of the nearby building. Their journey through a maze of twisting corridors and hidden alcoves led him to a room of exquisite beauty. The high, arched ceiling towered above them, sculpted with skillful precision. The sheer height of it suggested a sense of endless space, while the ornate patterns that danced across its surface added a touch of regal elegance.

Almond-shaped slits served as the room’s exclusive illumination source, inviting slender beams of golden sunlight to cascade inside. The warm rays painted patterns of light and shadow on the room’s surfaces. A refreshing gust of wind caused the light drapes to billow gently. It brought a faint scent of distant citrus groves mingling with the musty smell of old stone. Mosaic tiles in numerous colors and with complex geometric patterns dressed the walls from floor to ceiling.

Seated at a table in the center of the room were the dragon rider and a woman whose skin shimmered with the hues of the water, hinting at the texture of fish scales.

The woman with the glimmering skin nodded in greeting. “Welcome, Yasha. I am Mariam, queen of the Adira. We are delighted that you have arrived in Amaris. Another from your world, Fatiha, is already here, and we must unite both of you with great haste."

She turned her attention to Moirah and Louisa. "We are in grave danger. We believe Arielle, who is now in the thrall of Sephtis, is aware of the presence of the Yasha among us."

Moirah nodded slowly in disbelief, while Louisa banged her spear into the ground in anger.

The ocean queen looked between the women with sympathy. "I know how you must be hurt over her betrayal. Arielle, our conduit to the Divine, is no more. She is now Sathariel, and she is bent on possessing us and our world for herself. Tauheed imprisoned her within a capturing enchantment inside the castle at Heliopolis. But its strength is waning. The dome under which she and her forces are imprisoned will last only so long. It may have already deteriorated enough for her to break free."

Moirah looked grave. "So she is responsible for the taint that is creeping through the Jivanam trees. She has poisoned them with Resha."

The queen nodded. "We think her next move will be to go the Hayim. Sathariel will not dare come here because she knows it is protected. But it is likely she will see that the Jivanam tree in the citadel of the plains people is vulnerable despite their reputation as fearsome warriors. The city is also near the sacred site of the Creation of Amaris. I think that is a place she will strike for power. I believe Sathariel thinks harnessing the power of their Jivanam tree, so close to the birth of our world, as the only way she can evade imprisonment and thwart our efforts to save Amaris."

Harda continued the dire news: "The Hephaes have revealed that the key to imprisoning her lies within the rock of Sambandh, which holds great significance for you. The prison, known as the Fylakistone, which we need to use to capture Sathariel, can be formed only with the blood of the Yasha."

He smiled kindly at Jiyanu, who was looking between them. "That is you, in case you were wondering."

Jiyanu was confused, still trying to understand the bizarre set of circumstances that had led to him conversing with a dragon rider on what appeared to be another planet.

As Jiyanu's mind whirled, Harda continued: "Sathariel knows that by capturing one of the Yasha, she can prevent the creation of the prison that could hold her."

Moirah and Louisa exchanged concerned glances. Moirah was calm in her response. "This is very troubling news. Thankfully, we possess the incantations to protect the rock from her."

Louisa's eyes burned with anger. "Mother of Salama! How can you be so calm? This Sathariel is going to try to destroy us! We must fight her!"

Harda held up a hand in a plea for calm. "That's not all," he added. "Hana has discovered that Sathariel now has the opportunity to enter the Yasha's world through a Thura Gate that has opened between the two realms. We must seal the gates and create the prison without delay."

The gravity of the situation left even Jiyanu speechless. Moirah rose with determination. "We will commence the incantations to create the Fylakistone. Our teaching outlines the steps required for its formation."

Moirah smiled, her eyes lighting with warmth. "Our teachings foretold that the Sambandh was always more than just a protector of our race. This was handed down to us from elder to elder."

She began to sing in a low melodic tone:

> *"A prison crafted to contain the looming threat,*
> *That seeks to shatter all held dear, with regret.*
> *Yet, to complete this task and forge their defense,*
> *They require the blood of another, a vital essence.*
> *The unification of Amaris, a realm intertwined,*
> *Shall bring together the forces needed to bind.*
> *For the fate of Amaris lies in this grand design,*
> *To create from the Sambandh the Fylakistone, our ultimate lifeline."*

The queen stood, placing a hand on Moirah's. "May the Divine guide our path. We will provide all the support we can so that you may successfully bring the creation of the Fylakistone to fruition."

Chapter 33

The last few hours had left Cosmo in a bewildered daze. One moment he'd been at a historical monument, following a talking hummingbird. As if that weren't strange enough, he had then been transported through the universe to an entirely different world he knew nothing about.

Cosmo's sphere had crash-landed into a barren landscape. The tiny bird had guided him through the wild and rocky desert, its terrain a testament to the fierce elements it had once endured and withstood.

The land had unfolded before Cosmo in spectacular formations of burnt-orange and deep-crimson hills, their colors so vivid under the sun that they seemed almost otherworldly. The small bird led him over a series of deep gulches and winding arroyos, showing him where he could get water. And all the while, it had been explaining why Cosmo had been brought to Amaris and this mission he must undertake.

To say Cosmo's mind was blown was an understatement.

As he had made his way across ancient riverbeds that bore witness to waters long since dried, he had tried to make sense of it all.

As the sun had started to dip below the horizon, it was then, at a distance, when Cosmo first glimpsed what seemed like an apparition: a city emerging as though it were a part of the land itself. It was built entirely of sandstone, carved straight out of the living rock and nestled in the protective embrace of a monumental cliff. The cliff dropped away stupefyingly into a vast plateau stretching unbroken for miles, swallowing the horizon and merging with the sky.

It was here the hummingbird had brought Cosmo to Charaka, who had introduced himself as the leader of the Hayim.

As he tried to wrap his head around this mind-bending journey, the bombshell was dropped—not only was Cosmo to help thwart an evil queen's quest for this world's domination, but his own planet was now also in jeopardy because of this power-obsessed monarch.

And to do his part, he had to give up his own blood, as did two other people from Earth, who were apparently here as well. Somewhere.

He pressed his lips in a thin line as he tried to make sense of it all. *Is this a nightmare or something really cool that's happening right now?* He couldn't decide.

"Cosmo, are you all right? I know this is a lot to take in." Charaka smiled in sympathy as he secured blades in strategic locations on his body.

Cosmo couldn't help but wince at the thought of the potential discomfort of having such sharp weapons thrust into places that were downright dangerous and painful to conceal. That passing thought provoked his sense of anxiety at exactly how his blood was going to be extracted when the time came to "seal the deal" and put an end to this evil being called Sathariel.

If the knives Charaka carried were an indication, it could get very unpleasant. *I've never liked needles, never mind anything bigger*, he thought ruefully.

"This blood thing," he started, and swallowed apprehensively, "are you sure you need me? I'm from another world. Surely I wouldn't be suitable? I mean, will my blood do the trick?" *Maybe I can get out of it?*

"What runs through your veins is no different from what runs through me or the other races on Amaris," the Hayim leader confirmed as he adjusted his weapons. "We are fundamentally the same beneath our exteriors and all descended from the same creation, the same Divine. While there are, of course, differences in your blood, there are also similarities. You have been sent to us. There is no reason to think that you wouldn't, how you say, do the trick."

Charaka stumbled slightly over the phrasing, which Cosmo guessed was obviously foreign to him. Charaka rose, smoothing the feathers and braids in his long, dark ponytail.

Cosmo's brow furrowed. "Why has this Arielle, or Sathariel, as she now is called, been able to seize control? Why would you need someone to speak to the Divine on your behalf? Can't you do it yourself? In my world, we believe everyone is created equal. You are the architect of your own design. You have the power to shape your own destiny. Some believe your own mind is powerful enough to make your chosen reality happen. There's a phrase, 'If you can hold it in your head, you can hold it in your hand.' You don't need someone to speak to your chosen divine power or higher being for you. You can do that yourself. We believe in direct connection to the Divine."

Charaka nodded. "We have this understanding of equality on Amaris—it is inherent to all of us. Yes, we also believe the Divine made us all equal, with the same core essence."

The Hayim leader turned and looked toward the horizon, sadness in his eyes. "However, as time passed, tolerance and acceptance diminished among our clans. Thus, the being that is now Sathariel was brought to assist with creating harmony. But she has forsaken us in a bid to fulfill her own dark greed and lust for power."

Cosmo nodded, trying to comprehend the enormity of it all. "Well, in my world, everyone has an opinion, and they all believe they're right. The loudest often drown out reason. And when it comes to physical appearance, it's a whole other ordeal. We're subconsciously pressured to conform, to look a certain way, to dress a certain way, to behave a certain way, or even to think a certain way. And yet all the time, we believe we have the freedom to express ourselves. It's exhausting."

Sympathy gleamed in Charaka's eyes as he acknowledged Cosmo's words. "Your world indeed faces challenges in its way. Maybe it is not so different from ours."

Cosmo couldn't help but laugh. "Oh, I'd say yours is very different, in many ways. For one thing, we don't have dragons and an evil queen bent on domination. But we definitely have power-obsessed people who believe their way is the only way. And they will destroy anything and anyone to get the control they want."

Suddenly, the gravity of the situation struck Cosmo. His eyes clouded. “I’ve been here only a short while, and I’m already being told I’m going to be thrust into a battle, fighting for people I don’t even know.” He shrugged his shoulders with exasperation. “How do I even know if this is my path? How can I trust you? What if you’re the bad one?” Cosmo pointed an accusatory finger at Charaka.

The Hayim leader locked eyes with Cosmo, his gaze intense yet understanding. The corner of his mouth quirked up. “Those are valid concerns, Cosmo. But what does your heart tell you? Do you sense that you are meant to be here? Do you believe in your soul that you’re fighting for what’s right? Trust can be earned through time and experience, but sometimes, in the face of adversity, we must rely on our instincts. The Divine challenges us when things appear dire or painful, pushing us to grow and discover our inner strength.”

Cosmo nodded, acknowledging the wisdom in Charaka’s words.

The leader of the Hayim continued: “In those moments, we can tap into our spiritual resilience, our steadfast belief. We tend to forget this when life is easy, but it’s during the tough times that our faith in ourselves truly shines.”

Charaka gestured for them to walk, and they ascended the winding path toward the pinnacle of the citadel, where faint light from the upper tier beckoned with flickering promise. Meandering through narrow city streets that twisted like a labyrinthine puzzle, Cosmo took in the vibrant sights and frenetic energy around him. He saw women preparing for battle, their movements swift and measured as they readied themselves with astonishing focus and intent. They gathered in groups, talking earnestly among themselves, while others worked on crafting or repairing armor.

"Where are the men?" Cosmo asked, noticing that there were none to be seen.

Charaka smiled with pride. "The women of the Hayim are our fiercest warriors. They lead us into the charge. They take war very, very seriously."

"They certainly look scary." Cosmo looked at the women's arms covered in elaborate sleeves of tattoos. Intricate ink designs were etched into their skin, each mark telling a story of strength and survival. And the women's hair was shorn close to the scalp on either side, with braids adorned with feathers and beads in the middle.

"They are engaged in the sacred ritual," Charaka said as he pointed to two women who Cosmo guessed weren't much older than him. He watched as they painted patterns onto each other's faces.

"The designs they craft are not mere decorations," Charaka explained as they continued to walk through the winding streets. "They are symbols of their identity and prowess as they prepare for battle. See how their eyes are accentuated with vibrant pigments? That is to showcase their indomitable fiery spirit."

Cosmo noted that, like Charaka, the women's attire was a blend of practicality and aesthetics. They were also assembling an arsenal of weapons—daggers, throwing knives, and other lethal instruments—each carefully selected for its unique role in their survival.

“I definitely wouldn’t want to come across them on a dark night.” Cosmo grinned. Despite the ferocity of the women’s appearance, a purposeful serenity surrounded them.

Charaka smiled again with pride. “For them, Cosmo, it shows their dedication to their resolve to succeed in the task ahead—beating Sathariel and her dark army.”

Suddenly, two scouts rushed past, on their way to deliver messages, and Cosmo took in the children watching attentively from the doorways and open windows, eager yet apprehensive. He was riveted, already beginning to understand the unseen order within the apparent disorder.

If only my dad were here! He would love this! The intensity of the purpose-filled streets was exhilarating, alive with the anticipation of those who knew what awaited them.

“Qualea is our home, but we roam the vast plains,” Charaka remarked as they walked, his hands now clasped behind his back. Occasionally he would nod in acknowledgment to someone who raised their hand in greeting or more formally bowed. “As a people, we find solace in the freedom of movement. However, we understand the importance of a central belief unifying us. Even when we’re thousands of miles apart from those we hold dear, our love and shared convictions keep us connected.”

Cosmo nodded. “We have something similar where I come from, but sometimes we misuse our shared beliefs as an excuse to do harm. Faith is vital, but how we interpret it can cause immense problems—war-size problems.”

“I understand. Here, on Amaris, we must safeguard our right to believe. We cannot allow a being like Sathariel to rob us of that freedom. The ability to choose, to speak our minds, and to make our own decisions—it's a precious right. Losing it would be the death of the Hayim, of all the clans, not just physically but mentally. For us, it would drive us to madness, being unable to roam where we desire and follow our path."

A sympathetic smile crossed Cosmo's lips. "I understand. In my world, there was a time when we couldn't leave our homes, see our loved ones, or bid farewell to those we lost. People's anger grew, and mental-health struggles intensified. We need connection, physical touch. Being able to do that is a great gift, one that fuels us as a race."

"Indeed," Charaka agreed. "And isn't that simply love? Imagine living in a world devoid of care, nurturing, kindness, respect, and love for one another. That is precisely what we face on Amaris. That is what we must fight against together. And that is why you must stand with us to preserve these rights—for all of us."

Chapter 34

The grand throne room of Heliopolis, once a beacon of the Elutheros's radiant light, now pulsed with the oppressive darkness of Resha. Sathariel stood at its center, her crimson robes trailing like spilled blood across the marble floor. She had seized this city from King Damianos and Queen Gerlinde, bending its sacred stones to her will, but her triumph was marred by a gnawing unease, which was related to more than just the dome under which she was currently powerless.

She had already questioned Viera, who had remained tight-lipped—a decision that had cost the Divine Interpreter her life. Sathariel's skin prickled with the ripple in the fabric of Amaris—it had stirred her senses—a disturbance in the delicate balance of Ruach and Resha that signaled an intrusion. *What is it? What caused the change? It was no mere fluctuation; it's a signal, a warning that something, or someone, has breached our world.*

The nagging thought in her mind kept pulling her back to the Yasha Prophecy, but she had to be sure. Sathariel's eyes narrowed as she gazed into a pool of dark liquid, a scrying mirror she had crafted. Its surface rippled, offering fleeting glimpses of the world beyond: the Jivanam tree in Qualea, the Vanavashtha in Myrkvior, and the faint silhouettes of three figures.

Who are you? Their purpose remained shrouded to her. *Are they warriors sent by the Divine? Or mere mortals, pawns in a game I could easily crush?* The pool offered no answers, its visions fragmented and elusive.

Sathariel's fingers twitched, nails digging into her palms as frustration boiled within her. "The Divine dares to challenge me," she hissed through the empty hall. "But I will not be undone by His schemes. If these Yasha are His weapons, I will break them before they can strike."

She clapped her hands, and a Malevolent was immediately hovering at her side, its skeletal form cloaked in shadow, its eyes glowing like dying embers.

"What stirs in Amaris? I sense a shift, a fracture in the Divine's precious order. What do you know of these intruders?" she demanded. "Speak, or I will tear the truth from your essence."

The Malevolent sounded like bones grinding against stone. "They are the Yasha, my queen, foretold in the ancient prophecies. Three from a distant world, bearing blood like ours but different. The Thura Gates awakened for their arrival, the ancient portals. They were guided by the Ruach through the Jivanam trees."

Sathariel's breath hitched, a cold fury rising within her. The Vanavashtha, those ancient trees that anchored the clans to the Divine, were a thorn in her side. Their roots stretched deep into Amaris, channeling the Ruach, and they would resist her Resha-fueled influence.

"How did they cross into our world?" she demanded, cutting through the oppressive silence. "The Thura Gates were closed, their enchantments woven by the Divine Himself."

If the Yasha had entered through a Thura Gate connected to the Jivanam trees, it meant the Divine was meddling directly, sending these interlopers to thwart her ascent. But she would not be outmaneuvered. Not by the Divine, and certainly not by three mortals from another world.

The Malevolent's breath rasped in icy curls. "We know little else, save that they are protected by Tauheed, Queen Mariam, and the other clans—the Vanavasin and the Rehmat."

Sathariel's lips curled into a sneer. *Prophecies. The Divine's favorite tool, woven into the fabric of Amaris to inspire hope and bind the clans.*

As a former Kaluduta, she had once revered such words, but now they were chains she sought to shatter.

"Prophecies are nothing but words," she spat. "But if these Yasha are tied to one, I must know its meaning. The clans will rally behind them. I need more than whispers."

The Malevolent bowed its head, trembling under her gaze. "The answers lie in Naraka, my queen."

Sathariel would have to return to Sephtis, and she did not want to be in further debt to him. Her bones chilled.

With a wave of her hand, she summoned a vortex of Resha, its dark tendrils coiling around her like a serpent. The air crackled with energy, sigils on the walls flaring as she stepped into the portal.

The throne room vanished, replaced by a howling void that tore at her senses. Sathariel's crimson robes whipped around her, hair streaming like flames as she navigated the descent into the abyss, a test of will and power.

The void gave way to the entrance to the cavern of black stone that swallowed the light. The Malevolents guarding the threshold bowed, their cloaked forms visibly trembling in her presence.

She entered the palace, her steps barely making a sound in the vast, torchlit hall. The walls were etched with scenes of suffering, the air thick with the wails of the damned. At the hall's end loomed Sephtis's throne. His presence was overbearing—glowing eyes piercing the gloom as he regarded her.

"Sathariel," Sephtis drawled, his words like nails on metal. "To what do I owe this visit? Have you grown weary of your stolen city so soon?"

Sathariel inclined her head, her tone measured but firm. "My Lord Sephtis, I come seeking knowledge. Three strangers, the Yasha, have entered Amaris through the Thura Gates. The Malevolents speak of a prophecy tying them to my downfall. I must know the truth of this Yasha Prophecy, and the Koimeterion holds the answers."

Sephtis's laughter was a low rumble, cold and mocking. "A prophecy, you say? The Divine's little riddles amuse me. Knowledge comes at a price, Sathariel. What will you offer me?"

Her jaw tightened. Sephtis's games were tiresome, but she had anticipated his demand. "Name your price," she said, raising her chin. "But know this: The Yasha threaten your dominion as much as mine. If they succeed, Amaris will slip from our grasp."

Sephtis gestured, and the floor before the throne shuddered, revealing a spiral staircase descending into darkness. He motioned her toward it. "Beware, Sathariel. The scrolls are guarded by the shades of fallen Kaluduta, bound to protect their secrets. Even you may find them...challenging."

Sathariel descended the staircase, the air growing colder with each step. It was a crypt of ancient stone, its walls lined with shelves of scrolls that pulsed with faint light. Shades materialized as she entered—ethereal figures with translucent wings, their eyes hollow with sorrow. "You are not welcome here, fallen one," one whispered, its voice a mournful song.

Sathariel raised her hands, Resha crackling around her. "Stand aside, or I will burn your essence to ash." The shades lunged, their spectral forms wielding blades of darkness, but Sathariel was relentless. She unleashed torrents of dark energy, shattering their forms and clearing her path. At the crypt's heart, she found another scrying pool of dark liquid.

"Show me the prophecy," she commanded in a low growl that groaned through the stone crypt. The pool's surface shimmered, and an image formed—a fragment of an ancient parchment, its edges frayed, its script glowing with the faint light of Ruach. The words were written in the sacred tongue of the Kaluduta, a language she had once spoken as one of their kind. Her heart tightened, a fleeting pang of her former life, but she crushed it with a surge of Resha-fueled rage:

> *"When the great darkness falls, it will come by the hand of one once favored by the Divine.*
> *Only those like us, three in kind yet from distant worlds, can stand against the endless night.*
> *Their blood, their beliefs—akin to ours.*

They come to save Amaris from the grip of shadow.
Through the union of ancient relics, forged from the dawn of time, shall we summon them and reignite the radiant flame.
Then shall the great darkness be bound by the Fylakistone, the Divine's gift of a prison to protect that which he created."

Her breath caught. The prophecy named a great darkness, which she assumed was her. But it also revealed the Yasha's purpose: their blood, unique to their world, could forge the Fylakistone, a prison to bind her.

The pool flickered, revealing glimpses of the three, and spoke directly to her of the Yasha's strengths and weaknesses. A boy haunted by loss, his eyes wide with fear yet burning with determination, stood in Qualea's citadel. Another young man, his spirit scarred by rage, walked among the Rehmat in Salama, his resolve a dangerous spark.

Then there was a girl, resilient yet burdened by doubt, who was in Myrkvior, guarded by the Vanavasin. Sathariel's gaze lingered on each, her mind dissecting what she saw. *They are young and untested, their unity fragile. I can exploit that.*

"They are the Yasha," she murmured with venom. "Their blood binds the Fylakistone, but only if they unite. If I sever their connection, the prophecy fails."

Her eyes gleamed as she pieced together the mechanics of the prophecy. The Yasha's power lay in their shared blood, a unique essence from their world that resonated with Amaris's lifeblood.

The Thura Gates, anchored by the Jivanam trees, had brought them here, and those same gates could be her weapon to trap them.

Sathariel's laughter was a sharp, chilling sound. *A prison? For me? The Divine underestimates my power if He believes that three children can cage this fallen angel. I will not allow them to unite the clans. If their blood is the key, then I will spill it before they can wield it.*

She ascended the stone steps to the throne room, where Sephtis was waiting for her, his face shrouded in a darkness of his own making.

"Lord Sephtis, the Thura Gates are the key. If I control them, I can cut off the Yasha's escape, trap them in Amaris, and crush their hope. The Hayim hold the strongest gate in Qualea, do they not?"

The sound that emanated from the throne was menacing: "The Thura Gate in Qualea is ancient, forged at the Creation. It is the anchor of all gates. If it falls, the other gates will weaken, severing the connection between Amaris and their world."

Sathariel's smile was a blade, sharp and cruel. "But there is the other possibility. I can use this opportunity to take their world as well. Why not take both?"

Sephtis gave a low chuckle. "Your vision is grand, Sathariel. It may be possible. But I cannot see into other worlds. You will take this step on your own. But I *will* enable you to destroy the gate if necessary. Then you will cut off the Yasha from where they came."

Sathariel nodded. "Then Qualea will be my target. The Hayim are wanderers, scattered and proud. Their leader, Charaka, is cunning but overconfident. If I strike at their heart, I can seize the gate and break the Yasha before they unite. And I can use this to take more than just Amaris."

She turned to the throne and spoke in a reverent whisper: "Lord Sephtis, hear me. The Yasha threaten us both. Grant me the power to shatter the Thura Gate in Qualea, and I will deliver Amaris to you once I have taken this other world for my own."

The shadows around the throne undulated, and Sephtis's voice slithered through the air, the tone scornful. "Bold words, Sathariel. But the gates are woven with the Divine's essence. To destroy them, you will need more than your Resha-fueled wrath."

Sathariel strode to the center of the hall, refusing to believe she could be overcome. Raising her arms as tendrils of Resha coiled around her, dark and sinuous, she prepared to return to Amaris. The air took on a constrictive consistency, the walls glowing with an eerie crimson light. "Obscura, heed my call!"

The creatures came without warning, a convulsion of leathery wings and gnashing jaws erupting from the rotted darkness. The shapes were immense, night-black forms with the proportions of eagles but none of the grace—each wingbeat a convulsion, each hooked talon gleaming with a viscosity that suggested venom, not blood. Their jaws—unhinged with every shriek—were lined with fangs so densely packed that there was room for neither tongue nor mercy. The queen screamed again: "Malevolents, rise!"

The ghastly creatures gave a soul-sucking keen as they rose together, a deathly glow emanating from the hoods of their tattered garments.

"We descend upon Qualea to shatter the Thura Gate. The Yasha will kneel or they will burn."

The Resha surged within her, an intoxicating rush of power that drowned out the whispers of doubt. The Divine had cast her out, but she would rise as Amaris's queen, and the Yasha would be the first to fall.

Chapter 35

Sathariel was in a race against time to reach the Hayim before her adversaries could thwart her plans. The prospect of possessing not one but two worlds filled her with a greedy anticipation. These realms would become her very own playgrounds, where she could manipulate and control the lives of countless souls.

The enchantment binding her within the Heliopolis palace was no more. It had dissipated into the ether, as she had predicted, when the twin moons had risen into the sky. With her armies at her command, she would march toward the Hayim capital and seize Qualea.

Sathariel had forsaken her former self. She now served a new master—her anger and bitterness toward the Divine fueling her relentless pursuit. The remnants of her soul resembled a barren landscape, scorched and devoid of any light.

But there was still the tenuous connection between her and Tauheed, which had been forged deeper than she had ever realized before she had embraced her new destiny. She had thought it would be a hindrance, but Sathariel soon realized it was something she could exploit, even though it was painful to her.

While he remained unaware, she had tapped into his thoughts and emotions, a connection he had gifted her through their love for each other.

She could sense Tauheed's moments of elation and fear. And she had been connected to his dread and concern when he realized the danger posed by the Jivanam tree, a gateway to another world. While his fear of her intentions pierced her like a knife, at the same time, she relished that the one who had once loved her now feared her.

Sathariel cast aside any lingering regret, determined to utilize Tauheed's ties to her advantage. Her plan would unfold, using his connection as a crucial piece in her twisted game. Now, her primary objective was to reach Qualea before Tauheed could. If he sought a fight, then a fight he would have.

Ahead of her, in the distance, Sathariel could see the grand silhouette of Qualea. As she leaned on her scepter, she was hardly aware of the chill that always accompanied the sunrise. She stood resplendent in her shimmering battle armor, reflecting the first rays of light.

Sathariel took a slow breath, her gaze shifting to the Dark Forces behind her. The Malevolents lazily circled above her army—some who had chosen to follow her willingly and others who had been forced into service.

She was mounted atop a large silver wolf. The beast emitted low, guttural growls as it sniffed at the air. Sathariel moved away from the front line and fixed her eyes upon the city. Doubt gnawed at her, teasing her resolve.

Whispers in her mind, sinister and beguiling, reassured her. "You were never meant to achieve greatness by following the Divine. He had no grand plans for you."

Sathariel cast her mind back to a time when she had reveled in walking among the people of Amaris, bearing the Divine's love in her heart every day. It had once been an honor to relinquish her wings and serve as the vessel of the Divine's message, as she had believed she was chosen for a purpose greater than any other Kaluduta. As Arielle, she had seen her mission as a loving one, to bring the people of Amaris closer to the Divine. But now she believed the door to her previous life had been slammed shut, leaving no way back.

"There is always a possibility of redemption," a voice gently interrupted her thoughts, cutting through the chaos within her mind.

Sathariel started, realizing the words were not her own. "There is always an opportunity to seek forgiveness. If you open your heart, truly repentant, the Divine will welcome you back."

In the dim light, Sathariel discerned the silhouette of the Kaluduta Malakai, the Divine Messenger's presence offering a glimmer of hope. But then she remembered their last meeting.

"When we were last in company, you clarified that the possibility of redemption was highly unlikely," Sathariel spat, her tone filled with defiance. "And yet now you tell me that isn't the case?"

"It is not my role to convince you of anything, Sathariel." Malakai's gaze was soft. "You possess free will, and only you can determine which path to follow."

But the messenger's words burned like fire. "I am here to tell you that though you believe the door is closed, it remains open. If you open your heart, seeking forgiveness with genuine intent, the Divine will grant it. The purity of your heart and soul will be recognized. No one is forsaken unless they willingly abandon the possibility of return."

Tears welled in Sathariel's eyes, but she fought to suppress them. "What could you possibly know? I was abandoned. Left all alone. When I needed the Divine's guidance, it was absent."

Malakai's expression turned sorrowful. "But the Divine was always present. The enemy of the Divine is self-pity, and it is the enemy of your own strength as well. All you had to do was ask for support. Even in the depths of darkness, when everything seems impossible, open your heart and ask for the help you need. It will come, perhaps not immediately or in the way you hope, but it will come."

Sathariel shook her head, attempting to block out Malakai's words. "I did ask, and I received no response," she said bitterly.

"All good things take time," Malakai reassured her. "Strength is forged through adversity. Did you consider that you would emerge stronger, with more faith, by enduring difficulties? That you would have the capacity to aid others through their pain?"

Malakai's words pierced her thoughts. "Trusting in dark moments is challenging, as is believing that light still exists. But it does. There is never a time when there is no way back; if you approach the Divine with true regret and a desire to change, an honest and pure heart will guide you toward a brighter future."

Torn between conflicting emotions, Sathariel's soul and mind were being pulled in opposing directions. Deep within her being, she yearned for the love and kindness she had once bathed in daily. Yet anger and resentment surged within her, reminding her of her power and the pain of her abandonment.

During their last encounter, Malakai had declared there was no way back. Now, the messenger spoke of an opportunity to return to the light. What did it all mean?

The Kaluduta answered her question: "It means, Sathariel, that the Divine wishes to give you one last chance. He would rather avert the terrible chain of events your actions are about to unleash—the death, the bloodshed. You have free will. You are being given the choice to use it for good. You think you are lost when you are not. It takes much to be irreversibly consumed by darkness. Even the gravest of sins can be forgiven if one approaches the Divine with genuine remorse," Malakai explained, expression filled with anguish. "I sense within you that you are not completely lost. There is still a chance for you to turn away from the path of darkness and walk back into the light."

Tears streamed down Sathariel's face, a physical manifestation of her internal struggle. Yet thoughts of resentment and defiance resurfaced, intertwining with her anger. She recalled the voices in her head, whispering deceitful promises. They had urged her to believe that her power was a gift far greater than the love of the Divine.

Narrowing her eyes, Sathariel steeled herself. Her mind was made up. "You have made your case," she declared, standing tall and facing Malakai directly. "If the Divine truly desires my return, let him come rather than sending you as his so-called emissary."

She lifted her face to the sky. The clouds swirled above her, reflecting the turmoil within her heart.

"Hear me now, Divine," she cried out with pain and defiance. "If you had truly loved me, you would never have abandoned me to this fate. I reject your offer and all that you represent."

The Kaluduta gazed upon Sathariel with profound sadness, mouth set in a resolute line. "So be it," the Divine Messenger murmured, words tinged with regret. "So be it, Sathariel."

Raising her scepter high above her head, Sathariel laughed with bitterness. "Let me show you, oh, *Divine,*" she drawled, emphasizing the title with contempt. "Let me reveal the gifts I have been bestowed, the gifts you withheld from me." With a forceful strike, she thrust her scepter into the ground, and in an instant, lightning surged from it, crackling into the sky as it skittered upward in a vivid display of power. Extending her hand forward, she balled it into a fist, channeling the unleashed energy back into her fingertips from the air around her, and directed them toward Malakai. The power and electricity struck the celestial being in the chest, and the Kaluduta let out a visceral scream of agony.

A sneer twisted Sathariel's face as she channeled her frustration and anger, with the potency of the ancient force she wielded. *"Obscurum invocare, quod vivit deleo,"* she uttered, her words laden with a death curse.

Malakai's form glowed white-hot before erupting in a cascade of blinding light, a clash of white and dark energy. The very essence of Ruach, the pure force of goodness, which permeated every molecule of his being, was obliterated.

Sathariel doubled over, the exertion and the immensity of her action consuming her. She breathed heavily, every cell in her body absorbing the strain. She pushed herself upright as raindrops began to touch her face. Starting as a gentle pitter-patter, the rain quickly transformed into a torrential downpour. Thunder cracked across the sky, as if the heavens themselves wept in grief.

Chapter 36

The sun hung low over Qualea, bathing the Hayim's sprawling capital in a golden glow that belied the tension gripping its stone walls. Cosmo stood in the citadel's central courtyard, sneakers scuffing the packed earth.

The Hayim moved around him with purpose; a low hum of urgency filled the air. Charaka had taken Cosmo under his wing, and he knew he should be relieved. But as he stared down at his jeans and hoodie, which were stark against everyone else's flowing robes, Cosmo could only think to himself, *I'm an outsider*.

"I'm going for a walk," Cosmo shouted toward Charaka, who turned from his deep conversation with a warrior.

The Hayim leader nodded and waved. Cosmo wandered toward the citadel's outer gate and massaged his temples. *Maybe a walk will ease the thudding in my head.*

Suddenly, as he approached, a whoosh of wind swept through the street he was standing in, carrying the scent of ash and leather. He saw the Hayim around him glance up. Cosmo followed their eyes and froze, his breath catching as a massive shadow loomed over the gate.

A dragon—its scales a shimmering tapestry of sapphire and obsidian—towered before the entrance, wings folded like sails against its muscular frame. Its eyes, molten gold with slit pupils, gleamed with an intelligence that sent a shiver down Cosmo's spine.

The creature's head was adorned with spiraling horns, and its tail, as thick as a tree trunk, coiled lazily, tipped with a barbed spike that glinted like polished steel. Smoke curled from the beast's nostrils, and when the dragon shifted, the ground trembled beneath its clawed feet.

Cosmo's mouth fell open, wonder drowning out his fear. He had seen dragons in movies, but this was no CGI creation.

"Gideon. That's what he's called." A Hayim warrior standing close to Cosmo whispered the creature's name with reverence.

Gideon was alive, raw, and majestic. His scales caught the sunlight, refracting it into a thousand tiny prisms that danced across the courtyard. Each movement rippled with power, the muscles beneath his hide flexing like a living mountain. Cosmo's fingers itched to touch the beauty of that skin, the warmth of those scales. But the dragon's gaze pinned him in place, both terrifying and mesmerizing.

A figure clad in leather armor, a longsword strapped to his back and a bow slung across his shoulders, jumped down to the ground and placed a casual hand on Gideon's hide.

He was broad-shouldered, with a weathered face framed by a tangle of dark hair. His eyes, as sharp as Gideon's, scanned the growing crowd before settling on Charaka, who was striding toward him. Cosmo edged closer, curiosity overriding his nerves, catching snatches of their conversation.

"Deklan." Charaka's greeting was gruff but warm. The dragon rider managed a smile, but his expression then turned grim.

Cosmo's stomach twisted. This dragon could only be here because Sathariel, the fallen angel whose name sent shudders through the Hayim, was coming for *him*—or at least for the gate that had brought him here. He glanced back toward the Jivanam tree in the courtyard he had walked from, its branches swaying as if warning of the danger.

Charaka's jaw tightened. "What I don't understand is, why Qualea? The Thura Gates are now scattered across Amaris."

Deklan gestured to Gideon, who snorted, a puff of smoke rising. "The gate in Qualea is the anchor, forged at the Creation. Harda learned from the Vanavasin that its roots tie all gates together. If Sathariel destroys it, the Yasha will be trapped, unable to return to their world or help us. Harda sent Gideon and me to warn you and bolster your defenses. Sathariel's forces—Obscura and Malevolents—are amassing. She'll strike soon, likely by nightfall."

Cosmo's heart raced. Nightfall was just hours away, the sky already bruising with dusk. He looked at Gideon again, marveling at the dragon's calm strength. Its scales seemed to shift colors with each breath, first glinting emerald, then deep indigo. Cosmo imagined riding such a creature, soaring above Amaris's plains, but the thought was quickly eclipsed by fear. He was no warrior—just a kid who had stumbled into a prophecy.

He watched closely as Charaka nodded, his eyes scanning the citadel. "We are already preparing for the attack. The Hayim are no strangers to battle, and with Gideon's fire, we'll hold the gate."

Deklan smirked. "Not just Gideon. Harda is on his way with several other dragon riders. I am the first wave of the reinforcements. If Sathariel wants war, she's got it."

Charaka smiled and gave a triumphant laugh. “By the Divine! With the dragons here, she will have her work cut out for her!” He grabbed Deklan’s forearm and turned to Cosmo, still smiling. “Come here and let me introduce you to Gideon, Yasha. He’s very intrigued to meet you.”

Cosmo shuffled forward, acutely aware of Deklan and the dragon watching him, both with curiosity. Up close, Gideon’s warmth radiated like a furnace, his breath a low rumble. Cosmo’s knees wobbled, but he managed a shaky nod.

“This is the boy?” Deklan asked, his tone skeptical. “One of the Yasha from the prophecy?”

Charaka placed a hand on Cosmo’s shoulder. “He is. Cosmo, Deklan and Gideon are allies. Harda trusts them, and so do I. Stay close and listen.”

Deklan studied Cosmo, then softened. “You’ve got courage, kid, being here. Gideon and I will keep you safe.”

Cosmo managed a weak smile, his eyes darting to Gideon. The dragon tilted its head, as if assessing him, and Cosmo experienced a strange connection, like the creature understood his fear. He wanted to ask a thousand questions—how Gideon flew, how Deklan bonded with him—but Charaka’s command cut through Cosmo’s thoughts.

“To arms!” Charaka bellowed, rallying the Hayim. “Fortify the gate! Archers to the ramparts, spearmen to the courtyard. We hold until dawn.”

The Hayim sprang into action, their movements precise despite the looming threat. Cosmo watched, awestruck, as warriors hauled wooden barricades to the gate, their muscles straining. Archers climbed to the ramparts, stringing bows with arrows tipped with glowing runes. In the courtyard, spearmen drilled, their weapons gleaming in the torchlight. The Jivanam tree pulsed, its roots glowing faintly, as if lending strength to the citadel.

Deklan led Gideon to a cleared space near the gate, the dragon settling with a thud that shook the ground. Cosmo followed, unable to resist. The rider nodded to the dragon, his face glowing with pride. "He's the fastest. We flew through the night to reach you."

Cosmo nodded, his eyes wide. "He's...incredible. I've never seen anything like him."

Gideon rumbled, a sound like distant thunder, and Deklan grinned. "He likes you. Dragons sense heart, Cosmo. You're scared, but you're here. That's enough."

Cosmo's chest tightened, Deklan's words stirring a mix of pride and fear. As the Hayim worked, he found a quiet corner near the Jivanam tree, sitting with his back against its trunk. The citadel buzzed with activity, but Cosmo was alone, the prophecy's burden crushing him. Sathariel was coming, and he was just a kid, not a hero like Deklan or Charaka.

His hands trembled as memories flooded back—memories he'd tried to bury. The earthquake, the ground splitting beneath his feet, his mother's hand slipping from his as the house collapsed. He could still hear her, calm even in chaos. Tears pricked his eyes, and he hugged his knees, whispering, "I'm scared, Mom. I'm so scared."

A shadow fell over him, and Charaka crouched beside him, his dark eyes softening. "Cosmo, talk to me. Share what is troubling you."

Cosmo wiped his eyes, ashamed. "I'm scared, Charaka. Sathariel's coming, and I'm no fighter. Back home, there was an earthquake. My mom...she didn't make it. I couldn't save her. What if I fail here too? What if I let everyone down?"

Charaka's hand rested on his shoulder, steady and warm. "Listen, boy. Fear is a shadow, like Sathariel's Resha. It's real, but it can't hold you unless you let it. You survived that earthquake, and you're here, in Amaris, carrying a prophecy. That's not failure; that's strength."

Cosmo shook his head. "But I'm not enough. I'm not like you or Deklan or...or Gideon. I don't belong in a battle."

Charaka smiled with sympathy. "None of us are born for battle, Cosmo. I was a wanderer once, like my father before me, dreaming of open plains, not war. But the Divine called me, as He called you. You're one of the Yasha, chosen for a reason. Your blood, with Jiyanu's and Fatiha's, can forge the Fylakistone to bind Sathariel. That's your path—not fighting but enduring."

Cosmo sniffled, the words sinking in. "What if I can't?"

"You will," Charaka said firmly. "You're not alone. The Hayim stand with you. Deklan and Gideon stand with you. The Jivanam tree, its roots deep in Amaris, stands with you. You'll be safe, Cosmo."

Deklan approached, overhearing the exchange. "Charaka's right. Gideon and I will guard the gate. Sathariel's forces won't breach us. And you, Cosmo, you're stronger than you think. The prophecy chose you for a reason."

Cosmo looked between them, then at Gideon, whose golden eyes seemed to nod in agreement. The dragon's presence, solid and unyielding, grounded him. He thought of his mother, her courage in those final moments, that spark of resolve. “Okay,” he said with more certainty. “I’ll try.”

Chapter 37

The wind howled through the jagged peaks of the mountains, carrying a chill that seeped into Fatiha's bones. She pulled her cloak tighter, her breath misting in the thin air as she huddled closer to Lexi, Tauheed, and Hana on the back of Axelia.

The dragon spiraled lazily down, maneuvering the gale with care as the stony ground of the mountain loomed up at them. Axelia landed with precision on a narrow ledge carved into the cliff face.

As Tauheed and Hana slid gracefully down despite the strong gusts of wind, Fatiha grimaced. The path was slick with ice and littered with loose stones. Below, a chasm yawned, its depths swallowed by shadow. Fatiha's heart pounded, not just from the climb but from the pressure of their mission. "I didn't sign up for mountain treks."

"It's not far," Hana said breezily. She turned to look up at Lexi. "Will you wait?"

The dragon rider nodded. "Axelia needs to hunt. We will need her strength for what we will face at Qualea. I will be here when you return."

She gave them a salute, and Axelia pulled her body low to the cliff, bunched her muscles, and took off with a powerful down-sweep of her wings.

Fatiha braced her feet to stop herself toppling over in the backwind from the dragon's takeoff. She swallowed nervously. They were heading to the Taura's stronghold, a hidden fortress nestled in the heart of the mountain, to convince the reclusive clan to join the fight against Sathariel. The prophecy's burden was a stone in Fatiha's chest, and doubt gnawed at her. *Can I, a girl from Earth, really help save Amaris?*

Tauheed led the way, his broad shoulders cutting through the wind, his blade gleaming at his hip. Hana followed, her Vanavasin cloak blending with the rocky terrain. Fatiha admired them both—Tauheed's staunch resolve, Hana's quiet strength—but next to them, she was out of place. Cosmo was with the Hayim in Qualea, Jiyanu with the Rehmat in Salama, and here she was, the third Yasha, stumbling through a world she barely understood.

"Keep up, Fatiha," Tauheed called over his shoulder, shouting over the gale. She nodded, swallowing her nerves. "I'm trying," Fatiha muttered, her boots scraping against the stone. She glanced at Hana, who offered a small, encouraging smile. "Do you think they'll listen to us?" Fatiha asked, her words nearly lost in the wind.

Hana's expression sobered. "The Taura are stubborn, bound to their mountains like roots to earth. They've stayed neutral in clan wars for centuries, guarding their domain above all else. But Sathariel's threat is different. If we can make them see that, they'll join us."

Fatiha wanted to believe her, but the Taura's isolation was apparently legendary. Hana had explained to her that while they did pay some heed to being involved in the global affairs of Amaris, their stance was always the same. Taura first and last. They were a race of bloodthirsty fighters who were protective of their resources and home within the Mountains of Elphis. When they did trade, the Taura drove hard bargains. If they refused to be part of the plan, the clans' unity would falter, and the prophecy might fail.

The path widened, revealing a massive gate carved into the mountainside, its surface etched with taurine motifs of axes and picks, precious gems and stars. Two Taura guards stood before it, clad in armor of stone and steel, faces hidden behind horned helms. Their axes glinted in the fading light, and Fatiha's stomach twisted. They looked more like statues than men, unyielding and fierce.

"State your purpose," one guard rumbled, eyeing them with distrust, brandishing a spear.

Tauheed stepped forward, undaunted. "I am the Divine Interpreter Tauheed, with Hana of the Vanavasin, and Fatiha, the prophesied Yasha. We seek an audience with Chieftain Tamanka to speak of Sathariel's threat to Amaris."

The guards exchanged a glance that indicated their cynicism. "The Taura do not meddle in the affairs of the other clans," the second guard said. "Why should we hear you?"

Hana was calm but firm. "Because Sathariel's Resha will not spare your mountains. She seeks the Thura Gates, and none will stand if the clans do not unite."

The first guard snorted. "Elphis is our shield. No enemy has breached our fortress."

Fatiha's chest tightened. She wanted to speak, to say something profound, but words failed her. Tauheed's jaw clenched, but he nodded. "Then let your chieftain decide. Will you deny us entry?"

After a tense pause, the guards stepped aside, the gate groaning open to reveal a tunnel lit by glowing crystals. Fatiha followed Tauheed and Hana inside, her heart racing. The air warmed as they descended, the tunnel opening into a vast cavern that stretched so high, it was impossible to see the ceiling. The Taura's stronghold was breathtaking—stone halls carved with intricate reliefs, bridges spanning chasms, and a central plaza where a massive Jivanam tree glowed with faint light. Its roots wove through the stone, a reminder of the Divine's presence in the heart of the mountain.

Taura moved through the plaza—their forms broad and muscular, their skin weathered by mountain winds. Some glanced at the newcomers with curiosity, others with suspicion. Fatiha avoided meeting the prying, curious eyes on her, and she shrank into her cloak.

They were led to a great hall, its ceiling studded with crystals that cast a starry glow. Chieftain Tamanka sat on a throne of polished granite—his beard braided with iron rings, his eyes as sharp as flint. Flanking him were elders, whose faces were etched with distrust. Fatiha's pulse quickened as Tauheed stepped forward, his presence commanding.

"Chieftain Tamanka," Tauheed began, bowing slightly. "We come because of the threat of Sathariel. Her Resha corrupts the land, and she seeks the Thura Gates to trap the Yasha and seize our world. We ask the Taura to join us in this fight."

Tamanka leaned forward, his voice a low growl as his eyes burned into Fatiha. "Ahh, the Yasha. The Hephaes told us of this." He then turned to Hana, and his lip curled into a sneer. "You are lucky, priestess. They told me they granted you the stone they guard; otherwise, I would have to take your head."

Hana bowed. "I am eternally grateful for the generosity of the Taura, and the Hephaes, for enabling us to use the stone for the greater good."

The chieftain leaned back in his throne, stroked his beard, and snorted. "The Taura have no quarrel with Sathariel. Our mountains are our fortress, our Jivanam tree our shield. Why should we risk our kin for lowland wars?"

Fatiha's heart sank. The Taura's isolation was more than physical; it was a creed. She glanced at Hana, who stepped forward. "Sathariel's Resha does not respect borders, Chieftain Tamanka. Your mountains may stand, but for how long? If the Thura Gates fall, no clan will be safe."

Tamanka's eyes narrowed. "Our gate is intact. It is your concern, not ours. We guard our own."

An elder, her hair streaked with silver, spoke up. "The Yasha Prophecy speaks of saviors from another world. Yet I see only a girl, untested and afraid." The elder's gaze fixed on Fatiha, who flinched. "Why should we trust her blood to save us?"

Fatiha's cheeks burned, shame and anger warring within her. She wanted to shrink away, but Tauheed cut through the tension. "Fatiha is named by the Divine. Her blood, with that of the other two Yasha, can forge the Fylakistone to bind Sathariel. But we cannot succeed without the clans' strength. The Taura's might could turn the tide."

Tamanka nailed Tauheed with his stare. "Prophecies are wind. The Divine abandoned us long ago. We trust in stone and steel, not promises."

Fatiha's hands were sweaty. She hated being powerless, a pawn in a game she didn't understand. She stepped forward and swallowed in apprehension. "I'm not a warrior," she said, meeting Tamanka's gaze. "I'm scared, and I don't know if I'm worthy. But I've seen Sathariel's darkness. It's not just the lowlands—it's everywhere. If you stay here, it'll come for you too."

The hall fell silent, the elders exchanging glances. Tamanka's expression softened, but only slightly. "Brave words, girl, but words don't win wars. Our kin have died in clan feuds. Why spill blood for strangers?"

Tauheed was passionate and unyielding when he spoke. "Because this isn't a feud, Tamanka. Sathariel serves Sephtis, Lord of Naraka. She's already taken Heliopolis, corrupted its light. If she claims the Thura Gate in Qualea, she'll trap the Yasha and unleash Resha across Amaris. Your mountains won't save you when the Jivanam tree withers."

Hana nodded, her tone urgent: "The Vanavashtha are weakening. In Myrkvior, our Jivanam tree's roots are tainted. The Taura's tree is strong, but it won't stand alone. Join us, and we can protect the Ruach, the lifeblood of Amaris."

Tamanka toyed with the rings in his beard. "You speak of unity, but the clans are fractured. The Hayim wander, the Rehmat feud, and the Elutheros mourn their lost city. Why should we trust this counsel?"

Fatiha's heart raced. She saw the doubt in Tamanka's eyes as he considered his people's safety. But they were counting on her, even if they didn't know it. "Because we're trying," she said, stronger now. "I'm here, even though I'm terrified. Tauheed and Hana left their homes to fight. We're not perfect, but we're fighting for Amaris. If you don't help, Sathariel wins, and everything you love—your mountains, your tree—will fall."

An elder scoffed. "A child's plea. What of the Hephaes? The stone giants, our guardians. Can they not stop her?"

Tauheed shook his head. "The Hephaes are mighty, but Sathariel seeks domination. If she succeeds, Yasha can't return to their world, and the Fylakistone can't be forged. We need your warriors, your axes, to stand with us in Qualea."

Hana seized the moment. "Exactly. She's vulnerable there, but only if we act together. Your warriors could flank her forces, protect the gate while the Yasha unite. Without you, we're outnumbered."

The elders murmured, their skepticism waning. Tamanka studied Fatiha, his gaze piercing. "You speak from the heart, Yasha. But trust is earned. What proof do you offer that this prophecy is true?"

Fatiha hesitated, then reached into pocket, pulling out the small glowing ball, which she had taken from the bubble when she had come through in Myrkvior. It shone with what she now knew was Ruach, its light steady despite the hall's shadows. "This came from the craft that brought me here," she said. "It's tied to the prophecy, to the Divine. I don't understand it all, but I know it's real. Sathariel wants to destroy it, to trap us. Help us stop her."

Tamanka rose and walked toward her, hand outstretched. Fatiha gave it to him, and the Taura leader examined it, the light reflecting in his eyes. “Rare indeed...Ruach made into a tangible reality.” He handed it back, his words softer. “You’ve shown courage, Fatiha. But my people fear loss. Convince me their sacrifice won’t be in vain.”

Tauheed stepped closer. He was barely containing his frustration. “I’ve seen Sathariel’s Malevolents. I’ve seen the desecration of Elutheros and its people. I have borne witness to the damage the Obscura can do to a dragon. A dragon! She won’t stop until Amaris is hers. But with your weapons, we can drive her back to Naraka. Refuse, and your mountains will become your tomb.”

Hana added, “The Divine chose the Yasha for a reason. Their blood binds the Fylakistone, but their hope binds us. The Taura are Amaris’s shield. Will you let that shield rust?”

Tamanka was silent, his gaze distant. The elders whispered together in a low hum. Fatiha held her breath, her doubt warring with hope. Finally, Tamanka raised a hand, silencing the hall. “You’ve spoken well,” he said. “The Taura value strength, and I see it in you three. Sathariel’s threat cannot be ignored. We will send warriors to Qualea to guard the gate and face her. And wherever else you need our support. But know this: Our trust is hard-won. Fail, and our support will be forever withdrawn.”

Relief washed over Fatiha, her knees weak.

Tauheed bowed. “Thank you, Chieftain Tamanka. Your warriors will be our anvil, the Yasha our hammer. Together, we’ll crush Sathariel.”

Hana smiled, her eyes warm. "Amaris thanks you. We'll meet you in Qualea. We will return to Lexi and Axelia, who are waiting for us."

As they left the hall, Tamanka looked at Fatiha, his gaze no longer hostile but curious. She was still scared, still unsure, but for the first time, she believed she was a Yasha.

Fatiha emerged, blinking into the light, to see Lexi leaning casually against Axelia's side. They had been brought out through a secret exit from the mountain, and the guards had told the dragon rider exactly where to wait for them.

Her eyes were shining. "You had success! Well done! Now we have the Taura on board."

Fatiha smiled back, the grin so wide on her face, it looked like it might split. Tauheed and Hana couldn't conceal their joy either.

Tauheed laid a hand on the dragon rider's shoulder. "We must take Fatiha to the safety of Salama, then head to Qualea as soon as possible. Can you do that?"

"It's not me that's making the flight." Her eyes went vacant for a moment, and Fatiha realized she must be speaking to Axelia.

Lexi refocused on them. "Yes, Axelia can do that. She had her fill of mountain goats while you were away."

The dragon harumphed a retort, her breath curling into the air in tendrils of steam. Lexi laughed. "You have your ride, Yasha. Let's get you to safety and go join the other forces to see whatever this battle holds."

Chapter 38

As night fell, the citadel glowed with torchlight, the Hayim's preparations complete. The ramparts bristled with archers; the courtyard was lined with spearmen. Gideon stood at the gate, his scales shimmering like a beacon. Deklan mounted him, his sword drawn, a warrior born of sky and flame. Cosmo stood beside Charaka, his fear tempered by the strength of those around him.

The sky above transformed into a swirling canvas of deep gray and ominous black as unnatural clouds gathered with eerie intent. They twisted and contorted, forming bizarre and unsettling shapes that loomed overhead. A distant rumble rolled across the heavens, a low and menacing growl, the ground trembling as Sathariel's forces approached.

Cosmo, shivering in the icy air, looked up toward the city walls. Deklan perched with Gideon, who guarded the entrance to Qualea. Farther back, other dragons that had arrived just an hour earlier were interspersed at intervals on the craggy battlements of the rock-hewn city, their tongues tasting the air. All knew they were on the cusp of a fierce battle.

Cosmo's heart raced, his short sword—given by Charaka—like a toy in his hand. As one of the Yasha, he was meant to save Amaris, but in truth, he felt out of his depth in a world of what were akin to magical forces and war.

But despite the foreboding, there was still a buzz in the city, especially with the arrival of the reinforcements. Charaka had been overjoyed when a flank of Taura had come storming out of the rocky cliffs above Qualea.

How they had managed to travel hundreds of miles in a matter of hours was a mystery to not only Cosmo, but to Charaka and the rest of the assembled troops as well. But there was no time to question it as they prepared for the battle.

He was then dumbstruck all over again when he was introduced to Harda, the towering Caelum Bellator dragon rider, who had arrived with Mariam, the queen of the Adira. Hours later, he had met Tauheed, Hana, and Lexi, who had told him all about Fatiha and Jiyanu, the other Yasha. They'd come from Salama, where they'd left Fatiha to meet Jiyanu in safety, and to rally the Rehmat.

He found himself wondering what they were like, these other people from Earth. *Are they scared and confused like me? Or are they special? Are they better than me? What do they look like?* Cosmo had tight pang of jealousy that they were getting the chance to bond while he was standing there facing certain death. He examined the blade Charaka had given him and weighed it between his hands, admiring as it glinted in the light of the torches.

Shouldn't I find this all kind of exciting? Why am I so scared? Cosmo shook his head. This was no computer game, no virtual landscape where he could respawn after a defeat. He'd spent countless hours lost in digital worlds, navigating mazes, slaying beasts, solving puzzles. Those games had been his haven, a place where rules were clear and rewards were certain. Now, thrust into a real-life saga more perilous than any game, he found his past preoccupations laughably inadequate. The truth stung—he'd thought his virtual battles had prepared him for anything, but facing real danger, he realized how naive that was.

Thoughts of his father flooded his mind, unbidden, carrying a rush of mixed emotions. He wondered if his father even noticed his absence. Since his mother's death, his father had retreated into work, a shadow lost in papers and meetings. Cosmo's heart ached for the man who'd once played games with him, offering hugs after a tough loss. That man was gone, leaving Cosmo to face this alone. A pang of longing hit him, but he pushed it aside. Amaris needed him, and he had to focus.

A light touch brought him out of his thoughts. He looked up from the blade to see Queen Mariam, her smile warm and reassuring. "You're braver than you know, Cosmo. The prophecy names you, and we'll fight to protect you.

"Your blood, Fatiha's, Jiyanu's—it's the key to the Fylakistone. Sathariel wants you captured to stop it. We won't let that happen."

Mariam was gentle but firm. "Cosmo, Sathariel is approaching. We must protect you and prevent her from taking you."

She stepped closer, her armor glinting like fish scales, and placed her palm on his chest, her touch warm. "You are the special power, Cosmo. Your very being—you are the power. Treasure your uniqueness. Everything you experience that is different or unusual about yourself—that makes you special. And that is your power. We will defend you. You have nothing to fear. You will be united with Fatiha and Jiyanu soon. Remember, we need you, Cosmo; we need all of you to overcome Sathariel. And now, she is a threat to both our world and yours. We will fight to the death for your survival and protection and that of your home."

Cosmo gave her a trembling smile. Who would have thought his life would veer so drastically from school, games, and home? This was stranger than any fiction, more intense than any game. A spark ignited in his heart. As daunting as this was, it was an adventure, a call he hadn't expected but was ready to face. In that moment, a quiet resolve solidified within Cosmo. He was ready to play the most important game of his life.

Charaka broke the moment. "To the ramparts. Sathariel's forces are near. Cosmo, stay with Tauheed and Lexi. Harda, Mariam, join the dragon riders."

Cosmo followed Tauheed and Lexi, his heart pounding. The air grew thick; a metallic taste tinged his tongue. He glanced at the dragons perched on the battlements, their eyes fixed on the horizon. They stood as still as stone, sensing the Resha's approach.

Cosmo rolled his shoulders as the atmosphere became heavier, each molecule leaden. Pressure began to build between his ears, and Cosmo pulled at his earlobes to relieve it.

Tauheed gripped his shoulder. "Steady, Cosmo. Sathariel's Resha is pollution with its power, but we're stronger."

Lexi nocked an arrow, her eyes scanning the darkness. "You're the prize, and I don't miss. Stay near me."

Cosmo nodded, his blade shaking in his hand. He heard the hiss between the dragon riders: "Resha is here." They shifted uneasily in their leathers.

Axelia, who had been poised in a crouch, rose up on her haunches and let out a bellowing roar. As one, the other dragons mirrored her, hissing through their sharp teeth, mouths gaping.

The riders, who had assumed the flight position, brandished their weapons. Harda raised his sword aloft. “She’s here. Prepare for the onslaught. For Amaris!’

The dragons took to the skies, their mighty wings creating a wind that forced Cosmo to the ground, hands now over his ears as the sky filled with the sound of roaring.

And so it began.

Chapter 39

An epic clash of light and dark was raging. Qualea had become an apocalyptic panorama as Sathariel tried to take the city. Once pure and sweet, the air now reeked of sulfur and searing flesh, making each breath a battle in itself. Overhead, dragons roared as they swirled amid the gray smoke, their fierce orange flames raining mercilessly upon the Legion troops, each gust of fire causing the doomed to shrivel like dry leaves in a roaring bonfire.

Cosmo watched, dread pulsing through his veins as he watched from his vantage point. In the early stages of the battle, it had seemed as if the forces of good had seized the advantage—Sathariel's soldiers were being reduced to mere embers beneath the dragon's flames.

But it soon became clear the dragons' fiery onslaught wasn't the end for the Dark Forces. Like a twisted miracle, the blackened corpses of Sathariel's army staggered back to their feet. Their bodies, charred and broken, somehow found the strength to continue fighting. And with that force, they breached the city walls.

Witnessing the horrific scene, Cosmo, who had been rejoicing in their advantage, had the horrific realization creeping over him. He had seen this many times in his games.

"Can they not be killed? Why are they not dying?" he asked, with fear and bewilderment.

Tauheed and Hana, tasked with protecting him from the cataclysmic clash by using a magical shield, grimaced.

"The power of Resha sustains them," Tauheed responded, beads of sweat on his brow. The exertion of maintaining the shield was taking its toll. "It will take more than dragon fire to destroy their essence completely. We need more weapons crafted from avinash, the celestial metal that can destroy the Dark Forces. But only the Taura, who mine it, have blades forged from the material, save a few of the Vanavasin who have joined us..."

Mariam pointed toward ominous shadowy trails spiraling into the air. "That is Resha escaping from them. When that vapor ceases to rise, they are truly gone. The avinash is the only substance we possess that can truly eradicate the creatures of the dark."

The Hayim showered deadly arrows upon the Obscura, another creature that Sathariel had recruited to her cause from the depths of Naraka, that were trying to maul the troops from the air with their poisonous claws. They swept down, emitting blood-chilling screams as they entered the fray. A rake from their claws was deadly.

Taura soldiers were engaged in ruthless hand-to-hand combat with the relentless Legion ground troops. The battlefield was a chaotic scene, a savage dance of life and death.

Then Cosmo noticed that the Malevolents had formed a protective circle around Sathariel. He turned to Mariam, suspecting something terrible was about to happen. "What are they trying to do?"

Mariam grimaced. "I think they are trying to create a path for her to get to us and the Thura Gate."

She looked up toward the top of the city, to the garden where the Jivanam tree was. "So, it is thus. Sathariel is planning to use the portal to reach your world. Taking ours is not enough." Her words sent a shiver down Cosmo's spine. The terrifying possibility of their enemy's victory loomed ominously, casting a dark shadow over the atmosphere. The tension was palpable, as if the air itself had thickened.

"We have to stop her from reaching the gate," Cosmo declared, with determination.

Mariam looked at Hana, her piercing blue eyes reflecting the raging fires around them. "Can she use Resha to get there?"

Hana sighed, her words uncertain. "I do not know. We have never seen anyone wield the power of Resha as she does. Her strength is unlike anything we have faced. I am not sure if our troops can hold her back."

Tauheed looked at the two women. "I will go to her and see if there is any way I can reason with her."

Hana and Mariam exchanged glances. "I think the moment for that is way past, Tauheed." Mariam placed a consoling hand on his shoulder. "Hana and I will take Cosmo to the Jivanam tree in the garden. That way we can protect him and protect the portal within it."

Tauheed set his lips in a firm line and summoned Ruach. "I cannot give up on believing she will see what she is doing is not the way." He closed his eyes and prepared to confront Sathariel.

Chapter 40

Meanwhile, Sathariel, the epicenter of their fear, pressed forward, using the Malevolents as a shield against the onslaught of her enemies. She knew she was near the Thura Gate.

Her attention was diverted by the appearance of the Kaluduta Natanael.

"We both know I'm not going to be stopped by you," Sathariel said. "I'm too powerful now. You have grossly underestimated my ambition. This city, this world and others, will be mine."

The Kaluduta sighed heavily, and Sathariel saw pity in the messenger's eyes. "The Divine wants no harm to be done to those he has blessed. The direction you are taking is fueled by hostility."

Sathariel laughed. "Let me demonstrate to you how hostile I can truly be." With that, she summoned Resha to her. The air around her crackled with energy, and with a sweep of her arm, she unleashed it on Natanael.

The Kaluduta was thrown to the ground and left writhing in pain. The messenger's eyes flowed with tears of blood. Natanal managed to get up on one elbow despite the agony the celestial being was clearly experiencing and spoke to Sathariel with conviction.

"Arielle, do you think you can win this war? You have started something that will span across eons and cause more harm than good. You embrace your darkness, and it will destroy you if you are not careful."

The queen cast an artificial look of sympathy at Natanael and uttered harshly, "Do not call me by that name! Gone is the name Arielle, never to be uttered again. I am Sathariel now, and not known by the title given to me by the Divine."

Her words were laced with vitriol as she continued: "I realized that the Divine would never approve of my ambitions. He named me the Lioness of God yet wanted me to remain nothing more than an obedient cub, following his commands without question."

Natanael lay on the ground, blood now flowing from the messenger's mouth, gasping for air and trying to speak, the celestial being's life force slowly ebbing away. The Kaluduta's words were almost unintelligible. Sathariel leaned forward and brought her face closer, listening.

"Your desires will be in vain. You are looking for something without considering the hope and love that lie at the core of all things and all beliefs."

Natanael suffered through the pain and struggled to stand. Despite the damage to those beautiful wings, the messenger opened them wide and stared up at the sky. "I will not let you take my life, Sathariel."

The queen shielded her eyes as a blinding light consumed the Kaluduta, and Natanael simply ceased to exist. The air around her was filled with tiny glowing specks that sparkled, a million minuscule sparks of light, impossible to count. She let out a triumphant laugh, her lips curled into snarl.

The quiet voice of Tauheed, her former love and confidant, broke through the chaos as he muttered her name.

With sorrow, Tauheed, who had witnessed the scene, gazed at Sathariel. "You know your way can't succeed. Your power comes from death, not life."

Sathariel turned incredulously, her face twisted. "You dare to come to me as a vapor, a projection, Tauheed? Are you not brave enough to be here in your physical form?"

The queen erupted into anger. Holding her scepter aloft, Sathariel thrust the staff downward with a mighty force, causing hundreds of fissures to open in the hard ground. Her arms outstretched toward the sky, she screamed in fierce rage, "I will send you back whence you came, Tauheed! And prepare for me to overcome your pathetic efforts to stop me."

The Divine Interpreter gasped and doubled over as Sathariel forcefully pushed him back to the city with the power of Resha, his body disappearing into nothingness.

The Malevolents surrounded her, and Sathariel shut her eyes, pushing out into the ether with her mind for the enticing touch of Resha.

Sathariel reached out and ascended onto the spiritual plain. She was suspended above her physical being, surrounded by her Malevolents. She could see the darkness whirling and flowing within herself and them. Sathariel regarded them, weighing her options. She surmised that if she drew on their stolen sustenance and combined it with her own, she could transport herself to the

Jivanam tree in the garden. But she did not know if it would leave her with enough power to combat any threat she might face upon arrival.

She was not sure if she could pinpoint the tree's exact location. But Tauheed, by coming to her as a projection of himself after she had killed Natanael, had enabled her to discover exactly where he was in the city. And she guessed that was where he would be heading after he apparated back within the city's walls.

How stupid, she thought, sensing his fear. *What a futile bid to change my mind.* Tauheed was visible to her now on this plane. Behind him, she could see the branches of the Jivanam tree shimmering tantalizingly, imbued with the power to take her from one world to another. And there she could also see the Yasha. For those brief moments Tauheed had been in her presence, she had scraped across his mind and discovered what she needed to know—the one currently being protected in Qualea was Cosmo. She smiled, relishing the prospect of victory that lay before her. It was her one chance to seize the realm of her foes.

Sathariel understood the price she needed to pay to reach the Thura Gate. It meant sacrificing one of her Malevolents, draining it of its life force to supercharge her own. But she didn't hesitate. The end justified the means. To her, the Malevolents were but tools, replaceable if necessary. She breathed and reentered her body.

With a swift movement, she reached out, gripping the nearest Malevolent by its wrist. "Now it's time for me to take your power back, and you will help me become the conqueror of more than just Amaris," she declared with a steely resolve, her call rising over the clamor of battle. As she inhaled deeply, the street was filled with the petrifying screams of the Malevolent as it was sucked dry of its life force. The power engulfed Sathariel, filling her body with electrifying energy. Her eyes rolled back as she reveled in the darkness, a cry of ecstasy escaping her lips.

Chapter 41

Cosmo's eyes widened in horror as a woman who he knew could only be Sathariel materialized in the garden. She outstretched her arms and opened her palms, and dark light poured from her as she pushed forward.

He cowered as, in a bid to stop her, Mariam ran forward, creating a sword and shield of water. But it was no match for Sathariel's power. The queen laughed at Mariam's efforts. With a flick of her wrist, the weapons disintegrated into droplets.

The force of Sathariel's Resha had cast Mariam aside, and Cosmo looked up with a sinking heart to see the queen of the Adira's face contort in disbelief and horror. "Everybody get down! She's forcing her way through the Thura Gate! She's not come for you, Cosmo. She's come for your world!"

Cosmo flung himself to the ground as Sathariel ran toward the tree with a scream, a rictus grin of triumph etched on her face as she was engulfed in a metallic light. A sound akin to a sonic boom filled the air as she flung herself at the trunk, which warped and spun as the Thura Gate opened. The shockwave of Sathariel's passage through the portal sent up a choking cloud of dust and debris.

Cosmo gasped for air and gingerly pushed himself up from the grass, which had withered to a dull, brittle brown. His ears were ringing, but he could still sense a terrifying silence within the garden walls. Beyond, Cosmo noticed that even the sound of the battle seemed more muted. He watched Mariam rise to her feet, coughing violently as she fought for breath. A horrible truth dawned on him as the air cleared and the others rose. Sathariel was no longer on Amaris. Which meant she was on her way to Earth.

Chapter 42

The golden domes and spires of the Rehmat palace shimmered in the sunlight. The air was calm, and the only scent was the smell of the water splashing from the fountain, accompanied with the intensity of the blooms in the garden. Fatiha sat beneath the Jivanam tree with Jiyanu. How was it, she mused, that three teenagers from Earth had found themselves in a different world with the daunting task of saving its people from an impending catastrophe?

Their bond was curious, to say the least. Jiyanu and Fatiha should have been divided by language and culture. But on Amaris, a planet that seemed to breathe magic, they understood each other flawlessly, their words seamlessly translated by the very air. It was delightful, in a strange sort of way, but also mystifying, like most things in this new world.

Right now, though, Fatiha was aware of the silence that filled the air between them—neither an awkward silence nor a comfortable one. It was a silence that carried the responsibility thrust upon both of their shoulders, and the countless lives that hung in the balance. It was a silence teeming with the unsaid, the space between words brimming with thoughts and emotions too complex to explain.

Finally, Fatiha spoke: "I've been trying to figure it out, the reason why I was chosen, why I was brought here. What makes me, a regular teenager, qualified to save an entire planet? Because I was cheated on and dumped? It hardly seems relevant."

Her words lingered in the air, and she was shy and embarrassed by the raw honesty of her confession to Jiyanu, someone she had met just hours ago. But he compelled Fatiha to be truthful. *What do I have to lose?*

She was surprised and slightly hurt when he let out a loud laugh. But the wry smile on Jiyanu's face made her realize it was a genuine laugh, which spoke to her of his understanding. "I can relate," he said, and as fast as the smile appeared, it faded, his face paling at what Fatiha could only imagine was a result of Jiyanu's own memories bubbling to the surface.

His voice wavered as he continued, eyes clouding with a far-off sadness. "I've been nothing but a disaster since my mother was taken from me. I've messed things up for myself, for everyone around me. I saw my father take my mother's life. It's something that haunts me even now..."

His words trailed off, and the air between them became thick with the ghosts of their pasts. Fatiha's heart constricted in sympathy, her gaze never leaving Jiyanu's troubled face.

"I thought the end of my world was when my boyfriend cheated on me with my best friend," she confessed, in a whisper against the vast silence that surrounded them. "It seems so petty now, compared with what you've been through. But back then, I thought there was no greater betrayal."

At this, Jiyanu looked at her, his eyes stormy with empathy. "You forgave them, didn't you?" he asked, tone hushed yet clear.

Fatiha nodded, her gaze steady. "I did. It was hard, but holding on to that anger…it was like consuming poison yet hoping he would be affected by it. I didn't want to be that person."

Jiyanu's gaze drifted to the engraved archway of the palace, his expression thoughtful. "And now we're here, two people from Earth, planning to save an alien world from an evil queen."

"That's right," Fatiha replied, her gaze mirroring Jiyanu's determination. "And you know what? I believe forgiveness is our secret weapon. Sathariel expects us to retaliate to her hatred with our own, to fight her darkness with darkness. But what if we surprise her? What if we confront her darkness with our light?"

Jiyanu crunched his eyebrows together, mulling over her words. "You think forgiveness can defeat her?"

Fatiha rubbed her chin and crinkled her nose in thought. "Not forgiveness alone. It's the love, unity, and compassion that comes with it. That's what can defeat her."

Jiyanu was silent for a moment, and Fatiha realized he was pondering her words. Then he sighed. "Back on Earth, I thought my world ended when my father killed my mother. I've lived with the rage, the injustice of it all. I've dreamt of revenge, of making him pay."

Fatiha watched his eyes darken, a storm of anger raging in them. Then in a moment, it shifted, and she saw the pain. She reached out a hand and placed it lightly on his shoulder, her heart aching for his turmoil. *Love and hate. You can't have one without the other.*

"But that's not who you are, Jiyanu. You're not your father."

He looked at her, his eyes reflecting the torment of his past. "I've been struggling with that. Every time the anger rises, I fear I'm becoming him. But I don't want to be."

Fatiha's tone was exasperated but firm. "You're not him, Jiyanu. You're here, trying to save a world. Your anger doesn't have to control you. You can overcome it and let that fuel you, give you the strength to fight."

Jiyanu stared at her, silver lining his dark eyes, and she could see he was struggling to process what she was suggesting—the way out from his own self-flagellation, an escape from his own prison of guilt. "You really believe that, don't you?"

Fatiha nodded. "I do. And I believe in you, Jiyanu. Together, with Cosmo, we're going to save this world. With our own light."

Fatiha let her hand drop and slid next to Jiyanu so that their shoulders were touching. The silence of the palace grounds, which enveloped them both, was now companionable and not so terrifying.

She allowed the enormity of their task to sink in. Yet, amid the shadows of the daunting mission, there was a glimmer of hope. *Our pasts do not define us.*

A warmth bloomed in Fatiha's gut, and her skin tingled. When she turned to look at Jiyanu again, he was smiling.

Chapter 43

Sathariel's body spun out of control, senses jarred with vertigo and sickness as she somersaulted through the woven fabric of space and time. Dizzying hues of interstellar beauty whirled past her in a dazzling blur. Her mind was a tempest, swirling with questions and doubts. Would the powers she wielded so commandingly on Amaris hold true in this alien world? The unsettling unknown of it all compounded the intense pressure building in her chest as she rocketed toward another galaxy, another dimension, another era.

Suddenly, with a brilliant shard of light, she was violently ejected from the cocoonlike sphere she'd been encased in. Plunging through the other side of the astral portal, she crashed onto the solid ground of Earth with an unceremonious thud.

Every bone in her body seemed to scream in protest at the rough landing. She lay there momentarily, curled up in a tight ball, her face uncomfortably pressed into cool earth. Gritting her teeth, she forced herself to rise, dusting herself off as she straightened her attire, grimacing against the lingering pain.

She surveyed the unfamiliar environment—a bleak landscape dotted with dark, towering silhouettes of stone structures. Myriad shining stars punctuated the black-velvet canvas of the night sky.

But for the distinct otherworldly aura in the air, she could have mistaken the scene for Amaris.

Flexing her fingers experimentally, Sathariel closed her eyes, drawing in a slow, measured breath as she reached out with her senses, searching for the familiar hum of Resha's power. *Are the energies different here?* Even if they were, the strange buzz in the atmosphere told her that magic was not foreign to this realm.

Carefully, she moved farther into the maze of buildings. Rhythmic chanting, a call to her from a distance. A magnetic pull of curiosity tugged at her, compelling her to follow the noise.

Chapter 44

Back on Amaris, with Sathariel's absence, her Malevolents had vanished as abruptly as they had appeared, as if their purpose had been solely to escort her to the Thura Gate.

Those corpses that had been animated after death by her power, dropped like stones so they could finally enjoy the bliss of eternal sleep. The Legion soldiers that remained had put down their weapons, gripped by uncertainty.

Cosmo struggled to overcome his rising sense of panic. He focused on his breath, counting to four as he inhaled and exhaled.

"How do we get her back? What's she going to do?" His face was full of apprehension as his wide eyes darted from one face to another.

Hana's touch was soft on his arm, a comfort amid their collective dread. "She is not a problem for your world to deal with, Cosmo. Believe that, somehow, this will be figured out, even though right now, it seems like there is no solution."

Chapter 45

Guided by the hypnotic cadence of the chant, Sathariel found herself drawn toward the heart of the cavernous buildings. The sound wove an invisible path until she stepped into a chamber of grand proportions.

The flickering warm glow of countless candles bathed the chamber, illuminating the austere beauty of the ancient stones. Their soft light transformed the space into a constellation of earthen tones, an array of fiery oranges and deep, velvety browns.

Rows of men, their figures swathed in robes of a dark-orange hue that mirrored the burning candles, lined the room. Their heads were shaven. As they chanted in unison, their voices flowed like a river of sound, resonating within the chamber's confines in an unrecognizable language.

At the forefront of this congregation knelt a man clad in garments as white as freshly fallen snow. Slowly, he lifted his eyes, locking them with Sathariel's.

Sathariel broke the room's rhythmic chant with a snarl of indignation. "Do you not recognize who I am? I am Sathariel, hailing from the world of Amaris, and I claim your world as my own!" Her proclamation rumbled with menace through the hallowed hall, a challenge that chased the stone pillars.

The silence that followed was as deep as the void of space, the previous symphony of sound reduced to a deafening quietude. The man in the white robe held her gaze, his face breaking into a serene smile that held a touch of sorrow.

"Good evening, Sathariel. We have assembled here at the Borobadur Temple, and have been anticipating your arrival." He spoke in a calm murmur. The tone was gentle—not in defiance but in resignation.

"We?" Sathariel spat, disbelief seeping into every syllable, eyes wide with defiance. "What world is this I am in? How can I understand you?"

The man simply returned her scorn with a calm, collected nod. "You are standing in a sacred space. The veil between worlds is thin here, and this place is imbued with a miraculous power that enables us to hear one another in our own tongue."

The man extended a hand toward the shadow. "Pastor Alexandra," he called in a soft tone. A woman emerged, her attire unlike anything Sathariel had ever seen. As she moved, a glint of silver caught Sathariel's attention: a cross, hanging from the woman's neck, reflected the soft glow of the myriad candles that flickered throughout the hall.

From the opposite direction, another figure began to take shape out of the shadows. The man's face lit up with recognition. "Imam Ghazi. Like us, he has been waiting for you."

Sathariel balked, her confusion morphing into unease. "What sort of illusion is this?" she spat, words ringing through the cavernous space. "Are you the Divine's lapdogs? Your attempts to deter me are futile. I wield the power of Resha."

Yet another pair of figures slipped out from the shadows, holding a large ring of pure gold between them. Fused with an intensity that was impossible to ignore, their eyes affixed on Sathariel like magnets.

With that serene smile still adorning his face, the man, dressed in loose robes, introduced himself: "I am the monk Aikyaa, this is Rabbi Zohar and Daoshi Guang. Like all of us, they have also been anticipating your arrival."

Aikyaa rose to his full height, his robes rustling against the ancient stone floor, and reached out to the golden ring. He motioned for Pastor Alexandra and Imam Ghazi to join him. "You underestimate the extent of your Divine's reach, Sathariel. Despite the differences in our perceptions of his nature, his divine splendor, we stand united when it comes to threats against our existence."

Sathariel's heart hammered in her chest. Something was not right. The familiar, comforting power of Resha seemed distant, unreachable.

"You are on consecrated ground, Sathariel. Your dark powers are impotent here," Aikyaa continued. "This temple, constructed at the veil, was built with protective mechanisms."

Imam Ghazi stood in the dimly lit room, his face partially obscured by shadows, yet his expression remained stern and composed. "Our God wears many faces and answers to many names across our cultures. Yet he is the same as your divine."

Pastor Alexandra, standing opposite him, nodded in agreement. Her eyes were steady, reflecting a deep-seated belief as she responded: "One thing we all agree on, even you, is that the battle between good and evil remains constant, no matter where we are in the vast tapestry of this creation. We must ensure the triumph of light over darkness."

Their voices came together, filling the grand chamber with a rhythm of unity, and though Sathariel did not understand the meaning, the sounds of the language and the haunting melody struck her heart deeply.

> *"Duratmanam nihantu bhumyaam, yaatra prapanna sa.*
> *Lokan rakshatu Dharmatah.*
> *Punaragamanam kriyaat, svargam prapnuyat shaantim.*
> *Vishwasya hitamichhantu, sarvabhutahitam."*

"Your power is useless here, Sathariel." Daoshi Guang's words hung in the air like final death knell. "On Earth, we have fallen victim to our own misunderstandings and manipulations. Tonight, we put aside our divisions and unite to banish you. We do this for the collective well-being of our world."

The golden ring in their hands began to glow, the energy radiating from it making the air thrum with anticipation. Sathariel's senses were overwhelmed by the potent vibration of their words, the discordant harmony gnawing at her like claws scraping across her soul. She crumpled to her knees, a piercing wail breaking free from her.

The orange-robed monks were like a wave of fire to Sathariel's eyes, and she shielded her gaze, wincing. They added their words to the refrain, a powerful mantra in the grandeur of the chamber. Sathariel knew she, a looming figure of menace, had been rendered small and defenseless. She was a marionette whose strings had been cut, unable to resist as Rabbi Zohar and Aikyaa approached and fitted the golden ring around her neck.

The pressure engulfed Sathariel. It was an unbearable, monstrous wave that threatened to crush her. She doubled over; her silent screams pulsated in the hallowed space. Then her bones stretched; an unseen hand had seized her. Sinews and muscle were abruptly pulled backward with a force that squeezed the essence from her body. She was propelled through the shimmering portal. The last of her screeching cry lingered in the room, a fading remnant of the force that had once threatened to consume Earth.

Chapter 46

A radiant flash of light pierced the gloom, and Sathariel emerged next to the swirling, pulsing portal in the Hayim citadel. Her eyes flashed with fury, her aura shimmering ominously. A raw, guttural scream tore free from her throat, ripping through the garden.

"You dare?" Sathariel seethed with rage, every syllable a hiss. She was filled with fury at those who had just banished her and those here on Amaris who sought to stop her.

She spun around and stared at the group, then pulled off the collar around her neck in fury. "You dare to challenge me? You will pay. Oh, how you will pay!"

She realized she was no longer in the temple and was back on Amaris. *No matter, now I will take this world as I was destined.* Sathariel's scepter materialized in her hand, and she held it high, eyes mirroring the cold gleam of the metal. Sathariel's lips pulled back in a snarl. "Now comes the full scale of my wrath. I will bring the relentless might of Naraka down upon you. You will learn to fear my name!"

She slammed her scepter down into the soft earth. A harsh crack emanated outward, and a shockwave of power rippled through the air. Darkness swelled around her, and the Malevolents appeared from the shadows, their forms grotesque and twisted, eager to carry out their master's commands.

"Capture the Yasha, the boy from the other realm," she roared, incandescent. "Sacrifice yourselves if necessary, but bring him to me unharmed. His life force must remain intact," she instructed, words an icy whip cutting through the air.

Hana's skin prickled as Sathariel gathered Resha. The smells of smoke and fire imbued the atmosphere. Fear and dread knotted in her stomach, a pit of worry opening up as she turned to Mariam, whose eyes screamed the urgency of the situation. "Mariam, you must take Cosmo," she warned. The ocean queen, alongside Tauheed, braced herself as the Divine Interpreter reached out to pull Ruach toward him in retaliation. The air, as if heeding his actions, crackled, and the tang of salt, rain, and moss threatened to overwhelm the acrid scent of Sathariel's pull on Resha as he dug into the very force of nature.

Hana glanced at Cosmo, whose wild glare reflected his descent into fight-or-flight mode. The anxiety building in him was palpable, and Hana realized he could see no way out.

She watched in horror as Cosmo, seized by panic and clearly without thinking, began to run. His fear was driving him away from the safety of his protectors.

"Stop! Stop running! We can protect you." Hana's cry of horror pierced the air, filled with desperation and frustration. But it was too late. Cosmo was too far gone, his fear driving him to rash actions. He took off at a sprint.

Hana looked upward, searching the darkness for Harda and Lexi. But they were entangled in their own fight with Malevolents and Obscura, who had returned to the battle the moment Sathariel had come back to Amaris. The sky was teeming with clashing forces, flames, and acrid smoke. They were too far to reach the fleeing Yasha.

Hana's heart turned to ice as a dark shadow fell over Cosmo, a Malevolent's gruesome form taking on solid shape from the swirling darkness. The creature was fueled by Sathariel's bitter fury and the promise of an ultimate prize. Its claws reached out with an unquenchable yearning, a deep hiss emanating from the recesses of its hood.

Tauheed cried out in anger, and Hana searched deep into her soul for the pure energy of Ruach. The scent of roses and forest leaves began to bloom in her nostrils as she pulled the energy toward her.

Four more Malevolents, their dark forms taking shape, filled the air with the oppressive presence of Resha, the maleficent force providing a fountain of darkness for Sathariel to siphon. Their presence, as well as the power of Resha they provided, enabled the evil queen to create a barrier between Hana, Mariam, Tauheed, and Cosmo, who had frozen mid-sprint, held in the grip of dark power.

The Vanavasin priestess sank to her knees as Sathariel channeled the energy provided by the Malevolents' proximity and flooded her, Mariam, and Tauheed with constricting pain. Hana's teeth rattled in her head, and her bones were pushed the point of snapping with the force. *Too slow! I cannot fight it. I cannot pull enough Ruach in enough time.*

She heard Tauheed gasp as he clutched blindly at his throat. Resha pressed down upon every molecule in Hana's being. She saw Tauheed's knees hit the ground as he strained against the onslaught being brought upon them. "She has brought the Malevolents to give her the power she needs to take Cosmo," he choked out. "But I don't know if they alone can give her the supercharge she needs to imprison him."

Queen Mariam emitted a strangled cry. "If they cannot, she will take all of her troops' life force as well. She will take them all." Tears welled in her eyes.

Sathariel's laughter rang through the garden, harsh and guttural. "Mariam, you are wise despite your demise. With my Malevolents, I can channel their superior Resha to capture the Yasha. And yes, that, with the other troops I command, will provide me enough dark energy to do everything I need, hold back your pathetic attempts at using Ruach to prevent me, and take this boy for my own. You won't stop me."

Hana watched, powerless, as one of the Malevolents moved to the paralyzed form of Cosmo, and the deathly cold breath washed over his face. Even from where she was, pinned by her knees to the ground, Hana could smell the foul stench of decay, the creature's hiss to Cosmo audible. "Your soul, Yasha, is a sweet taste on my tongue," it sneered with malice and hunger.

Cosmo sank to the ground. She saw the crippling sadness descend upon him, the breath of the Malevolent leaving him weak and disoriented. She knew that breath would drain him; all hope was being sucked out of Cosmo, leaving him hollow.

"Do not kill him!" Sathariel commanded. With a determined glint in her eye, she uttered a powerful incantation. Her words rung out across the garden: *"Protego ergo sum!"*

Hana watched as Sathariel's body was engulfed in a bloodred darkness that ate up every pinprick of light as she drew on the power of Resha. In the sky beyond her, the dense crimson fog began to roll toward the battlefield outside Qualea from the garden.

From her vantage point above the city, Hana could see Sathariel's troops fall to their knees as the clouds made their ominous descent toward them.

As they were swallowed up in the mist, the sound of gasping and choking filled the air as Sathariel drained her army's life force with her demand for Resha's energy. Disoriented dragons roared, their keen sight obscured by the thick fog.

"What is she doing?" Tauheed gasped to Hana through the choking fog, his eyes wide with horror.

Hana's silver-lined eyes betrayed her fear. "Sathariel can draw on Resha only in those who have sworn fealty to her to imprison Cosmo. She's using her army to give her the power to transport herself back to Heliopolis with Cosmo! Curse her!"

There was a gigantic thunderclap and a boom, which pushed Hana's body into the ground. When she opened her eyes and peered through the evaporating gloom, Sathariel, Cosmo, and the Malevolents had vanished without a trace.

"Oh...oh...Divine." Hana stumbled over the words as she tried to stifle a wail.

The tears that had been held in Queen Mariam's eyes were now streaked down her face.

Hana clung to the final question hanging ominously between them: “How do we stop her now?”

Chapter 47

In the disorienting aftermath of Cosmo's abduction by Sathariel, Jiyanu had traveled with Fatiha and the Rehmat, Moirah and Louisa, to Myrkvior.

They had told him that their destination held within its tree-lined walls a seed of hope. It was a place to confer with the enlightened Vanavashtha, to construct a plan of action, and to mend their wounds.

Jiyanu now sat in the main hall as the Council of the Clans convened; voices were hushed and somber. His admired the grandeur of the thick tree branches that were interwoven into the structure they were meeting in, which was suspended high above the forest floor.

He was thankful for Louisa filling in both of them on who was who. The leaders, who he had been told were usually at one another's throats, now appeared to have forgotten their differences.

"It's amazing what having a common enemy can do," he said to Fatiha, who was also drinking in their surroundings, eyes wide in wonder.

The corner of her mouth turned up. "Yep. It's a shame that it takes a war to make that happen."

Amid the murmuring in the hall, he watched as Tamanka rose from his chair. The Taura leader climbed onto the ancient wooden table around which they had gathered. Tamanka's words projected through the vast room, painting a grim picture that held his audience captive. "We were lucky not to have too many losses at Qualea," he uttered, his lips in a grim line.

"But that is a small victory in comparison to us losing Cosmo. The Hephaes have shared with us the chilling revelation that Cosmo has, as we suspected, been taken by Sathariel. He is being held prisoner in the grand throne room of Heliopolis. Sathariel herself is watching over him."

Louisa cut through the murmurs with a questioning tone: "How can they possibly know that?"

Tamanka's eyes met the Rehmat leader's, hard and brittle, a battle of wills in the quiet. He pulled himself up and puffed out his chest. "The Hephaes, the children of the earth, share a bond with the very rock and stone of our world. When Sathariel invoked Resha to warp the walls of the palace and turned it into a prison for Cosmo, the Hephaes sensed the ripple through the stone's memory. Remember, the Taura sculpted that palace from Elutheros's single stone."

A begrudging nod of acceptance was Louisa's only response. The unsaid apology hung in the air, adding to the tension.

Moirah, a calming presence amid the friction, took to her feet. She was not afraid to speak the hard truth they all needed to hear. "The triad of Yasha is essential to forge the prison that can contain Sathariel. Without the blood of the other world that Cosmo carries, that prison will crumble. Our mission now is a rescue—a rescue that will determine the fate of our world."

"Our path will be fraught with Malevolents and Legion soldiers," Tauheed announced, his expression dark.

"We also have to contend with a Resha-bound Cosmo in the heart of the enemy's fortress. Not to mention the imposing presence of Sathariel herself. To liberate him, we must overcome all these obstacles, and remember: We must not kill Sathariel. Her life is inexplicably tied to the Vanavashtha, and through them to Amaris itself. Her death could spell our doom."

Jiyanu listened as the discussion turned to strategies, each option mulled over, dismissed, restructured, and reassessed.

"Could we replicate their previous rescue of Lexi?" Tauheed suggested.

"The risk is high," Harda responded. "The castle is a labyrinth, bristling with enemies and guarded by Malevolents who can sense the slightest ripple of Ruach. We need an element of surprise, a way to reach Cosmo unnoticed."

Jiyanu looked to Hana, who suggested a daring approach. "We could use the roots of the Vanavashtha to infiltrate the palace. With the Hephaes's aid, we can carve a path through the rock, a secret passageway into the throne room."

Tauheed nodded. "If we can pull Cosmo through the gateway, I can hold off the Malevolents just long enough for our escape."

The room fell silent as the daunting prospect sank in. Mariam chimed in on the plan that seemed to be taking shape: "What if Sathariel has weakened Cosmo? What if he doesn't have enough strength left after being drained by the Malevolent? I am sure

Sathariel will make it practically impossible to rescue him. She has too much to lose."

Hana rubbed her neck in thought. "The other issue could be that Cosmo has been tainted by the power of Resha from being exposed to the Malevolent and Sathariel. He is also not from here, and the very fabric of Amaris is on high alert. The goodness of Ruach could see him as a threat, and the very walls of the passageway opened up by the Hephaes to rescue him could close on his body, killing him during the rescue."

The tension broke as Tauheed suggested, "Perhaps we could take another Yasha with us to guide him. If Jiyanu or Fatiha go through with us, they will have already forged a recognizable bond with the earth. Then it will recognize Cosmo as a friend and not a threat."

"I find it highly annoying they're talking about us like we're not here," Jiyanu whispered to Fatiha, who rolled her eyes.

"Yeah, it's kind of rude, considering we're the ones supposedly saving them!"

Jiyanu stifled a laugh and nudged Fatiha in the ribs.

Moirah got to her feet and carefully pulled a silk cloth out of the folds of her robes. She gently uncovered a bangle, a shimmering blend of gemstone and metal.

Jiyanu leaned forward slightly, craning his neck to see it. "What's that?" He raised his eyebrows at Fatiha.

She raised her finger to her lips as she looked at Jiyanu and turned her attention to Moirah, who addressed the council.

"This is a precious relic from the old days of the spirit people. It is an aid to protect the wearer from harm. An artifact gifted by the

Taura to the Rehmat in times when our relationship had no strain. It holds the potential to safeguard Cosmo. This will create the bond you need. It is mined from the same mountains that bore the Hephaes."

Jiyanu jumped as Moirah turned her attention on him and Fatiha. "Would one of you be willing to help us rescue Cosmo?"

Jiyanu swallowed his nerves and urged his words to ring clear. "Absolutely. If it helps save your world, then I will do it. I trust you will protect me." As he closed his lips, Jiyanu thought he sounded a lot more confident than he felt.

Jiyanu's face bloomed with heat. But then, the boiling anger that so often spilled out of him began to simmer. His heart was ablaze with a burning purpose, which overshadowed the tormented memories that always threatened to consume his spirit.

That recurring vivid nightmare, the haunting image of his father's murderous rage and his mother's life extinguishing in his arms, was not churning so violently inside him.

Jiyanu was no stranger to pain, to the rage that festered from profound loss. But here in Amaris, he had found something he'd thought he had lost—a reason to fight, a purpose.

His inner voice spoke clearly. *This is my chance. A chance to turn this pent-up rage, this pain, into something meaningful. I may have been a victim once, but I refuse to be a prisoner of my past. I will fight.*

The pledge carved a path before him, a path brimming with peril yet gleaming with the promise of redemption. And he was ready to stride upon it. This was his purpose, and he embraced it wholly.

Harda rose in solidarity. "The dragon riders will lend their wings to this cause. We can draw away the Malevolents and create a diversion while you infiltrate the palace."

Moirah added: "Our final challenge is returning him and the other Yasha to our capital. While we can use the Vanavashtha to enter through the Jivanam tree, it must be destroyed before you leave the palace. Though Sathariel is not using it as a portal now, because she cannot, it does not mean she will not try again."

Tamanka stepped forward, a secretive smile playing on his lips. "I suppose," he started, his tone full of suspense, "it's time I shared a Hephaes secret with you all."

The hall waited on his words with expectation. "Hidden beneath the world we know, concealed from prying eyes, are the Durara Gates. They are a network of passages that weave together places distant and disconnected, like threads in a vast cosmic tapestry."

The room fell into stunned silence, all eyes fixed on Tamanka.

Harda let out a sigh and then a guffawing laugh. "Tamanka, so that is how you managed to get the troops to Qualea faster than dragon flight. You kept that quiet."

The leader of the Taura smiled smugly at the dragon rider and winked. "Long-distance travel without the dangers of the surface world. That's what they offer," he said, the corners of his mouth lifting into a more pronounced smile. "We have one such gate that will enable you to leave the palace in Heliopolis and return to us. They are also woven with protective enchantments. Any creature imbued with Resha cannot enter."

Jiyanu, who had been holding his breath, let it out in a slow *whoosh.* Now he was less intimidated by the task that lay ahead. The burden of their mission seemed to ease ever so slightly.

Hana broke the silence, her smile full of gratitude. "You have no idea, Tamanka. This...this could change everything for us."

Tauheed's face was full of relief and gratitude. "Indeed, Tamanka. Our thanks won't be enough." Murmurs of agreement filled the room like a calming tide.

Mariam raised her voice in a prayer of protection: "So, it's settled. Hana, Tauheed, Jiyanu, and I will make the journey. May the love and blessing of the Divine be with you." She turned to Jiyanu and Tamanka. "We are forever in your debt."

Chapter 48

In the secretive hush of night, Jiyanu, Hana, Mariam, and Tauheed emerged from the confines of the Durara Gate into the grounds of the castle in Heliopolis. The overpowering aroma of damp earth clung to them as they stepped into the faint silver glow of the moon, which had turned the landscape a silver-gray.

Waves of anxiety washed over Tauheed in a never-ending tide. Next to him, Mariam and Hana, who stood side by side, blinked in the moonlight, eyes wide and skin the color of ash. Cosmo's hands were clutched tightly, knuckles white with tension.

A cold shiver ran down Tauheed's spine as he saw the same fear mirrored in their expressions.

The Vanavasin priestess rolled her shoulders, and Tauheed could see tension in her jaw. She broke the stifling silence: "We must act, and swiftly. The sooner we extricate Cosmo from this place, the better. The heinous force of Resha, unleashed within these palace confines, is poisoning everything."

Mariam pointed toward the skies. "Look there. Our reinforcements." Above them, the indistinct shapes of dragon riders steadily approached the palace, their massive wings slicing through the air with barely a sound.

Anticipating their approach might be heard, Hana had cleverly crafted a cloak of silence to mute the sounds of their approach, including the dragons, as they neared the city. She beckoned them and they moved toward the wall, looking for the point where the castle and rock seamlessly merged. Bending down, Hana ran her hand along the stratum. She found the place that indicated where the rock from which the walls were sculpted stopped.

She beckoned to Tauheed, Mariam, and Jiyanu, gesturing for them to stretch out their hands to touch the surface. Hana began to recite an incantation:

> *"Prakaram gachchha, atal drishyam bane.*
> *Apaarata ko chhodo, bhinnata se samane.*
> *Antariksha gate, pathik anant mein. Sthirata ko bhedo, chale hum preet mein.*
> *Yatra siddhi devo, hum hain atithi teri prame."*

As the ancient words flowed, the stonework trembled. Tauheed held his breath as it transformed, revealing the ghostly visage of one of the Hephaes, its eyes and mouth materializing as if from a fog. Its silent gaze held them. Tauheed exhaled and caught Mariam looking skyward, panic etched on her features.

"Wait...Wait..." she whispered urgently. Before Mariam could complete her sentence, the skies exploded into a fiery spectacle, spirals of flame painting the canvas of the night sky in vivid shades of burnt orange and red. The silhouettes of the dragons danced within this inferno, their aerial ballet punctuated by the sudden emergence of the Malevolents around them.

"Now! Now!" Mariam's command sliced the silence. As if on cue, the stone giant's mouth yawned open, revealing an abyss of unknown depth.

"Through here," Mariam beckoned, pointing to the passage that would lead them inside the castle.

Tauheed took the lead with hesitant steps, and they all entered the yawning void, leaving the moonlit garden behind. He could not believe that through the Hephaes's mouth, they were walking through a tunnel the creature had made due to its ability to turn solid rock to air.

"How has it done that?' Jiyanu spoke quietly with a slight tremble.

Tauheed turned behind him to see the Yasha's face, eyes wide and frightened. "You have nothing to fear. The Hephaes *are* the rock."

The deep tones of the mountain giant filled the air around them. "We can move through the rock, be the rock, and change the rock. We are as one. As long we can hold Sathariel and Resha at bay, the passage will remain intact."

Jiyanu visibly swallowed. "I'll try not to think about the fact one of us could end up getting sandwiched into the stone if for any reason Sathariel discovers us and gets the upper hand."

The Hephaes rumbled forward through the tunnel it had forged, its colossal form a symphony of grinding stone and echoing vibrations that reverberated through the very marrow of the earth. The giant's body, hewn from the mountain's ancient granite and veined with shimmering quartz, seemed to dissolve and reform with every thunderous step, blending seamlessly with the surrounding rock as if it were an extension of its own essence.

One moment, its craggy face—etched with deep fissures that mimicked the wrinkles of timeless wisdom—emerged from the jagged walls, eyes that glowed faintly, like embedded geodes catching a stray beam of torchlight, fixing upon the travelers with a gaze that spoke of secrets.

Then, just as suddenly, the features faded back into the stone, vanishing like a mirage in the desert heat, only to reappear moments later in the uneven floor beneath their feet, where the ground rippled subtly as if breathing, then in the vaulted ceiling above, where stalactites twisted into the semblance of a stern brow or a gaping maw.

The air grew thick with the scent of damp earth and mineral dust, particles swirling in the wake of the giant's passage, coating their skin and filling their lungs with the raw, primal taste of the mountain's core.

The Hephaes had sculpted this passageway and the winding corridor ahead from its own substance, carving through solid rock with effortless might, yet it remained intrinsically bound to its very fabric.

The Hephaes's deep tones filled the passage it had created. "I can sustain this passage for only so long. Sathariel's power is permeating these castle walls. You must hasten."

Tauheed did not need any encouragement to press on. The heat inside the passage escalated. Despite his successful efforts to quell his anxiety, a fresh wave of sweat broke out on his forehead. Tauheed glanced at Mariam, who appeared visibly uncomfortable.

"I'm a fish out of water in this stifling heat," she confessed, her tone lined with exhaustion. Hana turned to reassure her and held out a hand to assist the queen, steady and confident.

Tauheed smiled with sympathy. "You're within the stone giant's very essence. The Hephaes brings the primordial heat of the Elphis mountains, forged at the dawn of Amaris. Not much farther—the intensity of Resha is growing in strength. We are almost at the end."

But even as he spoke, the passage they were walking through, created by the Hephaes, began to narrow and rise, taking on a threatening aspect.

The Hephaes exhaled through the walls, a sigh and a command. "Stop! Stand together."

Tauheed was now staring at a dead end. *Maybe the Hephaes can sense it.* "Is it a trap?"

"I will go first," announced the stone giant, booming. Tauheed turned to Hana, his hand extended in a plea for support.

"Hold my hand, and we can channel the power of Ruach together," he proposed. With her free hand, Hana reached out and grabbed Jiyanu's wrist, grip steady and reassuring. "We must stay linked to pass through the entrance to the palace itself." She nodded for him to connect with Mariam.

The queen of the ocean people placed her hand on Jiyanu's shoulder. The wall in front of them began to ripple and distort, twisting into liquid. They pressed forward, and plunged into the unknown.

Tauheed walked through the wall of what was now water, into Sathariel's throne room. The queen was otherwise occupied, her gaze fixed on the chaos unfolding outside the window. Her hand was outstretched, the very air around her crackling with power. Clearly, she was controlling the Malevolents, who were currently locked in aerial combat with the dragon riders. *Just as we planned. The distraction worked!*

He cast his gaze around the room. There, shackled in the dark chains of Resha, was Cosmo. His eyes were devoid of spark, dulled by his prolonged imprisonment and torment. "Let's do this while she's distracted," Tauheed whispered, just audible above the sounds of the ongoing battle.

He gestured for Hana and Mariam to draw on Ruach. The chains encircling Cosmo began to glow as they chanted their incantation under their breath. His vacant eyes flickered as he recognized the familiar voices.

Tauheed looked at Cosmo's vacant face. *Why do you not see us?*

Hana let out a gasp of realization. "It cannot be. Sathariel is using him! She's channeling his life force. Quickly, Jiyanu, you must put the bangle on him. The power of Ruach does not recognize him as its own. It sees him as a threat, the antithesis of what is good. If you put the bangle on Cosmo, the Earth will see him as its own. That's the only way to break her control."

Barely hesitating, Jiyanu sprinted toward Cosmo and yanked his limp wrist. With a swift movement, he thrust the bangle onto his arm. The sudden disruption of her power flow alerted Sathariel, who spun around to face the intruders, her face contorted in fury.

"How dare you!" she shrieked, her hands glowing with the promise of an imminent attack. But before she could strike, Hana and Tauheed countered with a blast of their own, redirecting the flow of Resha and absorbing its dark energy. Meanwhile, Mariam clutched Jiyanu's wrist tightly, and together they unleashed a powerful blast of Ruach, hurling Sathariel off her feet.

"Hephaes, open the passage!" Tauheed commanded, his words taut. Behind him, the stone wall of the throne room started to shudder, a doorway slowly forming on its surface. He watched with no small degree of satisfaction as Sathariel, sprawled on the floor, roared in anger. She staggered to her feet.

As they disappeared into the tunnel, the entrance continued to close behind them, and Tauheed heard Sathariel's frustrated yell. The last thing he saw was the queen dashing toward the wall, fists raised to pound on it. But he knew the doorway had vanished.

Even though there was a stone wall separating them, Tauheed still heard her muffled cries. "I will make you pay for this!" came her scream, which bounced off the walls of the now-deserted throne room.

Inside the tunnel, Tauheed led their group back toward the Jivanam tree. Mariam and Jiyanu dragged a barely conscious Cosmo between them.

The passage was filled with the presence of Hephaes, laced with agonizing pain. "She's trying to bind me! Hurry!"

"Mariam, Hana, we must use Ruach to keep the passage open and absorb the Resha Sathariel is using to close the tunnel. The Hephaes won't have enough power to stop Sathariel's binding and keep the passage open," Tauheed instructed.

Hana and Mariam gave a firm nod, sweat beading their brows.

Looking over his shoulder, Tauheed saw the passage collapsing behind them, the path they had taken gradually vanishing. With a sickening dread, he questioned whether they would make it out alive. “Keep moving,” Hana panted. “I’ll hold her off.”

Chapter 49

Cosmo was half awake and full of confusion. *Where am I?* The narrow confines of the passage were rekindling dormant fears, the claustrophobia that had haunted him since the earthquake.

His memories flooded back. Being trapped in the rubble. Being buried alive with his mother for two agonizing days.

Cosmo's mind replayed the desperate rescue, the bitter triumph of survival tainted by the tragic loss. This was the profound tragedy that had sparked his father's obsession, setting him on an unending journey to understand the connection between physical matter and the elusive realm "beyond the veil." The burial of his real life in his archaeological work.

Cosmo's heart thundered against his ribs, a frantic metronome demonstrating his fear. He knew he was on the precipice of a massive panic attack, his worst nightmare materializing around him. Cosmo's breath hitched in his throat, pulse racing with adrenaline.

Tauheed's strong arm wrapped around him. "You've got this. Just breathe. Remember, you're not alone. We're here with you," he soothed. With a gulp, Cosmo attempted to steady himself as he struggled to bring his galloping heartbeat under control.

A shimmering light appeared in the distance, signaling the end of their grueling journey. Gathering all his remaining strength, Cosmo, with Jiyanu, Mariam, and Tauheed, hurried toward the light, with Hana bringing up the rear. As he emerged from the tunnel into the clear night, the sky above Jiyanu was illuminated by the fierce battle between the Malevolents and the dragon riders.

Each fiery explosion was a grim reminder of the danger they were in. It was the scene of a nightmare that left a bitter taste in Cosmo's mouth.

He turned to see Tauheed, Jiyanu, and Mariam emerge into the garden. Exhaustion painted their faces. He watched Tauheed and Mariam as the aftershocks of fighting the Resha began to hit them. Doubled over, dark energy seeped out of them in waves. Tauheed dropped to his knees, mirroring Mariam's actions. Their bodies convulsed, violently expelling the consumed Resha, the darkness dissipating into the cool night air.

"Where is Hana?" Cosmo turned and asked Jiyanu.

The scene that followed would be etched into his memory forever. The outstretched arm and the horrified expression on Hana's face as she emerged from the stone wall, only to be sucked back in. The sight left Cosmo frozen as the dragons roared above.

Mariam's ragged breaths and guttural cry filled the air, which reeked of sulfur. "We've lost her. We've lost her."

Tauheed, hands braced on his knees, looked up at them and wiped his mouth, removing the traces of vomit from Resha. His eyes were filled with anguish. "No time—she is part of the rock now. We have to leave her.'

Cosmo's heart broke into a million pieces. *She did this for me. Another life on my conscience. Another life I could not save.*

Mariam's eyes shimmered with unshed tears. "She will be honored by the mountain people and her own for her sacrifice."

Looking up at the tumultuous sky, Cosmo could see one of the dragons clearly wounded, struggling against the relentless Malevolents. The situation was dire and time was running out.

"We must run for the Durara Gate. NOW!" Tauheed's command cut through the tension, leaving no room for debate. "Go ahead of me. I must destroy the tree."

Cosmo scrambled toward the end of the garden with the others. There, on the left of the entrance to the main gate, was the barely perceptible carving at the base of the rock wall.

Jiyanu's call was urgent: "This is it, Cosmo, this is it!"

Tauheed opened his hands and let forth Ruach from his fingers and wove it around the tree. The ropes of light grew taut, and in a snapping motion, he pulled the Jivanam out of the soil. A sigh of pain echoed through the air as the tree was wrenched up from its roots.

He then interlaced his fingers and drew his palms together. The tree burst into white-hot flames. Panting, Tauheed then turned his attention to the wall. With a gesture, he used Ruach to make the base of the stonework fall in on itself, revealing an opening they could squeeze through and a flight of stone stairs.

Cosmo swallowed. *More confined spaces.* Tauheed gestured for them to enter the gate. "This will last only a short time. We must get back to the Vanavasin. Then we must get you to the spirit people before Sathariel gets there herself."

Chapter 50

Sathariel paced back and forth within the grand throne room. The flickering torches cast dancing shadows across her face as she seethed with fury. *How dare they! How dare they take the boy from me!*

A surge of anger reverberated through her veins. *I will not allow them to create a prison that will strip me of my power.*

Pausing for a moment, Sathariel took a deep breath, her mind racing with possibilities. *How can I prevent my capture?* An idea began to form within her mind, a desperate plan to turn the tides in her favor.

She addressed one of her Malevolents, which had waiting in the darkest recesses of the throne room. "There is only one way I can think of to prevent my capture. That rock of Sambandh, the one the Rehmat have created to imprison me. I must destroy it."

Sathariel shook her fist at the heavens, her anger directed toward the Divine. "You think you can stop me? You are mistaken. I have more power to draw upon than you can ever imagine!"

She beckoned the Malevolent closer, its presence both captivating and unsettling. "You have served me well, but I need you for one final sacrifice," Sathariel whispered with a sinister edge. "I must speak directly with Sephtis. He will possess the key to prevent my imprisonment, to enable me to destroy the rock of Sambandh."

The creature hovered before her, a sinister glow the only light to indicate the remnants of a face. "Show yourself to me," she commanded.

The Malevolent obeyed and revealed its terrifying visage. Sathariel stared into its scaled, reptilian features, fiery white pupils flickering with an otherworldly light, skin so thin that every plane of its skull was etched through the membrane. The sight would have instilled horror in the hearts of many, but Sathariel saw only an instrument of her desires.

"Thank you for your service," she murmured, almost tenderly. With a swift movement, she reached out and caressed the creature's cheek, her touch juxtaposing coldness and intimacy. "And now, you will make the greatest sacrifice of all."

Closing her eyes, Sathariel tightened her grip around the Malevolent's throat, her nails piercing its flesh. The creature hissed and let out a silent scream, its life force gradually draining away. Sathariel's body was engulfed in a swirling tornado of black mist as she absorbed the Malevolent's power, its essence merging with her own.

Looking up, she saw the King of Darkness. His twisted throne loomed ominously in the shadows. With reverence and a touch of fear, Sathariel dropped to her knees before Sephtis.

"Master, you have witnessed my struggles against the forces of light," she began, with a mixture of awe and desperation. "I know that you desire Amaris as much as I do. You yearn for revenge, just as I do, after being rejected and cast out by the Divine."

Sephtis leaned forward from his throne; his chilling authority seeped through the walls of the chamber. Sathariel shivered involuntarily, and it was as if a thousand insects crawled beneath her skin.

"I can provide you with the means to destroy the rock of Sambandh, but I cannot guarantee its success," Sephtis intoned. "But know this: If you fail, the prison they construct for you will become your eternal downfall. You may escape, but ultimately, it will hold you and be your undoing."

Sathariel's mouth hardened into a determined line as she stood tall. "I do not believe I will fail," she declared.

"Your desire is granted then," Sephtis responded. "Here is the trade. I will aid you, but your soul shall be mine, condemned forever to damnation. No return."

Sathariel saw the trade-off as a necessary means to an end. *This power bestowed upon me will make me invincible, capable of thwarting the forces of light.* The idea of eternal slavery did not concern her, for she was convinced she would find a way to manipulate her fate.

Sathariel knelt on the cold stone floor, her eyes wide with a fierce longing that burned with an inner fire. Her hands were clasped tightly in front of her, trembling slightly, as she gazed up at the shadowy figure towering above her. "Master, grant me the tools I need," she implored, every word dripping with an insatiable thirst for power.

Before her, a dagger materialized on the floor, its blade shimmering. "This dagger, when plunged into the rock of Sambandh, will shatter the stone and return it to the earth whence it came," Sephtis explained. "You must act swiftly before the Yasha have the chance to taint it with their blood. Do not let this happen."

Sathariel nodded, her gaze fixated on the gleaming blade. "Amaris will soon be ours. I journey now to avert my own demise. The people of Amaris must be prepared, for their new queen is about to ascend to her rightful throne."

With those words, she disappeared into a vortex of darkness, her destiny intertwined with the shadows that had become her allies.

Chapter 51

Jiyanu arrived back in Myrkvior, and immediately time became an enemy he could not afford to spare.

Harda, Lexi, and the dragon riders were recuperating from their clash with the Malevolents. Jiyanu knew they all faced the conundrum of how to get him, along with Fatiha and Cosmo, to Salama and the Sambandh rock as quickly as possible. The Durara Gates were the immediate solution.

Constans, the austere leader of the Vanavasin, had been dubious upon learning about the clandestine access to the gate in his citadel and wanted to at least know its whereabouts in his city.

With a touch of theatricality, Tamanka guided them to a long-forgotten storeroom in the citadel's kitchens. Concealed behind a hinged panel nestled in the rock face, he unveiled a spiral staircase descending into the heart of the gargantuan tree that formed a column for the citadel.

A gasp escaped Moirah. "How on earth were you able to carve out such a route?" she asked in awe.

Tamanka's chest swelled with pride. "Long ago, we found a way to control the caterpillars that fed on the heartwood of your trees. We used them as our janitors in the mines, removing the green debris. By guiding them up the tree's core, we converted it into a hidden passageway, giving us an inconspicuous way to monitor the world above."

Constans's stone-like countenance remained unreadable, yet the arch of his eyebrow hinted at amusement. "So, this was less about strategic advantage and more about mere curiosity, was it not?"

Caught off guard, Tamanka fumbled for words. "No, no, certainly not," he stammered. "We enjoy knowing about the world above. Our love for our subterranean home runs deep, but we also appreciate the importance of being aware of the world beyond."

Accepting the explanation, Constans signaled the group to descend into the wooden cavern of the tree trunk.

Meanwhile, Cosmo, Jiyanu, and Fatiha huddled close together, their murmurs barely discernible amid the rhythmic sound of their footsteps.

"Now we are all together again, let's address the big question. Why do you think we've all been brought here?" Fatiha asked.

Cosmo pondered her question. "Could it be due to my knack for outsmarting opponents in games? That's what this is—a game with far greater stakes."

Jiyanu offered his thoughts, lips pursed. "Perhaps it isn't about what we can impart to this world, but what it can teach us."

He turned to Fatiha. "When we were in Salama, you told me how broken you were after your breakup. You thought you were useless, unwanted. But look at you now! You're the linchpin in a battle to save an entire world. You matter."

A smile crept onto Fatiha's face. "Yes, you're right. I can make a difference."

The group emerged into a vast cavern. The sight that greeted them was breathtaking. A solitary stone archway, its edges dressed with mesmerizing engravings and cryptic hieroglyphs, stood majestically in the center. The ancient construct radiated an air of profound mystery, as if holding secrets that transcended time and space.

Tamanka stepped forward, speaking with reverence and pride: "The Durara Gates were forged with the power of the Mountains of Elphis and blessed by the Hephaes; these gates enable us to traverse time and space swiftly, reducing hours of travel to mere moments."

Constans couldn't help but smile. "So, Moirah, now you have discovered the Taura is also a secret gateway to your capital."

The Rehmat leader raised her eyebrow but said nothing.

Tamanka coughed awkwardly, his embarrassment evident. "Once we have imprisoned Sathariel, we will share our knowledge with all the Amaris clans, including all of the Durara gates' locations."

Constans unfolded his arms, his demeanor affable. "That is a gracious offer, Tamanka. This is for the good of Amaris, after all."

The leader of the mountain people mumbled under his breath.

Mariam interjected with a playful jab: "Ah, the trials and tribulations you land walkers must face. Creating secret gateways in our ocean realm would be quite the challenge!"

Mariam's words elicited laughter from the group, easing the tension. "Now, let's get moving. We must create this prison and banish Sathariel once and for all."

Cosmo, Fatiha, Jiyanu, Tauheed, Mariam, and Moirah stepped through the gate.

Chapter 52

In the heart of Salama, in the garden of the Jivanam tree, Louisa stood back, her contemplative gaze sweeping over the surroundings. Every detail had been meticulously planned, leaving nothing to chance. The weight of their world's fate rested on their shoulders, and Louisa was acutely aware of the magnitude of their task. She had immersed herself in ancient texts, delving into the wisdom of their ancestors, searching for an answer that would ensure their victory over Sathariel. She believed she had found it.

Only Moirah, her most trusted confidant, was privy to Louisa's backup plan, the solution she had uncovered in her relentless pursuit of knowledge. With a nod, Louisa signaled for a Rehmat warrior to approach, carrying the rock of Sambandh.

"You know what to do." Louisa's lips were in a grim line. "Return the rock to its rightful place in the shadow of the Vanavashtha sapling. That is where the battle will take place."

The warrior stepped forward, treating the rock with reverence. With great care, she lifted it onto a bronze plinth, revealing a perfectly symmetrical schism where Louisa had extracted the section required to create the Fylakistone. The once-smooth surface now bore the mark of their purpose.

In that moment, a hummingbird darted into the room, fluttering before Louisa's face. "They are nearly here, the Yasha," it chirped. "I've just received word that they will enter the palace in minutes."

Moirah retrieved the chest containing the fragmented piece of Sambandh rock. She glanced upward at the dragon riders circling in the skies, vigilant for any signs of Sathariel's approach.

Chapter 53

Cosmo, accompanied by Fatiha, Jiyanu, Tauheed, and Mariam, entered the garden. Louisa's smile was resolute as she raised her hand, beckoning everyone to gather.

He hoped they were on the cusp of thwarting Sathariel for good. Tauheed smiled at him, and then Fatiha and Jiyanu. "Now, we must take a drop of blood from each of you," he explained. "It will bind to the Fylakistone."

Moirah placed a chest open on the ground, which contained a segment of the rock of Sambandh. It glittered in the light, each facet swirling with a force ready to be harnessed into a prison to hold Sathariel's dark power: the Fylakistone.

The trio stepped forward. Tauheed, holding a knife provided by the Taura and crafted from avinash, gently made a small incision on each of their fingers. Cosmo winced. *There's that blood thing again.*

"Squeeze your finger, and let a drop of blood fall onto the stone," Tauheed instructed.

Cosmo followed his guidance. The droplets of blood shimmered. The stone began to crackle with electrifying energy, drawing the droplets into itself like a magnet.

Cosmo's gaze fixed on the stone. "It's happening," he exclaimed, pointing at the radiant artifact. "I think it's working!"

"You're right!" Fatiha's excitement was palpable. "I think we might have a fighting chance."

The power of Ruach surged through the stone, and a clap of thunder resonated through the sky.

Moments later, lightning sliced across the heavens as Sathariel materialized between Tauheed and the rock of Sambandh. Her face contorted into a snarl, and with a raised fist, she summoned the Malevolents to join her.

"I will not let you take victory from me!" Sathariel hissed, her stare burning into them. She shifted her gaze to the fragmented rock, and her eyes flickered with triumph. "You think I don't know how to stop this?"

Cosmo balked at her shout as Sathariel brandished a dagger and plunged it into the heart of the Sambandh rock. Slicing the rock in two with defiance, she then pulled it out, crowing with victory.

The sliced rock began to splinter and crumble under the force of her attack. A wave of desolation washed over their faces as they beheld the destruction.

"Now the rock of Sambandh is destroyed. The prison you have created for me is nothing!" She laughed at them with mock pity, baring her teeth. "For your Fylakistone to hold me, the rock of Sambandh must remain."

Fear pricked Cosmo's skin, a chill covering him. The air, filled with the remnants of Resha shattering the goodness of the Ruach from the stone, turned to the consistency of syrup.

Cosmo's heart constricted and his throat was dry. *What are we going to do? We've failed.*

He turned to Fatiha and Jiyanu. Fatiha's face was white, eyes wide with alarm. But with Jiyanu, defiance burned like an inferno from every pore.

Cosmo watched in horror as Jiyanu propelled himself forward into Sathariel's oncoming onslaught in a bid to shield the Fylakistone from further harm. He snatched it out of the chest.

The queen of darkness sneered, convinced that victory was within her grasp. But Moirah fixed her piercing gaze upon the queen. "The battle is not over, Sathariel. You are not the victor."

Cosmo watched, his heart in his mouth, as Moirah regarded Sathariel with a tinge of sadness. "Did you truly believe we would not do everything we can to overcome you?"

Sathariel's jubilation waned, confusion clouding her features. She stared at the radiant stone in Jiyanu's grasp, and Cosmo saw a creeping realization dawning upon her.

He was just as perplexed. Why had the Fylakistone not disintegrated? Why did it still exist?

Sathariel's icy smile froze upon her face, her expression contorted in disbelief. "Why has the prison not been destroyed?" Fury laced every syllable.

Her eyes darted toward Jiyanu, who still clutched the stone. Sathariel cried out in pain as fire seared through every sinew. The Fylakistone's power tightened like a noose around her neck, restricting her movements and sapping her strength. Burning, snapping, constricting. The fire was so hot, it was almost like ice.

Louisa stepped forward with a quiet authority. "The reason you are not freed, Sathariel, is because what you destroyed was not the true rock of Sambandh. It was merely a manifestation, a reflection crafted to deceive you. The real rock is hidden away, guarded by our strongest warriors in the depths of our citadel."

A tortured howl of agony tore from Sathariel's throat. "How dare you trick me!" she shrieked, unleashing fury like a raging bull. She turned away from them, muttering under her breath to Sephtis, seeking an explanation for her plight. Sathariel's gaze fixated on Cosmo, and as her icy glare permeated his soul, he glanced to see Fatiha and Jiyanu as transfixed as he was.

A wicked grin spread across Sathariel's face. Her eyes bored into his. "You may think you have captured me, but let us see if there is another way for me to break free from these bonds. My fate is tied to yours, but what if I take one of you down with me? If I am to be imprisoned, let us see if your death will give me release and more power." Before anyone could react, she brandished the blade she had used to split the rock of Sambandh and threw it with force at Jiyanu.

Time seemed to slow for Cosmo as the dagger hurtled toward its target. Jiyanu thrust his hands into the air to hold the Fylakistone out of harm's way. But it left his torso completely exposed, and as the dagger plunged into his chest, Jiyanu let out a guttural gasp. Blood spilled from his lips as he struggled to breathe. He crumpled to his knees.

Bile rose in Cosmo's throat, and every molecule of his being seemed to constrict.

Sathariel sneered in triumph, relishing her perceived victory. "So, now you may have me as a prisoner, but you have lost one of your own, Yasha. How careless of you," she taunted, her eyes gleaming maliciously, lip curling. Fear filled Jiyanu's eyes, overshadowing his face.

Cosmo rushed to Jiyanu's side, and his heart ached with despair. He cradled Jiyanu's face, hands trembling as he looked into his eyes. "Stay strong; don't give up," Cosmo pleaded, his grip firm, almost desperate. "You need to stay strong."

I will not cry. I will not let you see I fear for you. Like I did with my mom. I never let her doubt me or think we couldn't get out.

Mariam rushed to Jiyanu's side. The color was fading from his face, and his breaths grew shallow. She knelt beside him, her hands trembling as she grasped his fingers. "We can't let him go like this," she implored.

Cosmo looked at her and exchanged a silent understanding. At that moment, he made a decision.

He looked to Fatiha, who gently took Jiyanu's hand, careful not to cause him any further pain. Cosmo outstretched his own palm toward Fatiha, Mariam, Moirah, and Tauheed, and they formed a protective circle around Jiyanu.

Though his body sagged, his chest heaving with labored breaths, Jiyanu's spirit remained unbroken. His fingers dug into the stone. "I won't let her win." Sweat trickled down his forehead, and his eyes flickered with urgency. "I don't know how much time I have left. Do it quickly," he urged.

Cosmo looked at Fatiha, and they commenced their chant, their voices intertwining in the melodic harmony Tauheed had taught them on their journey through the Durara Gate. The air crackled with energy as their incantation enveloped the courtyard:

"Akin to our likeness, hailing from a distant world,
we are saviors against the eternal night.
Our blood binding, rescuing Amaris from the clutches of endless darkness.
We ignite the radiant flame, imprisoning that which has become the force of night."

Sathariel's face contorted in agony as the power took hold. A cascade of screams erupted from her lips as she convulsed, grabbing wildly at her hair, digging fingernails into her temples. Blood oozed between her fingers.

Cosmo's gaze dropped to the stone cradled in Jiyanu's hand. It radiated with pulsating shades of orange and red, exuding a powerful aura. The very essence of the stone was alive, resonating with raw energy.

Amid Sathariel's torment, her physical form began to fade. She grew increasingly transparent, her matter dissipating under the overwhelming power of the Fylakistone. A golden mist coiled around her, taking the shape of a serpent, its grip tightening.

Sathariel let out a final gasp of air, her hands raised above her head. "You will not keep me in this prison forever." Her eyes flashed with a deep, raw anger and hatred before she vanished into a radiant orb of light.

The orb floated toward Cosmo, who stood alongside Fatiha, and the glowing sphere eventually merged into the Fylakistone. As Sathariel became imprisoned inside it, Jiyanu's hand slipped from their grasp, his eyes fluttering shut as he released a final sigh.

Silence blanketed the courtyard, broken only by a keening sound that resonated through the air. The dragons cried out mournfully, paying tribute to Jiyanu's passing. The remaining Malevolents, who had observed the scene, vanished from sight.

"Where did they go?" Tears streamed down Fatiha's face as she sobbed uncontrollably.

Tauheed comfortingly rubbed her shoulders. "I believe they returned to Naraka. Without Sathariel, they have no purpose in this world."

Cosmo struggled to control his own grief, choked with emotion. "What about the Legion? What about all those who served her?"

At that moment, a gentle wind began to rise, and a being gradually took shape before them. Its wings shimmered with a kaleidoscope of colors. "It's one of the Kaluduta," Mariam whispered, her mouth falling open in shock.

Waves of kindness, peace, and calm washed over Cosmo, easing his grief-stricken heart.

"The Divine and the Kaluduta stand with you in your sorrow," the Kaluduta conveyed with compassion. "Jiyanu has made a tremendous sacrifice. But in his loss, you have given the people of this world a profound gift. Your actions will not be forgotten when you return to your Earth. Many blessings will be bestowed upon you."

Fatiha, consumed by grief, clearly couldn't help but express her anger. "But how does this help Jiyanu? He doesn't get to come back with us. He didn't ask for any of this. How is this a victory when he is gone?"

The Kaluduta regarded her with sadness. "The death of someone you care for is painful. You may not have known Jiyanu for long, but the bond you formed through this arduous journey was strong. He sacrificed himself for the safety and future of many others. There can be no greater way to live than to put others before oneself. While it is the end of his time with you, it is the beginning of eternity for him. Do not fear—he shall be richly rewarded in his new realm."

"What about those who know him back on Earth? What will happen to them? Will he be missed?"

"Time exists on different plains and is flexible," the Kaluduta explained gently. "The Divine will ensure a seamless transition. His disappearance will not be considered out of the ordinary. The threads of his existence will be carefully woven back into the tapestry of time to cover his presence, and his absence."

With these words, the Kaluduta retrieved the stone from Jiyanu's hands. "The Fylakistone is a prison to keep Sathariel confined and protect the world from her dark influence. You must safeguard it, Tauheed. Your people's lives depend on it."

Turning to Moirah, the Kaluduta bowed his head. "The rock of Sambandh is forever intertwined with your people and the Fylakistone, providing everlasting protection. In the days to come, it shall serve as a shield should the worst come to pass. It is your legacy and future to keep it safe."

With that, the Kaluduta vanished, leaving them all bathed in an air of both grief and hope.

Chapter 54

Cosmo and Fatiha grappled with the overwhelming sorrow of losing Jiyanu. Tears stained their cheeks as they struggled to comprehend the reality of his absence.

Mariam enveloped them both in her arms, offering comfort. "I wish I could find the words to ease your pain, but grief is a burden we all must bear. The loss of someone we love is a profound and terrible experience. But you will overcome it. The pain is raw right now. It will tear at your core. But you must hold on to the fact that it was not in vain. The pain of losing a loved one becomes even more unbearable when they are taken from us too soon."

Harda had joined them in the garden and placed a comforting hand on Cosmo's and Fatiha's shoulders. "Jiyanu made a courageous sacrifice. His memory will forever be etched in our hearts. We will never forget him."

Tauheed, who had taken the Fylakistone, gazed at its swirling depths. It was hard to fathom that Sathariel, she whom he had once loved, was now imprisoned within its facets.

He looked up, his gaze soft and tears in his eyes. "I understand the depth of your sorrow, but we must remember Jiyanu's valor. He gave himself selflessly."

He turned to Tamanka, who had just arrived through the Durara Gate. "Tamanka, can you fashion a sword, within which we can place the Fylakistone? I think that if we are able to create a blade from avinash, we can add another level of protection to the prison."

The leader of the Taura nodded. "With the help of the Hephaes, we can do that. I know they will want to ensure that she does not escape and put our world in jeopardy again."

He carefully took the stone from Tauheed. "We will also establish several secure locations to house it. Only a small circle of custodians will know its whereabouts at any given time. By constantly moving the Fylakistone, we minimize the risk of anyone attempting to free Sathariel. We can have a site within the Mountains of Elphis, and the Hephaes will be honored to guard it."

Mariam nodded in agreement. "In our oceanic capital, we shall create an equally impregnable prison. The essence of earth and water, bound by the power of Ruach, will hopefully ensure that Sathariel never escapes again."

They all raised their hands and spoke together. "And so, it is done."

Harda turned to Cosmo and Fatiha. "Are you ready to return to your own world?"

Fatiha's eyes glistened with unshed tears, and her lips pressed tightly together as she paused, searching for the right words. "Can't we stay a little longer? If what the Kaluduta says is right, we should be able to and not be missed, right?"

Tauheed smiled warmly. "Of course, why not? What did you have in mind?"

Fatiha's gaze brightened with a shy hope, eyes dancing. "It would be nice to see your home, and to have another opportunity to ride on a dragon, like I did to Salama. But this time not because I was about to be captured or killed by an evil force."

Harda nodded in agreement.

Cosmo leaned forward, his eyes alight with curiosity. "I would also like to visit your kingdom, Mariam," he said, both eager and hopeful. "If it's possible."

The ocean queen laughed. "I think anything is possible. It would be my pleasure to have you as my honored guests."

"Then it is settled," Tauheed declared. "The Yasha shall return through the Thura Gate once they have traveled across our world. And we will ensure that Jiyanu's sacrifice is truly honored."

Chapter 55

Cosmo awoke, and the reality of what the day would hold made his heart ache: Today he would return to Earth. He clenched his jaw. What awaited him back home? Would he arrive at the same time? Would his father still be there? A wave of excitement and trepidation washed over him as he estimated he had been on Amaris for around six months, although it was difficult to determine.

During his time in this mystical world, he had witnessed extraordinary wonders. Defeating an all-powerful evil queen had just been the beginning.

Side by side with Fatiha, he had experienced the grandeur of the endless skies unfolding before them as they took to the air upon the backs of dragons. As the wind had whispered past, tousling their hair and filling their lungs with the crisp scent of altitude and freedom, he had struggled to stop himself from crying with wonder. Cosmo remembered exhilaration and joy. He also took a moment to recall when they had overseen the creation of the mystical shrine, hidden beneath the surface of the magnificent lake of the Koimeterion. Nestled at its heart was a sacred space dedicated to Jiyanu, now remembered as a hero whose story would no doubt be passed down through the ages of Amaris.

Alongside the rest of the clans of Amaris, he and Fatiha had sung songs in a tribute to their friend's bravery, a testament to his courage. Jiyanu's name would be eternally remembered and eternally revered.

Another memory, however, shimmered bright in Cosmo's heart: when he had swum amid the resplendent array of sea creatures in the ocean.

Mariam had bestowed upon them the extraordinary gift of gills. The transformation had been peculiar, a tickling sensation at their throats followed by a new awareness of the ocean's pulse. It had granted them the freedom to dive into the aquatic realm without the need to surface for air.

His heart had raced as he'd glided alongside neon-bright fish and mesmerizing aquatic beings that seemed to be spun from moonlight and sea foam. Together, he and Fatiha had spent hours delving into the heart of the grand underwater palace and the mesmerizing citadel belonging to the elusive ocean people.

For several sunrises and sunsets, they'd spent time living, learning, and playing under the watchful eyes of the Adira. They'd learned the language of the currents, tasted the strange, salty fruits of the sea, and danced with the inhabitants of the palace.

Their grand adventure had finally culminated in the mystical Forest of Myrkvior. Here, amid towering trees and whispering leaves, they had listened to the tales spun by the ancient Vanavasin, learned the secret names of the luminescent flowers that bloomed under moonlight, and played hide-and-seek with the forest's playful inhabitants.

The magic that resided in Myrkvior had seeped into their skin, into their minds, into their hearts. It was an experience they would carry with them always.

A gentle knock interrupted Cosmo's reflection, and Fatiha entered the room, her face radiant with a bittersweet smile. "It's time to go."

Cosmo grasped her hand tightly, and together they made their way toward the Vanavashtha and the gateway that would transport them back to their own world. As they approached the glade, they saw Tauheed waiting for them, accompanied by Moirah.

"Once you have returned to your own world, we are going to separate the power of the Thura Gates. The only Jivanam saplings still in existence are those that reside in Salama and the Mountains of Elphis. We were able to stop Sathariel's rot when she was imprisoned, but we cannot run the risk of them being used for ill intent. The Thura Gates' power will be imbued in locations known only to the few."

Fatiha nodded. "Hmm, yes, I don't think we would be too keen if another Sathariel paid us a visit!"

Tauheed laughed, a smile playing on his lips. As they stood amid the tranquility of the surrounding trees, the whispering of the Vanavashtha filled the air with a ghostly murmur. "They bid you farewell," he told them softly.

"It will be so difficult to let go of this place," Cosmo said, his words trembling with emotion.

Moirah's gaze was warm and understanding. "Just remember to look up at the sky. We may be gazing upon different parts of the universe, but we still share the same vast expanse."

The group embraced tightly, savoring their final moments together. Tauheed gestured toward the portal. "Now, it is time. Time for you to return to your own world."

Cosmo nodded, gratitude and emotion welling up within him. "Thank you, thank you for everything. Thank you for allowing us to embark on this extraordinary journey."

Tauheed and Moirah clasped their chests as a salute. "May the Divine watch over you, Yasha. Travel safely across the cosmos."

Cosmo and Fatiha stepped into the Thura Gate. Cosmo's heart was equally filled with sadness and joy. It was time to return home.

There's more to this book than meets the eye. Every name tells you about their role in the story...

GLOSSARY OF NAMES

Amaris (Hebrew) — given by God

The Divine Interpreters

Shekinah (Arabic) — the manifestation of the presence of God; divine

Leader: Arielle (Hebrew) — lioness of God

Capital: Chinasa (Nigerian) — God answers prayers

Tauheed (Sanskrit) — unity

The Yasha (Hebrew) — liberated/saved

Cosmo (Indian) — universe

Fatiha (Arabic) — beginning

Jiyanu (Chinese) — building the universe

Forces of Light — Places, Portals, Sacred Objects, and Beings

The Divine (Latin) — of or like God/supremely good

The Divine (Sanskrit) — God/divine origin

Nidhana (Sanskrit) — destruction

Avinash (Sanskrit) — indestructible

Jewel of Aikyam (Sanskrit) — oneness

Durara Gate — portal to other worlds (Spanish) — it will last

Riyon (Indian) — immense beauty of heaven

Elnathan Prophecy (Hebrew) — the gift of God

Fylakistone (Greek) — prison

Goitera (Sanskrit) — enchantment

Hisoki (Lake of) (Japanese) — secretive

Jivanam tree (Sanskrit) — life force/life giving

Kaluduta (Arabic) — winged army of God/ sent by God

The Lake of the Koimeterion (Latin) — crypt

Malakai (Fijian) — messenger

Misham (Hebrew) — resembles God

Natanael (Hebrew) — God-given

Resha (Hebrew) — wicked; bad power; criminal activity

Riyon (Indian) — immense beauty of heaven

Ruach (Hebrew/Greek) — good power; breath of the spirit

Sambandh (Hindu/Sanskrit) — bound together

Theodore (Greek) — gift of God

Thura Gate (Sanskrit) — brave

Clans of Amaris

The Forest People — Vanavasin (Sanskrit) — forest dweller

Leader: Constans (Germanic) — steadfast

Capital: Myrkvior (Germanic) — murky wood

Hana (Hebrew) — favor and grace

Viera (Russian) — truth

Vanavashtha (Sanskrit) — one who gives up earthly life/roots

The Mountain People — The Taura

Leader: Tamanka (Indian) — Lord of Earth

Capital: Faesten (Old English) — fasten

Mountains of Elphis (Greek) — hope

Hephaes — God of Stone/Hephaestus (Greek) — stone giants

The Spirit People — Rehmat

Leader: Louisa (Latin) — warrior

Capital: Salama (Swahili) — safe

Moriel (Hebrew) — the Lord is my teacher

The Plains People — The Hayim

Leader: Charaka (Hindu) — wanderer

Capital: Qualea (Arabic) — fortress

The Dragon Riders — The Caelum Bellator

Leader: Harda (Germanic) — brave

Capital: Paracletes (Greek) — helper/comforter

Ananpal (Indian) — protector of peace

Lexi (Greek) — protector of humanity

Axelia (Greek) — protector of mankind

Deklan (Irish) — man of prayer

The Free People — The Elutheros

Leader: King Damianos (Greek) — to tame

Capital: Heliopolis (Latin/Greek) — city of light

Queen Gerlinde (Germanic) — rules with spear

The Ocean People — The Adira

Leader: Mariam (Arabic) — drop of the sea

Capital: Maren (Latin) — star of the sea

Kaimana (Hawaiian) — power of the ocean

Kano (Japanese) — hunting range

The Dark Forces

Leader: Sephtis (Persian) — eternal death

Capital: Naraka (Hindu) — hell

Sathariel (Hebrew) — fallen angel; side of God/concealment of God

Abaddon (Hebrew) — destroyer/angel of the abyss

Lael (Hebrew) — supporter of God

The Malevolents (Latin) — ill-disposed and spiteful

The Obscura (Latin) — shadowy/indistinct

IF YOU LIKED THIS BOOK...please leave me a review on Amazon!

And if you would like to read more about the world of Amaris, you can read *The Amaris Prophecies: The Rising.*

An evil queen. A shattered stone. A magic realm on the brink of collapse.

And two girls—one of magic, and one of Earth—are all that can save the worlds.

Njeri has always been gifted, preparing since childhood to become one of the Spirit people who channel the magic force that binds the realm of Amaris. But when she accidentally taps into the Ruach—an evil force that destroys rather than creates, and tears asunder what is best left bound—her mistake releases the greatest enemy Amaris has ever known: the wicked Queen Sathariel.

Now, the evil queen's shadow darkens the land. And the only way for Njeri to stop her is with the Fylakistone, a magical talisman that was broken in eons past and, if the pieces are reassembled, can imprison Queen Sathariel and save Amaris.

Joining forces with Chloe, a teenage girl transported from Earth to Amaris through a magic portal, Njeri will risk everything to find the shattered Fylakistone, to join the pieces and capture the wicked queen.

But Queen Sathariel has plans of her own. Plans that will turn the kingdoms of Amaris to war, its people to battle. Plans to shatter the world, and remake it in her own image...unless two girls can learn to trust each other, trust themselves, and halt the doom of *The Rising*.

If you love CS Lewis' *The Lion, the Witch and the Wardrobe*, Madeleine L'Engle's *A Wrinkle in Time*, or JRR Tolkien's *The Hobbit*, you'll adore acclaimed storyteller Zoe Nauman's *The Rising*—a young adult coming-of-age story like nothing you've never experienced. BUY NOW to get your fill of friendship, fantasy, and adventure!

ABOUT THE AUTHOR

Zoe Nauman is a journalist, copywriter, editor, and speaker who has worked with some of the world's most well-known publications and brands for over twenty-five years. She's an expert storyteller with a penchant for helping brands find their unique voice. As a journalist, she has interviewed some of the world's biggest celebrities, including Angelina Jolie, Nicole Kidman, and Lionel Richie.

A globetrotter by heart, Zoe moved from the UK to Sydney in 2008, living there for seven years while travelling to some of the most beautiful parts of Asia, including her beloved Bali. She now works in the US and the UK writing; corralling her three chihuahuas: Poco, Chika, and Enzo; eating olives stuffed with blue cheese; and running on the beach.

https://www.instagram.com/authorzoenauman/

www.ingramcontent.com/pod-product-compliance
Lightning Source LLC
LaVergne TN
LVHW090554110826
845146LV00001B/125

* 9 7 9 8 9 8 8 0 3 5 7 9 4 *